Also by Lou Iovino

Skybound

Data Mine

THE RARE EARTH TRILOGY

Inheritance

Reckoning

Praise for INHERITANCE

"An irresistible science fiction page-turner that will have readers openly weeping in places and applauding in others. This narrative is a masterclass in storytelling. While no novel is flawless, this little sci-fi gem comes close."

—BlueInk (starred review)

"Iovino does a marvelous job setting up his Rare Earth trilogy with this mesmerizing opener. A strong cast and a well-designed setting fuel this entertaining space opera."

—Kirkus Reviews

"This is a true science fiction novel. A tale of the human ambition to tackle and conquer new frontiers and to eke out a living in the deadliest of environments."

—Tulsa Book Review

"Rich, solid, working-class sci-fi. *Inheritance* is a gripping read, a moving portrayal of labor, and a promising start to the Rare Earth Trilogy."

—IndieReader (starred review)

"*Inheritance* is a witty and entertaining sci-fi thriller. The story is well paced, neatly organized and dynamic, with convincing multidimensional characters and a believable vision of the future astromining industry."

"A fast-paced, invigorating science fiction novel. With its palpable instances of sabotage and tragedy, *Inheritance* is an exciting, mystery-filled introduction to a new science fiction series."

"*Inheritance* is a far-flung adventure through space and memory, filled with a pining, bitter nostalgia and a focus on how the past influences the future, the future influences the past."

RECKONING

LOU IOVINO

RARE
EARTH
TRILOGY
VOLUME
TWO

A NOVEL

Copyright © 2025 by Lou Iovino

All rights reserved. Published by LAB Press, LLC, New Jersey.

Cover design by Damonza.

Station diagrams by David Lindroth Inc.

ISBN 978-1-7371746-6-0 (trade paperback)

ISBN 978-1-7371746-7-7 (e-book)

For my beloved siblings—one of you is our parents' second favorite, one of you is third, and, of course, neither of you is me.

"But there's a story behind everything. Sometimes the stories are simple, and sometimes they are hard and heartbreaking. But behind all your stories is always your mother's story, because hers is where yours begins."

—Mitch Albom, *For One More Day*

DARKSIDE STATION

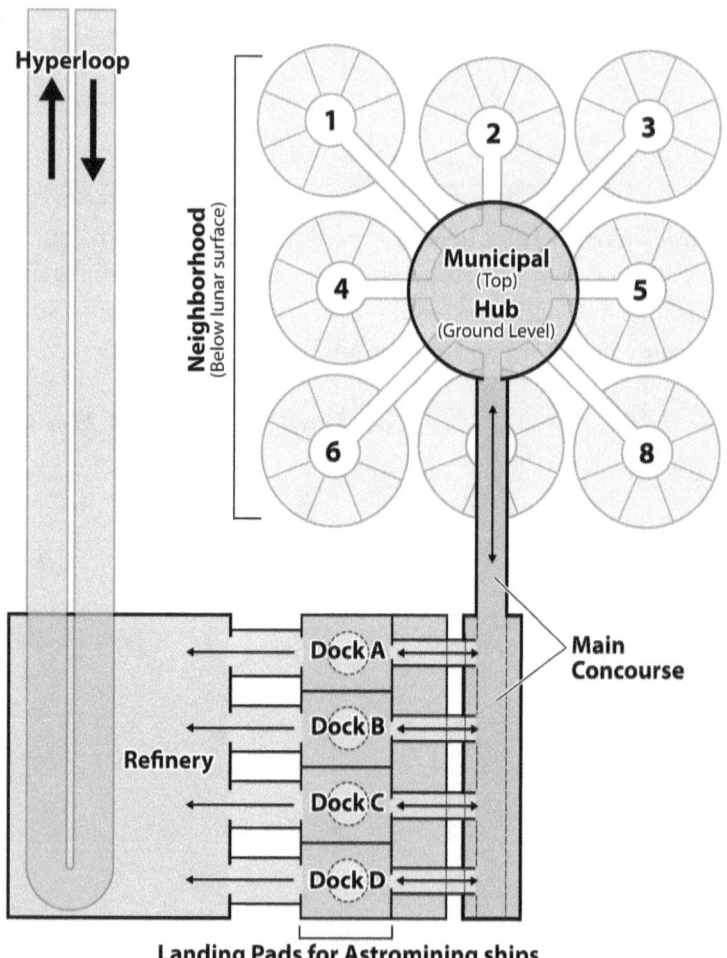

Hyperloop

Neighborhood
(Below lunar surface)

1 2 3

4 **Municipal**
(Top)
Hub
(Ground Level) 5

6 8

Main Concourse

Refinery

Dock A

Dock B

Dock C

Dock D

Landing Pads for Astromining ships
(Lifts lower ore containers to refinery access level
and crews to the Main Concourse)

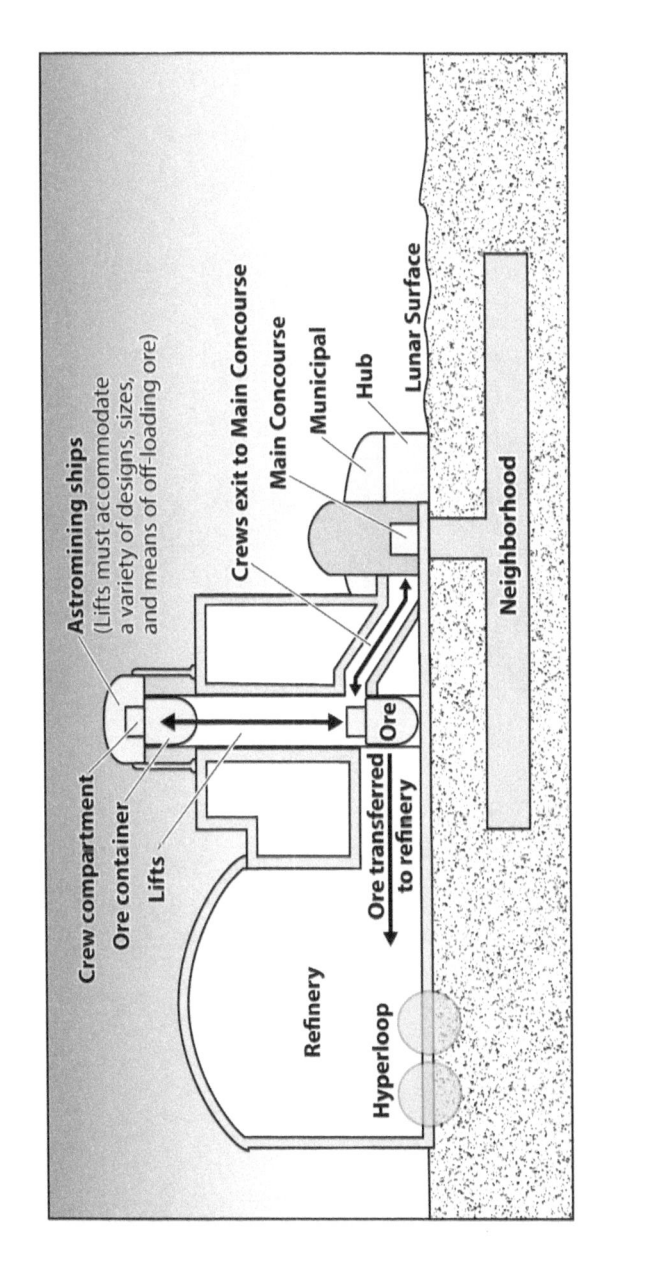

PART I

You and Me

Blood

I'M sure you're wondering why I did it.

Why I attacked the station and those ships. How I could do that to all those *innocent* people.

You want to know how I got here. Not *here* here, of course. I mean the bigger *here*. How I came to be this person, someone who could do such terrible things.

There's a lot you want to know. Where I've been all these years, what I've been doing, how I got started. Who I've been working with and when they found me, and when and how I found them. And for that matter, how did *that* even happen? You want to know why *this* and why *that* and why and why and why . . .

You see, I know you. It probably kills you to admit it, but it's true. I know you, and I know that now that you've discovered my secret, you'll agonize over these and so many other things I can't even begin to imagine. You'll turn these questions over and over in your head, again and again and again, trying to puzzle out everything and driving yourself crazy in the process. The unanswered questions will haunt you. They always have, and that's why I'm making these recordings.

I'm doing this for you.

But if I'm being honest, I'm also doing it for me.

Listen, I'd love to be able to sit across from you, look you in the eyes, and help you understand. But I doubt I'll get that chance. So instead, I thought maybe if I simply talk . . . just say out loud some of the things I've been holding inside. If I just come out with it all, and then figure out a way to get this recording to you, then maybe, in the end, you'll get a bit of what you need, and I will too. And then both of us can move on to whatever happens next.

I don't know about you, but I'm ready for that.

Anyway . . .

Where do I start?

———

I CAN'T GO ALL the way back to the beginning. Not yet. So how about this? Let's start with your *special* scar. You know the one I'm talking about. The frowny little half-moon scar on the bottom of your chin—the one you got right before sixth grade when you went over the handlebars of your ten-speed. I can't believe it's still there after all these years! Faded for sure, but unmistakable.

I'll never forget that day. You scared me half to death with the way you carried on. The whole street came out to see what happened. And my god, the blood! So much of it all over your shirt and shorts, right down to your flip-flops. You howled in the back seat of the Chevy all the way to the emergency room, and then even louder when they took you back. Eight stitches, was it? Nine? So long ago—a lifetime ago! And yet there it was today on full display, the souvenir from that summer staring me in the face as you kneeled over me in that maintenance conduit.

It was the perfect target.

Your teeth clacked together so hard I worried I'd chipped a tooth. As soon as the heel of my palm connected with your scar, your eyes got really wide, even wider than they already were, which was pretty hard to believe because only seconds before, you'd discovered I was the one you'd been chasing all over the station. I never really understood the saying "eyes wide like saucers" until that moment. Thankfully, they didn't stay that way very long. I couldn't bear what I saw in them. Shock, betrayal, surprise, anger, so many things contained in that single gaze. It was awful.

As your eyes fluttered closed, I guided you down to the floor so you wouldn't get hurt, made sure you had a soft landing. A tiny murmur escaped as your head lolled to the side, a small, red-tinged bubble on your lower lip all that remained of whatever you were going to say.

I have to admit, though, despite the awful circumstances, actually touching you after so many years was sort of electrifying. It satisfied something buried deep inside, scratched some sort of motherly itch. It was nice, all things considered. But you're too thin, Thea. Strong, no doubt. Hell, you were on me like lightning in that conduit. My cheeks and forehead still ache from where you crushed my goggles into my face. But it worries me. You're probably working too much or are under too much stress from being up here doing that damned job on that blasted ship. You have to take care of yourself, honey. No one else will. But I guess you know that by now, huh?

Anyway, as soon as I got you situated, I noticed the cut on your cheek. You flinched a little as I examined it, but I was careful not to wake you. Despite all the blood on your face, I was relieved to see that it was only an inch across maybe, no more. But make sure you take care of it. A little disinfectant, I figure, and a dab of liquid bandage is all it needs. But not the stingy kind. I know you hate that.

I did a quick scan of the rest of your body, too, and miraculously it didn't look like you had any other injuries. I can't swear to it, though, because I got distracted by the puffy cloud logo stitched on the pocket of your flight jacket, the Watts Astromining logo your father adapted from that picture you drew—the one that hung on the refrigerator until the day you left for Cambridge, drawn a lifetime ago on a rainy Saturday when we were all together, young and happy and still a family. Husband and me and baby made three. Those golden years before it all started to come apart. Before the business and the ship and the trips and the moon took over our lives. The endless trips that constantly took your dad away, leaving just baby and me, never again three.

I stared at that patch, couldn't tear my eyes away from it. For some reason I had a burning need to touch it—to touch the past, I guess. But as I reached out, a drop of blood fell off my thumb and landed in the center of the cloud.

The blood from the cut on your cheek.

My blood too.

You're my blood, Thea. Not just his, you know. Mine too. But as I knelt there and searched your face, your breath warm on my cheeks, I was reminded how easy it is to forget that fact. Your bushy eyebrows, wide nose, meaty earlobes. His and yours. Barely any of me in you, really. More dark brew than latte. Allies and co-conspirators in everything. He could do no wrong in your eyes. Home on shore leave or up here, it didn't matter. Sun shined out of that man's ass and you were always happy to bask in it.

Speaking of ends, boy that must have been something to behold. As the Alzheimer's grabbed on and he got sicker and sicker . . . all his usual filters stripped away, defenses down, charisma absent. Did you get to see the side he reserved for me and me alone? Catch a glimpse of the *truth* of the man, even if only briefly before it was over?

Is it wrong of me to hope that you did?

I thought about that as I pressed our family blood into the patch's fibers, turning the happy white cloud pink, then apple, then ruby red. Even as I was doing it, I didn't know why. It just felt right. But as I watched the *Zephyr*'s logo soak up every last drop, the lights in the conduit suddenly cut out, followed by a noise coming from beyond the safety door, which had sealed off the section of the conduit you and I were in—a fail-safe measure following the explosions.

When the lights flickered back on, I crept over to the door and listened. I heard the noises again, distant but louder, and there was no doubt. Someone was coming.

I knew that if I moved quickly, I could take advantage of the chaos all over the station. Use the mayhem to get to my safe space. If I could just get *there*, I'd be able to figure out what to do. But just as I was about to leave, your hand suddenly jerked, and you let out a ragged breath.

It seemed like you were starting to come around. I balled up my fist in case I needed to hit you again, which was unfathomable to me right then and still is. For there to be an *again*, there had to have been a first, which of course there was. God, I still can't believe I did that to you!

And then you said his name.

Elliott.

You know, I once saw you guys eating together in the Hub. He stole something off your plate, and you playfully swatted at him. He ducked out of the way and said something before he popped whatever he stole into his mouth, and you laughed. It was a big, hearty laugh too, not one of your forced or polite ones. A full-on belly laugh, and I could tell you were genuinely happy. I'm glad he made you happy, honey. And I know you'll never forgive me now that he's gone, even though it wasn't my fault. Not really, anyway.

But we'll get to that.

As I stood over you in the conduit, praying you wouldn't

wake up, you kept turning your head back and forth, muttering his name. It was like you were looking for him and couldn't find him. It felt like it went on forever, but in reality, it was probably just a few seconds. Then you let out a long, slow whimper and went quiet again. I counted to ten and was finally able to unclench my fist, let myself relax, and swallow down the bile that had risen in my throat. That is, until you said the next thing.

Mom?

I can't describe the feeling of hearing that word, that question. I wanted so badly in that moment to stroke your hair and tell you it would be okay. Tell you "Momma's here," like when you were a little girl and had a scary dream or when there was one of those big Texas summer whip-ups that would rattle the windows and scare the shit out of the dog.

God, why did you come here, Thea? He died, and you were free. Finally free of *both* of us. You could have gone anywhere and done anything. You're so smart and so capable. Why this? Of all things, why *this*?

After you said my name, I thought about staying there with you. I really did. I thought about turning myself in and being done with it—just being done with it all. I'd fulfilled my mission, I figured, so why not? What was left for me? That's how much hearing you say my name rattled me. I honest-to-God thought about leaving it all behind, but then another bang rang out from the other side of the safety door. People were closing in, and that's when my resolve evaporated.

The hard truth is . . . I wasn't brave enough to stay.

There was only one thing I could *actually* do—something I've done before.

Gently, so gently, like a butterfly kiss so I wouldn't wake you, I brushed my lips across your forehead. "I'm sorry, baby," I whispered to you. "I'm so sorry. But Momma's got to go."

Then I left you behind.

Hits and Misses

"Is there a G?"

"No," the woman says, her voice slithering out from behind a black mask, the slits of her dark eyes the only thing visible on her face. She brandishes her pencil and presses it to the paper, tiny bits of graphite flaking off as she draws a thick line. "Last one."

Thea stares at the paper.

_ o _ h e r.

She could have sworn the answer was *gopher*. The clue was "trouble under the ground." What else could it be?

And then it hits her. B-o-t-h-e-r. It has to be *bother*. Trouble under the ground is a bother.

"Is there a B?"

The woman with the pencil silently shakes her head and then draws the final leg, hanging the man. When she pulls her hand away, the stick figure swings from the crossbar, his little stick legs kicking and stick arms waving, until they don't anymore. Thea watches in horror as the hanged man's blank face darkens with grays and blacks, the colors beginning to swirl inside his circle head. Faster and faster they spin like a whirlpool as the woman cackles. The face maelstrom whirls and churns until the vortex begins to slow and the image resolves into a face, one Thea knows well.

She stares at Elliott's gray pallor and slack jaw, X's over his dead eyes. Then she tears her gaze away from the horrific image and looks back to the puzzle.

_ o _ h e r.

She chokes back sobs of anger and frustration as she looks up at the woman with the pencil. Her adversary. The hangman.

"What's the answer!" Thea screams.

The woman moves to fill in the two blank spaces, then stops. She drops the pencil and reaches for her facemask instead, tugging it off to reveal her identity.

"The answer is *mother*, of course," her mom says, a quizzical look on her face. "Honestly, honey, how'd you miss that?"

A white-hot fury fills Thea as she gazes at her mother's wry smile. She balls her fist, screams at the top of her lungs, swings—

And punches the interior of the maintenance conduit.

The stinger radiates down her forearm and across her triceps, bright pain in her knuckles and elbow quickly turning to cold numbness. Her eyes snap open and wildly scan the space. She twists onto her side, cradling her injured fist against her chest. Her head swims as she sits up, and that's when she notices the pain in her jaw and remembers why it's there.

She cradles her chin and probes her teeth with her tongue, relieved to find none are missing or damaged. Touches the cut below her eye and comes away with only a trace amount of blood on her fingertips, the cut starting to clot. Dizziness forces her to close her eyes and sit back against the wall. She hugs her knees to her chest and waits for her world to settle.

Maybe it was a hallucination. Some sort of synaptic misfire

or hypoxia-induced illusion, an aftereffect of oxygen deprivation during the catastrophe in the main concourse. Her eyes saw one thing and her brain transformed it into something else —some*one* else. That has to be it—it's the only thing that makes sense, she thinks, unable or unwilling to process the evidence to the contrary, the implications of which are too big to fathom. She vigorously, maniacally nods her head, trying to convince herself the explanation she's devised is the right one, fool herself into believing its validity. But it doesn't work, and the nodding turns into banging as she smacks her head again and again and again against the thick steel of the conduit wall, stopping only when one especially hard whack makes her surroundings go wobbly.

She blinks to steady her vision, and a gurgle in her stomach grows from an acidy belch to a wave of nausea as the truth takes hold. Sweat breaks out across her torso and back. She pulls off her flight jacket and tosses it aside, trying to cool herself, hoping it'll steady her twisted guts. But her efforts fail. The deep belches and blarghs transform into a howl, a throat-shredding scream as her stomach empties, bile-tinged spittle mixing with the tears streaming down her face and dripping off her injured chin.

"You! How can it be you?" she shrieks. "It's impossible!"

A supernova of emotion crashes her system. Pain spikes somewhere in the center of her brain—an actual pop that drops her to her elbows. Her sight blinks out then back again, fear suddenly replacing rage. Her heart beats out a frantic rhythm as she forces herself to breathe—counts her breaths, prays for calm, fights to remain present. Slowly, painfully, it begins to work. She can feel herself stabilizing, watches the tremors in her hands slow and eventually stop. But then the slick all over her body ices over and she begins to tremble.

She scrambles over to where she tossed her flight jacket moments earlier and is about to pull it on when she sees something that stops her short. Her eyes zero in on the *Zephyr*'s logo, the puffy white cloud now a murderous red. She examines the area around the patch and finds no other blood drips, streaks, or smears. It's only there on the cloud. She touches the fibers, and her fingers come away sticky. She stares at a bloody fingertip, understanding dawning. And it's at that moment that her entire body and soul go quiet, her resolve returning in the span of a single heartbeat.

"You did this," she says through clenched teeth, twisting the jacket in her white-knuckled fists. "It was you all along."

A bang rings out.

Thea freezes, listens. The sound comes again, a steady clanking, something metallic.

She drops her jacket and creeps forward to the junction, the one the saboteur—no, the one her *mother*—leapt out of before. She doesn't know what lies around the corner, so she approaches it cautiously. Peers around and sees the closed safety door, hears noises coming from the passage on the other side. The control panel on the adjacent wall is glowing a steady red, and she knows there's no way of gaining access to the controls without a passcode or access card.

She crawls forward, places her ear against the cold metal of the safety door, and listens.

The noises are getting closer.

She considers banging on the door, screaming that she's there and needs help. But then a different thought emerges.

What if it's her?

She scoots back around the corner, careful to make no sound. She crouches in a three-point stance like a linebacker, ready to drive at her mother again, determined to not let her get away this time.

She waits, fighting to control her rising anger.

There's a low beep, and she hears the safety door iris open.

Someone is heading toward her. She readies herself, twists

her back foot to ensure purchase on the decking so she can spring forward with full force.

But then a man's voice says, "We'll check this main, then head to the shed on four," and Thea's heart drops. She rests on her haunches, relief and disappointment washing over her, knowing she's lost her mother again.

The Municipal security officer comes around the corner, followed by a woman similarly dressed. Thea raises her hand, weariness enveloping her.

"Did you see—" is all she manages before the lead officer stabs out with his stun stick, striking her in the chest. A whip-like crackle accompanies a bright white spark that illuminates the conduit. The flash momentarily blinds her, and she feels herself falling backward.

The back of her head hits the floor.

As she stares up at the ceiling, a dark corona pushes in from the edges. Then the security officer's face is above her, staring down.

The face swirls and churns and then resolves into her mother's face, same wry smile as before. Same question on her lips as everything starts to go dark.

"Honestly, honey, how'd you miss that?"

3

Something in the Air

AFTER LEAVING YOU BEHIND, my only thought was to get to my safe space. My nerves were frayed and I really needed to stop for a little while, just let everything sink in, and come up with a gameplan. But maneuvering through the conduits was a lot harder than I'd expected. Safety doors closed off many of the normal routes, so I had to keep doubling back to find a way through. It felt like forever until I discovered an unobstructed passage that would take me where I needed to go. But just as I started to make decent progress, I heard something up ahead.

At first, it was hard to determine what the noise was over the constant mechanical whir. Damn conduits are like echo chambers. I closed my eyes and held my breath, strained my hearing until I heard the noises again, and my worst fears were confirmed.

Voices. And they were coming toward me.

I whipped around and started crawling back to the last junction, sliding my knees along the floor to try and limit the noise I was making. But it slowed me down, and the voices that were now behind me kept getting closer. I was just about to give up on trying to move quietly, hoping the ambient noises in the conduit might conceal my escape, when I reached an atmospherics access panel.

Based on the station's current occupancy of seven hundred or so, the air scrubbers need to be changed three or four times a year. That's why atmospherics panels are secured with four simple quick-release levers at the corners, unlike other less-frequently accessed panels that require a specialized nut driver —which I knew because of my job on the maintenance crew. That simple difference is what kept them from finding me.

I tugged and turned each lever, then gently leaned the panel against the wall next to the opening and peered inside. There was nothing janky, no alterations or foul-ups in the unit, so there was room for me. I scrambled into the space and replaced the panel, manipulating the spring mechanisms on the interior so that the levers reset. I had to squeeze past the oxygen scrubber housing and duck under its wiring harness, beyond which the space opened up wide enough that I could lie flat on the ground, making myself invisible to anyone who might peer through the grate in the access panel.

Then I waited.

I checked my watch; it had been more than twenty minutes since I left you. Way too long. My window was closing, and there I was, stuck hiding in the dark, waiting for the slowest people in the universe to make their way past me and keep moving down the conduit. Finally, I heard dull thuds, probably from hands and knees as they crawled, and snippets of a conversation. I could tell right away there were two of them— a woman and a man. I didn't recognize either of their voices, but everything was muffled by the walls and machinery around me, so there was a chance we knew each other—or more accurately, that they knew the person I had been pretending to be since I arrived at Darkside.

"You cut out. Say again, base," the man said, now very close to my location.

"Municipal wants all maintenance personnel out of the conduits," a filtered voice replied, and that's when I knew they were on the radio. The voices got louder as the two people paused right outside the access panel. The woman asked about the refinery, and the radio operator confirmed that there was a radiation leak, but that it was small and already contained. Hearing that, I almost gasped out loud. The helium processor I hit should have been spewing out massive amounts of radiation. And even if engineering had somehow managed to contain it right away, the explosion still should have contaminated the refinery with enough radiation that they'd have to close it down for decades. That's when I knew something had gone terribly wrong.

My heart was pounding so hard I worried the people on the other side of the wall might hear it. The male maintenance worker asked about the Hyperloop, and the person on the radio confirmed what I already knew: that inbound was in vacuum, but things looked good on the outbound track, which I'd made sure would remain operational so they could evacuate people to the shipyard.

"Muni's already got teams inside. You guys need to get back right away," the radio operator said, then asked where the two of them were. The woman said they were between Two and Three, and the operator told them to stand by.

The seconds stretched out, each one feeling more and more precious given the news about the refinery. I had to get out of that damned hole and find out what happened. I was already on thin ice with my leadership and had no idea how in hell I going to explain this fuckup.

Finally the operator came back on and told the two workers that she'd opened the safety doors between them and the shed on Two. The male maintenance worker gave a quick "Roger, out," then said to his partner, "Let's get the hell out of here," which was exactly what I was thinking too.

As I waited for the sounds of the two of them to fade, my mind raced. How in blazes did the team inside the refinery contain the fallout so fast? Did the reactor have a fail-safe I wasn't aware of? If it did, then at least this wouldn't be all on me. I had memorized the schematics my handler sent up, the ones they'd obtained from their mole inside the International Astromining Alliance. And yes, by now, it shouldn't come as a shock to anyone that we have people on the inside. I set the charges *exactly* where they needed to go for maximum damage. I couldn't imagine how radiation levels were in the green. I needed information, and more importantly, I needed to talk to my handler.

The problem was, the two workers were now going the same way I was—toward Cul-De-Sac Two. I figured I'd enter the Neighborhood there, then work my way through to my apartment. I couldn't follow too closely behind those searchers or they'd hear me . . . but any other route would take me far too long. So I waited, feeling my blood pressure rise with each passing second. Things were simultaneously moving too fast and too slow. Municipal was sending in people to hunt me down, and you were probably spilling my secret already.

And I was stuck hiding behind an atmospherics panel.

I waited another minute, then went back to the panel and peered through the grating. It was all clear, so I climbed back into the maintenance conduit and secured the panel behind me.

I had a long way to go, and I was already out of time.

———

THERE'S a maintenance shed atop the fourth building in each of the Neighborhood's eight cul-de-sacs. Only maintenance crew like me and certain Municipal personnel have access to the sheds and the conduits, so I wasn't too worried about running into anyone in the shed on Two—other than the two workers blazing a trail in front of me. But their conversation with station operations seemed to have lit a sufficient fire under their asses. I hoped so.

I crept to the edge of the hatch leading down into the shed as silently as possible, took a deep breath, then peeked over the edge. The room was empty. The workers had already moved on. I headed down the ladder, happy to be out of the confines of the conduits.

A massive workbench ran the length of the shed, its surface littered with tools, spools of wire, tubing, solder, fiber optic cable, chains, and various lengths of plastic and metal. Bins spilled over with screws, fasteners, ribbon cables, green electronic boards, 3D printing composite, and a hardware store's bounty of other odds and ends. I barely gave it a glance as I moved directly to the floor-to-ceiling display of the Neighborhood. Each building was lit with dozens of LEDs, almost all of which were glowing green, with only a few scattered reds—which meant I'd gotten the placement and yield of the explosives that breached the Hyperloop right. If I hadn't, the red would have been a whole lot more prevalent, and things would be a great deal worse for the residents. Casualties are inevitable in my line of work, of course, but the goal was always to cripple operations at Darkside while sparing the people. And that's the truth, Thea. You might not believe me, but I tried, I really did. Sometimes, though, shit happens.

Like that friggin' boxcar, for instance, getting blown into the main concourse. That thing wasn't even supposed to be there when the charges went off. Someone fucked up. I mean, the whole point of trains is for them to run on time, right? Someone should look into that.

I was about to leave, but then I thought about you and what you were probably telling Municipal. Giving them my name wouldn't matter, because you couldn't possibly know my alias. But my description . . . *that* could do me in. I needed a new look.

I scanned the bench's surface, then started pulling open drawers, looking for a set of shears or scissors, and ultimately settling on a greasy pair of tin snips. The sharp edges made quick work of my braids, which I buried deep in a trash bin. I was sure it looked like a hack job, but it was the best I could do under the circumstances. I then started opening the old-fashioned metal lockers on the wall. The second locker I checked had one of the bright red jumpers we wear on the job. It was a little long, but it worked fine after I rolled up the pant legs. I applied a bit of grease from the tin snips to my bruised and swollen cheeks for good measure, then headed for the door.

As soon as I stepped from the shed onto the building's roof, a wave of sound washed over me. The air felt electric. I let the door close quietly behind me, watched as the security panel next to the handle turned from green to red, then peered over the edge of the roof at the unfolding chaos.

A mob of people was in the common area below, surging toward Cul-De-Sac Four, which was blocked off by Municipal security officers and makeshift barriers consisting of benches, tables, even a kid's soccer net. Some officers had bullhorns and were screaming at the residents to stay clear of the barrier; others were brandishing billy clubs and stun sticks. But the crowd looked undeterred. Something had them desperate to get into that particular cul-de-sac.

Heads turned at the sudden blare of a maintenance truck's horn. The vehicle was moving slowly through the crowd, making its way, like everyone else, toward Cul-De-Sac Four. The crowd parted reluctantly, then surged forward in the truck's wake, filling in the space it had carved through the swarm of bodies. When it reached the barrier in front of Four, the officers quickly cleared a space wide enough to grant the truck access, then raced to replace the barrier before anyone could rush through the gap. Those who tried got a stun stick to the chest.

I tore my eyes from the scene, ran to the roof access door, and headed down into the building. The stairwell was empty all the way down, which perhaps made me reckless. As I spilled out onto the ground floor, I nearly collided with two men, one bleeding from a gash on his forehead.

I tried to act natural. I reached out as if I was going to help the man with the bloody wound, but he waved me off, so instead I asked what was happening outside. The man helping his bleeding friend gave me news I never expected to hear. The saboteur had been captured, found in one of the conduits above Cul-De-Sac Four.

I knew, of course, that I had not been captured. I traced a mental map of the twists and turns I'd made after leaving you in that conduit, and realized we'd had our tussle in the area above Four. And that's when I knew they found you . . . and thought you were me.

As I stood there, frozen with fear of what might be happening to you, the guy with the wound looked me up and down, his gaze flitting between my fucked-up face and hacked-off hair. "What happened to you?" he asked.

I snapped out of it and came up with a quick excuse, told him I was elbow-deep in a scrubber unit when the shit hit the fan. As he looked me over, I wiped at the grease on my face, purposely making it worse to cover my bruises, and avoided making eye contact, because right then every fiber of me was screaming to get away.

The other guy saved me. "Well, I'd steer clear of the bull-shit out there. Municipal's gonna start knocking heads, if they haven't already," he said, then led his buddy past me and up into the stairwell. As soon as they turned the corner and were out of sight, I tore out of the building—straight into a madhouse.

Blasts of unintelligible screeching from bullhorns mixed with shouts and screams from all corners of the Neighborhood. I now understood why people were rushing toward Four. Everyone wanted to catch a glimpse of the person who'd turned their lives upside down—or so they thought.

I worked my way around the fringes of the mob toward the south end of the Neighborhood, sticking close enough to the masses that I didn't stand out as the one fish swimming against the current. Just as the crowd between me and my destination started to thin, a shout went up from behind me, followed by the blaring of the maintenance truck's horn as it exited Four.

Everyone knew what it contained. Or more accurately, *who* it contained.

I knew the smart thing to do would be to ignore what was happening behind me and just race to my apartment. But the pure unadulterated vitriol, the abject hatred pouring off the crowd got the best of me. I couldn't just leave, which I know is ironic coming from me, of all people. But at that moment, all I wanted to do was protect you—to protect my baby.

I turned back. There was no chance of pushing through the crowd—not that I had any idea what I'd do if I could. But I spotted an overturned trash bin on the sidewalk, next to a light pole. I climbed on top of it, using the pole for support, and got line of sight over everyone's heads.

The maintenance truck was creeping through the crowd, its bed rimmed with security officers swinging billy clubs and stabbing out with stun sticks at the enraged residents who were beating on the truck's cab and quarter panels. Even from higher up I couldn't see into the truck bed, but I was sure you were there, wisely laying low. Ahead of the truck, other security guards were clearing a path to the common area, trying to get you out of the Neighborhood and upstairs to Municipal as fast as possible.

As I silently cursed the lynch mob, someone called out,

"Yo, Mae!" It took me a second to remember *I* was Mae. Up here, at Darkside, I'm Mae Green from maintenance.

It was my coworker Inky. She lives in my building. Her real name's Inga Somethingorother, but we call her Inky because she has albinism, and by the end of every shift she gets so cruddy she ends up resembling a Rorschach inkblot.

Inky was weaving through the crowd, elbowing aside anyone who got in her way. I climbed down and grabbed her outstretched hand just as she reached the light pole.

"You see anything?" she asked, thumbing back to the truck, and I told her I couldn't. She took in my appearance and asked about my hair with a smirk on her face, which confirmed my guess that it looked hideous.

"Just looking for a change," I said, running a hand over the nubs of my braids, then added, "That and too much gin last night, which is how I fell off the couch right onto my face." I pointed to my bruised cheeks.

"Been there," she said, seemingly satisfied with my shoddy explanation. I asked her if she was working that night, just to change topics. She told me she was supposed to but heard that Municipal was going to "put it all on lockdown."

I feigned a puzzled look and asked if she meant they were locking down the Neighborhood, which would have made sense given the craziness all around us. But before she could answer, another cry went up from the crowd. When it eventually died down, Inky told me Municipal was locking it *all* down —the whole station. "Get ready for some medieval shit around here," she said.

"Well, hell, then I'm gonna go take a nap," I told her, trying to act nonchalant to mask my exploding anxiety. I gave Inky a quick squeeze on her shoulder, knowing she had no idea it would be the last time we would ever see each other. Despite her being up here and helping to keep this infernal operation humming along, she was good people.

She gave me a small nod and let herself be swept toward the common area. I watched her disappear into the crowd, then hurried once more toward my apartment. I cast one last worried glance over my shoulder at the mob as I went, but I knew that at the moment there wasn't a thing I could do for you.

Like me, you were on your own.

4

Hints, Allegations, and Things Left Unsaid

THEA'S HEAD smacks down on the steel truck bed as the vehicle jumps the curb. Her eyes snap open. Shouts and screams fill the air. She blinks hard, trying to clear her fuzzy brain, desperate to understand where she is and why she's surrounded by these people dressed in black, yelling and pointing away from where she's lying near their heavy cap-toed boots.

A bottle arcs through the air and shatters on the truck's cab. She tries to protect her head from the falling glass but discovers she can't because her wrists are bound behind her back. She tucks her head against her chin and twists onto her side, which is difficult because her ankles are similarly bound. Her movement draws the attention of one of the people near her, who she now realizes are Municipal security. He turns and looks down on her, his face shield fogged over.

He grabs her collar and hauls her up toward him. "Don't you fucking move!" he screams into her face, then shoves her down again.

A starfield explodes in her eyes as her head once again bounces off the steel truck bed. She tastes copper from her bitten tongue. As she blinks away the stars and spits out a red-streaked glob, she watches the man who screamed at her seconds ago crack a woman across the head with his billy club. Blood flies from the woman's split skull as she teeters on the shoulders of the person who's raised her high enough to see inside the truck bed. The officer rears back, readying another vicious swing, but before he can finish the job, Thea kicks out with both feet and buckles the man's knee.

He wheels around and raises his blood-smattered face shield. A toothy smile breaks out on his acne-laced face as he glares down at her, his billy club still raised, now with a new target in mind.

Thea tries to stay his hand. "Wait, I'm the captain of the *Zeph*—"

The young officer's club comes down. Pain explodes across the crown of her head and through her shoulders. A black hole begins to materialize before her. She sputters, fights, claws against the pull, but it's no use. The void swallows her whole.

———

BURPS AND BLIPS OF SYLLABLES, then actual words materialize from somewhere deep and distant.

Contained.

Riot.

Cell.

Wordswordswordswords. None of them make sense. Just meaningless noise—

Murder.

Traitor.

Traitor, yes. That one . . . *that* one gets through to her. That's the truth of it, isn't it? The sum of it all, she thinks, the muzzle on her mind loosening its grip. She strains against the weight of her eyelids. Like bags of sand, sand left by the sandman to bring her a dreeeeam. He was the cutest that she'd ever seeeeen. Elliott and his moon beeeeeeam.

She feels like she's flying. And she thinks she must have been doing so for a long time, too, because her shoulders are so sore. She wants to find a place to land, so she forces her eyes open the tiniest bit to search for a tree. Any branch will do, just so she can rest a bit. But there are none. No trees, no branches. Just a scuffed floor, boots at the edges of her vision treading on dull gray linoleum. That's when she realizes she's being carried, her arms twisted awkwardly behind her. She feels pain near her ankles, the bindings cutting into her shins. Her neck spasms as she tilts her head up and sees a door with blinding white light shooting out of it, straight into her brain stem. She winces against the light and her head sags down too fast, so fast that her world swirls and the voices and the noises start to break apart, slipping from her as the pull of the void begins to take her under again . . .

Until the first slap.

She feels herself sliding sideways, but rough hands grab her shoulders and set her upright again, thumping her back against something hard. Pins and needles stab both arms as blood rushes back into them. She opens her eyes in time to see the palm descending. The second slap does its job, like a shot of adrenaline to the heart. She absorbs the blow, then turns and looks into the eyes of the pimply bastard from the truck that hit her with his billy club.

Spittle speckles her cheek when he yells, "Wake up!"

She can't wipe it away, her hands still bound behind her back. She's seated on a cold metal bench. "Where am I?" she asks.

"Fuck you," he says, just as the door behind him flies open and Gasira Achebe strides into the room.

She stops dead in her tracks when she sees Thea, then quickly pushes the young man aside and takes in Thea's injuries, focusing specifically on the matted blood atop her head.

"Undo her bindings," Achebe says to the man without taking her eyes off Thea's bloody skull.

"But ma'am—"

Achebe wheels around on him and repeats her command through clenched teeth.

The only color on the officer's pale face comes from the blossoming red in his cheeks as he takes out a pair of snips and cuts the zip ties binding Thea's hands behind her back. She really wants to rub her wrists and enjoy the relief pouring into her at being able to move her arms again, but she doesn't want to miss her chance as the young man kneels to cut her ankle bindings.

She drops an elbow on the top of his head, grabs the back of it, and smashes his face into the edge of the bench she's seated on.

He stumbles backward, clutching his crushed nose.

"That's for me and the woman you clubbed, you fucking animal," Thea says, glaring at the man around Achebe, who's inserted herself between the two of them.

"What are you talking about?" Achebe asks.

"Big man went to town on a resident before he turned on me," Thea snaps. "Go ask her yourself, assuming she isn't in the morgue."

Achebe turns to the officer. "Is this true?"

"Ma'am, they were out of control," he says, blood dripping through his fingers as he clasps his ruined nose. "I did what I needed to do."

Achebe reaches toward him and rips the bodycam off his vest. Waggling it at him, she says, "We'll see," and then dismisses him. He glares at Thea before leaving the room.

"Sorry about that," Thea says.

Achebe kneels down, picks up the snips the officer dropped

when Thea attacked him, and uses them to cut the zip ties around Thea's ankles. "Young and stupid. But I'm sure he's not the only one who went overboard down there. The whole station has been a madhouse since the explosions."

She sits on the bench next to Thea and looks at the caked blood mixed with her braids. "You probably have a concussion. I'm going to get a doctor to come take a look at you."

"I'll be okay," Thea says. "Tell me what's going on."

Achebe settles back against the wall so she's sitting in the same fashion as Thea. She looks equally exhausted.

"The helium-3 reactor the saboteur hit is destroyed, but the fail-safe we installed a few months ago worked perfectly. Radiation leakage was minimal."

"What about the people who were inside?" Thea asks.

Achebe doesn't answer, but the way she shakes her head gives Thea all the answer she needs. They're gone. "The damage to the main concourse is our biggest issue," Achebe adds. "It's pretty bad."

"I know. I was there when the boxcar crashed into it. Barely made it out before the safety door closed."

After a few beats, Achebe recovers from her shock. "Breach foam is holding for now," she says, "but until we can get outside and assess the extent of the damage, the Neighborhood, the Hub, and the docks are all locked down. I just issued a shelter-in-place order to all of Darkside Station."

"Can I call my crew?"

"Don't worry. I sent word that we have you." Achebe turns to face Thea directly, waits for Thea to meet her eye. "I'll get you back to them soon. But first . . ."

Achebe's demeanor sharpens, her gaze once again penetrating, per usual. That's when Thea realizes she hasn't addressed the elephant in the room. "You know I had nothing to do with this, right?"

"Of course," Achebe says, waving toward the door where

the bloodied young officer and the rest of the rumor mill is probably huddling. "But tell me how you ended up in the maintenance conduits."

As Thea stares into Achebe's dark eyes, the intelligence therein undimmed by the weariness etched everywhere else on her face, she is suddenly overcome with fear—an irrational, paralyzing, unwelcome fear about telling this person, this person who she respects and trusts, that her *mother* is the one to blame. As irrational as it is, she feels somehow implicated in her mother's crimes. The daughter of a murderer must somehow be tainted too, right? Does evil skip a generation, or is it buried too deep in the genes, an inescapable part of her own operating system?

She stutters, unable to form the words, overcome by conflicting emotions. Achebe rests her hand on Thea's thigh and gives it a gentle squeeze, but instead of steadying her, the gesture makes Thea feel worse, like she's letting Achebe down.

"Are you okay?" Achebe asks, concern or confusion, Thea can't be sure, in the woman's furrowed brow.

She sucks in a ragged breath, fights back her irrational guilt, musters her strength and conviction, and is about to spill everything when Brian Allgood bursts into the room.

Surprised, Achebe says, "Admiral, how did you get here?"

Allgood ignores the question as he strides toward them. Thea flinches in anticipation of some sort of attack and is stunned when he instead takes her hand.

"Are you okay?" he asks with concern, his eyes taking in the bloody and bruised sight of her.

Confusion replacing her trepidation, Thea tells him she's fine and slowly pulls her hand back.

"Admiral, I issued an order for everyone to remain put," Achebe says, not trying to hide the annoyance in her voice. "So tell me why you aren't aboard the *Bellwether* right now."

He grants her only a quick glance. "Because you're not in

charge anymore, Gasira," he says, then turns his attention back to Thea. "What were you doing in the conduits, Captain?"

"What do you mean?" Achebe says, cutting him off and hopping off the bench so that her two inches of height on Allgood are undeniable.

"The Alliance has finally had enough of your incompetence," he says. "They've put me in charge."

"Nonsense. Satellite comms are restricted. There's no way you've been in touch with the IAA."

"I have. Of course I have," he says, irritation pouring off him. "Your rules never applied to me."

Realizing the door to the room is open, Achebe walks over and shuts it, then turns back to Allgood. "This is preposterous," she begins, and it's clear she has more to say, but just then Brian Allgood's temper breaks.

"You can complain about getting fired later, Gasira!" he practically shouts. "Right now, I want to know what Captain Watts was doing in the goddamn maintenance conduits just minutes after the fucking world turned upside down!"

For the first time in Thea's experience with the woman, Gasira Achebe appears to be at a loss. She takes a step toward Allgood, some sort of retort poised on her lips, but then stops, crosses her arms, and goes silent.

Allgood turns his red face on Thea, his earlier concern for her well-being apparently a distant memory.

"Well?" he says, like a parent to a child caught sneaking in after curfew.

"I was chasing the saboteur," she says. "That's why I was in the conduit. I was trying to catch them."

"Are you sure it was the saboteur?" Achebe asks, exchanging glances with Allgood, who looks equally shocked.

"Yes, I'm positive," Thea says.

No one says anything for a few seconds, the air in the room

charged with anticipation. Finally, unable to bear the silence any longer, Allgood's exasperation gets the better of him.

"Did you recognize them?" he asks, moronically enunciating each syllable in the way people sometimes do when talking to someone who doesn't speak their language. And that's when Thea realizes Allgood's earlier civility wasn't born out of concern for her well-being. He only cared that she was okay because her not being all right would deny him the chance to win, to beat her, to put her in her place. Any foe not vanquished *by him* is a lost opportunity, and that's something he can't stomach.

Thea glances over at Achebe, Allgood's latest conquest, and makes a crucial decision—a decision from which there is no going back.

She glares at Allgood's smug face, slowly shakes her head, and says, "No. I didn't recognize them."

5

Dark Secrets

THE SCENT of Asaad's vindaloo filled the hallway. My mouth immediately began to water, and my stomach groaned. I can't tell you how many times I'd come home from a shift to find a tiffin waiting for me outside my door, fluffy naan in the top tier perfectly steamed by a generous portion of one of the sweet old man's delicacies. Utter perfection every time! And when I'd return the empty container, he'd pour us a few fingers of McDowell's and we'd shoot the shit, which I think was the real motivation behind his generosity. Space can be a lonely place. We'd drink our whiskey, and I'd tell him about the latest happenings in maintenance, and he'd entertain me with gossip he'd heard at the general store. Those nights drinking and laughing with Asaad were some of the best moments up here.

It would have been nice to taste my friend's cooking one last time.

As I reached my apartment, I tried to resist looking down the hallway, but my eyes were drawn to a loose piece of the yellow-and-red striped security tape crisscrossing Bobby's door —the tape meant to secure his murder scene. *My* murder scene.

You see, I'm a murderer, Thea.

Of course, that's not exactly news. Lots of people have died by my hand. Too many, to be sure. But every war comes with collateral damage—and yes, this is a war. It's a war for humanity's soul, and casualties can't be avoided. But Bobby Bean . . . that damned fool. I feel sorry for a lot of the deaths I caused, but I don't feel sorry about that one.

He tried to make a quick buck by selling that booby-trapped case of printer material to your pilot. Bobby didn't know what it contained or how dangerous it was, but still. He shouldn't have done it, and his greed and stupidity almost killed you. And it *did* kill Elliott, that poor man. Plus, after what happened to your ship, he could have connected me to the case. So something had to be done, and I did it.

My guts twisted as I stood there in the hallway, watching the security tape flap around in the updraft created by the building's ventilation system. I'll never forget the look on his face when I hit him, again and again. So much blood, all over the place, running all down the front of him as he sat there in that stupid chair of his. So stupid . . .

I don't know if it brings you any sort of comfort. Probably not. But please know that I made him pay for what he did.

———

I HURRIED to my bedroom closet and grabbed my go-bag from the top shelf, quickly tossing in an extra hoodie and some socks because my safe space runs cold. Then I ran to my bed and snatched my ID, some cash just in case, and my bottle of cloza-pine from the nightstand. I looked around and didn't see anything else I needed. But just as I was about to leave, I saw your nine-year-old face. That elementary school picture with the bright yellow *Keep Austin Weird* t-shirt and those blue jeans with the rainbow patch on the back pocket. Do you remember those? Man, what a picture! I kept it taped to the lamp next to my bed. It was the last thing I saw every night before I fell asleep. Your wide smile showing off a missing front tooth. My baby girl.

I couldn't leave it behind. I took the picture, then headed for the door.

———

YOU BIG-SHOT MINERS don't tend to slum it in the Neighborhood, so let me tell you a little bit about it.

The Neighborhood's eight cul-de-sacs are nearly identical. They're so similar, in fact, that the residents nicknamed them *the octuplets*. Sure, everyone does their best to try and individualize things so that their homes don't feel so cookie cutter, but if you step back from the largely cosmetic customizations, the entire residential construct is a case study in uniformity.

There are, however, exceptions.

Tenement Four of Cul-De-Sac Seven—my apartment building—is directly below the main concourse. In fact, it's the only residential building built beneath any part of Darkside Station. Some people claim that you can feel vibrations and hear the occasional loud noises from the main concourse, but this was my second year in that building, and I'd never heard or felt a damn thing. You know people, though. They'll do anything to make a case that they have it harder than the next guy.

There's something else unique about Tenement Four in Cul-De-Sac Seven—something that very few people know about. In the original station design, most of Darkside's critical systems were routed below ground to help shield them from regolith wear and tear and the occasional micrometeorite impact. But as the docks and refinery grew to meet the increasing demands of the industry, maintaining some of those underground systems became impractical. So about fifteen years ago, engineering decided to reroute some of the station's major systems like power and communications to the surface. As a result, a few of the original maintenance conduits weren't necessary anymore and were sealed off. But they're still there. And more importantly, most of the station's systems are still accessible from inside these abandoned conduits. They didn't bother disconnecting everything; in a pinch, after all, these systems could serve as a backup. Redundancy is the key to life in space. No, they simply shut off the lights and closed the safety doors.

This is why the New Muses landed me a job on the maintenance crew when they sent me here in the guise of highly capable mechanic Mae Green. It's also why they secured this particular apartment for me in the Neighborhood—for its access to these old conduits. Within them was a long-forgotten utility room, which I had turned into my safe room. That's the place I was now desperate to get to.

There was no one in the stairwell, and I made it to the roof without incident. As I walked to the maintenance shed, I wondered where you were, what you were doing—and if you were okay. By now you were probably up in Municipal, spilling your guts. Man, I'd love to have been a fly on the wall. What would you say? How could you even, I don't know, *explain* to them who I was? But I didn't get to wonder about it for too long because I was startled by a sudden spasm in my forearm.

I pulled back my sleeve and saw a quick burst of pink light from my tracker—the device my handler had placed there a lifetime ago on a remote beach before he sent me up here. The glow was there for a split second at most before going dark. I waited for it to happen again, but it didn't. Still, the fact that it *had* activated, even if only briefly, told me my handler was looking for me. I felt a wave of relief, and even more anxious to get to my safe room where I could make contact.

I rubbed the spot on my forearm where the tracker was buried, hoping my handler had a plan. I really don't know much about him. In fact, I don't even know his name. But I know he always has a backup plan.

I placed my thumb on the scanner next to the maintenance shed door, worried they might have already disabled my access. But the panel went from red to green, and I was able to go inside.

The lights in the shed flickered to life.

After engineering decommissioned the redundant conduits, they simply sealed the ladder leading up to the entrance inside one of the walls and placed the maintenance shed's lockers over top. As far as I was concerned, that only made things easier.

I opened my locker door and pushed my spare jumpers aside. Clips I'd installed on either side let me detach the back of the locker from the rest of the unit. I pinched the clips one by one, slid the metal to the side, and revealed the cut-away I'd made in the wall of the shed. The bottom rungs of the ladder were exposed, leading up to the entrance of the abandoned conduit.

The safety door sealing off the entrance to the old conduit is airtight—meaning there's no oxygen being pumped inside. Usually I'd simply open the door and wait for fresh oxygen to flow in from the shed, but today I didn't have that kind of time; I needed to find portable breathers. Every shed keeps a few on hand for emergencies, and it turned out there were three in this shed, but one had a rubber band around it and a sticky note attached that said "defective." I laughed when I saw it, because fixing it was probably on *my* to-do list at some point, and I'd never gotten to it. I dropped the busted one back into the drawer and took the other two.

I put on the headlamp from my go-bag, adjusting the straps

now that I'd cut off a bunch of my hair. When it was tight on my head, I slipped into my locker, closed the front door behind me, and maneuvered into the space next to the ladder. Then I reached back into the locker, rearranged my clothes so they hung normally, and clipped the back wall of the locker in place.

As I ascended the ladder, I rooted around inside the go-bag for my electromag popper—which was the whole reason I needed the bag in the first place. The black rectangular device's magnetic surface adhered to the sealed safety door with a click, and its only button glowed red. Light circled around the edge of the button after I pressed it, resembling one of those *processing* wheel animations on a computer. Then the device emitted a soft beep, and the button turned from red to green. The wings on the safety door irised open with a hiss, but only slightly—the device feeds the door just enough power to disengage. I had to pry the door open the rest of the way manually.

Once I'd climbed up into the abandoned conduit, I reached for the manual crank to reseal the door and nearly jumped out of my skin when I touched a spiderweb laced across the handle. What the hell are spiders doing in space, for fuck's sake! I pawed the webs away then pulled the sticky strands off my fingers like the strings of a popped bubble-gum bubble. The crank was grindingly slow, but steadily drew the blades of the door together. My electromag device then locked them in place once again.

I collapsed to the floor of the conduit, heart racing, clawing at my bag to get one of the breathers. The air was really thin, but my past forays in here had clearly left enough oxygen behind for space insects to thrive. I fumbled to get the breather over my headlamp, cursing myself for being so stupid and not putting it on first. Tears sprang to my eyes as I finally got it in place and took my first deep breaths.

Only then did I allow the sobs. I let it all crash in, everything that had happened in the last few hours.

The bombs.

The station.

My life up here, now over.

You.

I clicked off the headlamp and sat in the darkness—just sat in the safety of that secret place for a few minutes and let myself feel everything.

What did you tell them when they got you upstairs, Thea?

Are you in trouble?

Are they going to try to use you against me? Will you let them?

How much do you hate me?

My head felt like it was going to pop off. It was too much. I rooted through my bag, found my pills, and took one to help me calm down. Things have gotten better over the years, by the way. I still need my meds, but the episodes don't come as often, which I think proves that leaving Texas and your dad behind was the right choice. For me, anyway.

After a few minutes, I started to feel better, so I clicked on my headlamp and began the crawl to my safe room . . . and whatever would happen next.

6

Compromised

"HOLD ON, I want this part recorded," Allgood says, then opens the door and waves to someone in the hallway. Thea expects Achebe to intervene, but instead she walks over and fills a glass with water from the tiny sink in the corner of the room.

Achebe hands the glass to Thea, who takes a small sip and says, "Are you okay with this?"

"It's a good idea. Will be useful for the powers that be back home," Achebe replies.

"No, I meant with him taking over."

Achebe glances back at Allgood. "I don't have much of a choice right now. And frankly, Thea, we need this to stop. So if this is what the IAA wants—"

"Okay, Captain," Allgood says, cutting Achebe short as he steps aside to allow someone new to enter the room.

Darcey.

She races over and swallows Thea in a hug. "Thank God you're okay," she says. "When I heard it was you . . ."

Darcey pulls away and winces as she takes in Thea's injuries for the first time. As Darcey rises up to look at her crusty head wound, Thea examines her friend's face and sees the genuine concern written all over it. And for the first time since reuniting with her old classmate, Thea is happy that she's here. Which also makes her worry that she does indeed have a concussion.

"If you're done," Allgood says, waving Darcey to the space behind where he's taken up a seat next to Achebe.

Darcey meets Thea's eyes, and after a beat the two women nod to one another, coming to some silent agreement—a truce, or perhaps a new beginning. Only time will tell.

Darcey gets in position, aims her handheld at Thea, then tells her boss she's ready.

"This is Brian Allgood, Admiral of the Conglomerate Fleet, and I am speaking with Captain Thea Watts of the civilian operation Watts Astromining," Allgood begins, not bothering to include Achebe for the record. "Captain Watts, please tell us what happened."

They make her start at the beginning. Seeing the refinery explode from the *Zephyr*'s lift, fighting the mad rush of people trying to get to safety, nearly getting sucked out of the station after a Hyperloop boxcar ruptured the main concourse wall, and the obstruction in the Hub safety door that saved her life. They listen with silent, rapt attention as she tells them everything, until she finally gets to the part where the person she's identified as the saboteur shows up in the Hub.

"What did the saboteur look like?" Allgood jumps in after holding his tongue longer than Thea would have imagined was possible.

She reaches for the glass of water sitting next to her on the bench and takes a few sips, buying some time, trying to calm her nerves.

After a few more seconds, Achebe asks, "Captain Watts, was it a man or a woman?"

Thea sets the empty glass aside. "I couldn't tell. They were dressed in an all-black body suit with a face mask and tight-fitting skull cap."

"That's it?" Allgood says. "That's all you've got?"

Thea doesn't respond. The silence in the room grows sticky and thick. Achebe, Darcey, and Allgood trade glances as Thea stares at the floor.

She thinks about coming clean, knows this is her chance. She can easily claim to have been confused, blame her earlier memory lapse on her head wound. They're going to get her mother anyway. What's to be gained by concealing her identity? She's not even sure why she lied to Allgood in the first place, except that when she looks up into his reddening face, she simply doesn't want *him* to have her, suddenly can't bear the thought of it being him that could bring her mother to justice. In fact, she doesn't want *anyone* to get her mother, because *she* wants to be the one to find her—*deserves* to be the one to find her.

Achebe leans forward and lightly touches Thea's thigh, snapping her out of her trance. "Thea, are you okay?"

Thea nods to Achebe, then meets Allgood's penetrating gaze. "Sorry. I wish I could help."

As Allgood settles back in his chair, Achebe takes over. "Is there anything about this person that stood out at all?" she asks. "Every detail matters."

Thea hesitates under the guise of trying to recall more about the saboteur, then says, "They had a backpack of some sort, which they dropped when they took off running."

"A backpack?"

"I think that's what it was."

Allgood swivels and points to the man standing guard near the door, who then turns and leaves. "Did they say anything?" Allgood asks.

Fear ices up Thea's spine as she remembers her mother's words in the Hub as they were standing face to face.

Hi, Thea. I'm glad you're okay.

"Umm . . ." Thea says, picking up the empty glass and tipping out a droplet of water.

Taking the glass from her quivering hand, Achebe asks again if she's okay. Thea gives her a weak nod then turns back to Allgood. "I'm sorry, what was the question?"

"Did the person you encountered in the Hub say anything to you?" he repeats, once again leaning forward in his chair.

The room feels warm, too warm, and her head begins to swim. She grips the edges of the bench. "No, not that I remember."

"That's fine," Allgood says. "We can check the security feed from the Hub."

The room begins to swirl as Thea realizes her mistake. How could she be so stupid! Of *course* they'll check the security cameras—and see that her mother said something. Which will make them question everything else she's told them thus far. *It's over*, she thinks, swallowing down a flood of acid overrunning her stomach. She's about to confess when Achebe jumps in.

"There's no footage," she says. "We lost the cameras when the station temporarily lost power."

"Are you *kidding* me?" Allgood says. In an instant he's out of his chair, in Thea's face, slapping his hand on the bench next to her. "You're gonna have to do better than this, Captain Watts. You're the only one who saw this person. Think!"

In response, Thea lurches to the side, vomits on the floor, then goes limp. Allgood has to grab her shoulders to keep her from falling off the bench.

———

A *KERPLUNK* FOLLOWED by an ice pick in her deltoid snaps Thea back to consciousness.

A woman in light blue scrubs removes the autoinjector

from Thea's arm. "Easy, Captain," she says, placing the device back in a small black case. "It'll take a few hours before you feel like yourself again."

"What *was* that?" Thea asks, as Achebe helps her sit up. Other than the doctor, the two of them are the only ones left in the room, which someone has mercifully cleaned.

"It's a dendritic stabilizer," the woman says, hurriedly collecting her things. "You have a mild concussion and will need to rest a day or so. Unfortunately, we can't keep you here. We have more casualties than we know what to do with." To Achebe, the doctor adds, "I really have to get back," then exits the room.

Thea touches the top of her head and feels a dried blob of liquid bandage where the skin was split open.

"Sorry for the rush job," Achebe says. "Medical has got their hands full."

"Where're the others?" Thea asks.

Achebe helps Thea to her feet. "Back at the *Bellwether*, I presume." She holds Thea's arm as she shuffles toward a wheelchair in the corner. "The admiral instructed me to tell you that if you remembered anything else, you are to immediately contact Lieutenant Grey."

"Roger that," Thea says, then stops and turns to Achebe. "I'm sorry. The whole thing is kind of fuzzy."

"You've had quite a day. We all have. Maybe you'll recall more after you get some rest. I have a surface transport waiting to take you over to Dock D."

"Why a transport?"

"The concourse is still compromised."

Thea settles into the chair, thankful to be off her feet. "What about you?" she asks.

Achebe smiles at her, once again radiating the determination Thea has come to expect from her. "First, I'm gonna have a drink—a big one. Then I'm gonna talk to some people back home. Brian Allgood isn't the only one with influence back on Earth."

"I hope you're successful," Thea says. "I don't think people are gonna be happy about him calling the shots."

"Well, even if he is, I don't think it'll be for very long," Achebe says, steering Thea's chair out of the room. "Brian's a lot of things, but he's also relentless. He'll find whoever did this. And I have no doubt, he'll make them pay for fucking up his world."

———

THE CLEAR DOME slowly lowers into place, followed by a gentle burst of air as the vehicle becomes airtight. The interior glow changes from red to a warm yellow. "Prepare for departure," the autopilot says as the station's exterior doors gradually swing open. Seconds later, the transport crawls outside.

Thea is alone in the vehicle. Once it's clear of the station, she curls up on the bench seat, resting her cheek on the cool fabric. Despite the decreased gravity inside the transport, her body feels heavy.

"Destination in eleven minutes," the autopilot says.

She closes her eyes, giving in to the exhaustion weighing on her like a blanket. But she can't rest; her body's still buzzing from the medicine coursing through her. She turns onto her back and forces her eyes open with a whimper. Clusters of red, blue, and amber hull lighting break up the vast tapestry of the starfield above her.

The fleet.

Guilt presses down on her as she gazes up at the lights of the ships circling above her. An unrepentant liar's guilt. A backstabbing colleague's guilt.

A daughter's guilt.

Tears flow as she tries to measure the magnitude of her

deception, imagining the looks of betrayal and mistrust and contempt when they all eventually find out about what she did. Because they will find out. They'll find out it was her mother all along, and that Thea knew it—and lied about it.

And for what?

She forces herself off the bench and moves to the front of the transport, watching as it moves toward the docks. To the right, engineering drones zip above the roof of the main concourse, lasers beaming down as they scan the structure. Light from inside the concourse streams through the silicate glass walls and illuminates the pocked gray lunar surface, except for the section destroyed by the Hyperloop boxcar. *No— destroyed by my mother*, she corrects herself. She stares at the dark and damaged section and seethes with anger and confusion until it passes out of sight.

"Thea, do you read?"

Hearing Rory's voice on her handheld triggers a ragged sob, so instant and fierce that it hurts Thea's chest. She scrambles to pull the device out of her pocket and tap its cracked glass. "I'm here, Rory," she says, her voice thick with emotion.

"Oh, thank God! We're here too, Thea. All of us." Thea can hear Beetle's and Lola's cheers in the background. "Are you okay?"

Guilt, once again.

A captain's guilt. A friend's guilt.

"No," Thea says. No point in pretending. "Not yet anyway."

"I get that," Rory says. "Let's get you home."

Thea's throat seizes as the dam she's built inside herself shatters, the sudden release of emotions threatening to pull her under. She had started to think of this place as home and her crew as her family. Rory, Beetle, Lola . . . Elliott. The family she'd always wanted. For so long, her mother's absence had been at the center of everything bad in her life—the years of anger and sadness piled up and scarred over. She'd gotten used to the feeling of it. But after her dad died and she came here, she was finally, *finally* getting to the point where she could tuck it all away, forget about her mother and move on. And now . . . she's back. *My mother destroyed my old home and family, and now she's here to destroy my new ones.*

And worst of all, I'm helping her.

She pounds the seat. Howls at the stars. Screams at the universe on display all around her for answers, already in mourning for a life that she'd just barely begun to live.

By the time the transport rounds the edge of the station and pulls into Dock D's airlock, she's spent. The roar from the airlock pressurization procedure, the autopilot's voice telling her the cycle is complete, and the hiss of escaping air as the transport's dome opens barely break through to her. It's only when Rory lifts her out of the transport that she realizes she's inside the station again. He kisses her forehead while Lola and Beetle grab hold and the four of them hug. She wants to cry from joy and shame and exhaustion, but there is nothing left to give, nothing else to do but let Rory carry her home and tuck her into her bed.

Like her mother used to do, which ruins the moment.

Her mother ruins everything.

7

Communication

STANDING up after so long on my hands and knees was a relief. I locked the door behind me and immediately connected the communication terminal's bare wires to an old loader battery. To stay off operations' radar, I never fired up the safe room. Instead, everything I needed ran off power supplies I'd filched from here and there around the station.

I paced back and forth, encouraging blood back into my numb extremities, and after what felt like an eternity, the computer's home screen finally appeared. It takes a while because the machine routes through a twisted series of proxies to mask its location. A dialog box covered most of the screen, warning that satellite communications were restricted, which wasn't a surprise. Of course they'd locked everything down. But I had a way around that too.

My handler had sent me an old, tattered, fiftieth-anniversary edition of *Snow Crash* in his first care package from home. You know the book. You and your dad used to go on and on about it your freshman year of high school. I still remember sitting there at the kitchen table and listening to you debate, neither of you looking for a contribution from me despite the fact that I'd read the book too. But that wasn't unusual. By then, I'd given up trying to get into your "club," and you weren't letting anyone else in anyway.

The page my handler dog-eared starts the scene where the protagonist, Hiro, is talking to a character called the Librarian about the destruction of the Tower of Babel, the original info-calypse when man built a tower to heaven and God knocked it down. He gave us numerous languages to confound us, so the story goes, then scattered humans around the world as punishment for our hubris. Of course my handler picked that scene! It's perfect. How dare we put ourselves on God's level. The audacity of humans trying to exceed our Earthly bounds. And yet here we all are, doing it again. This time on the friggin' moon. Parable, fable, holy text. Cautionary tale. It doesn't matter. I wouldn't be here, doing these things, if only we'd learned the original lesson. Technology is our generations' tower, Thea, and it needs to be knocked down.

Don't believe me? Fine, I'll give you an example, one that should hit close to home.

Technology—in this case a so-called *advanced metacognitive system*—is why your boyfriend's first ship was destroyed.

Let me explain.

Our idea was simple: install a virus in the *Victor Hugo*'s systems designed to paralyze her tethering mechanism. It would seem like a mechanical issue, which would get the station's dock engineers involved. Then, as they fixed the issue, their diagnostics would become infected with a Trojan horse, and we'd gain access to the Darkside network. That's all we wanted. But no, the *Hugo*'s damn *machine brain* took over, triggering that terrible series of events and ruining months of hard work. Killing some folks in the process, too. Like I said, collateral damage happens, but in this case, it didn't need to.

It's just like *artificial* sweetener. We all know it's terrible for us, yet we suck it down, day after day, ignoring the damage it's doing. Rotting us from the inside out. It's the same with *artificial* intelligence.

And for the record, that's where I would have gone had you and your dad let me into your exclusive little debate club. That would have been, and still is, my argument. I think we could have had a good time talking about it, the three of us.

But anyway . . . enough of that.

I looked at the dog-eared page and started entering the first letter of each line, just going straight down the left margin. This sequence constituted the special encryption key, a one-time-use backdoor into the lunar satellite network. The backdoor, and the associated key, go back decades, all the way to the beginning of Darkside's expansion, when we had an operative working on the IAA's system architecture. No one else knew about it. But if it had somehow been discovered, somewhere along the way . . . then there was a chance that Municipal and the IAA could figure out where I was transmitting from, and maybe even where I was transmitting *to*, on Earth. They could locate my handler, or worse, find the Muses' home base. So this was a big risk. I thought about it, and all the other reasons not to play the card I was about to play, but came up short. I needed guidance from my leadership, so I typed the final letters from the book and hit the enter key.

A pop-up window filled the screen, indicating that the key was accepted and I'd gained access to the lunar network. I ran my sleeve across the dusty display and tapped the green telephone logo in the bottom-right corner of the window. After waiting a few seconds, per our protocol, I terminated the call.

I then turned my attention to making the safe room a bit more hospitable. I climbed atop a workbench in the corner, reached up to the ceiling into a cluster of webs, and grabbed hold of a steel crank, the white paint on its handle chipped and flaking. It's a battle every time, but eventually the mechanism yielded, and I was able to move the handle, the flow of air increasing as I spun it twice around. The vent tied into the core ventilation system that supplied the docks and main concourse, which was why I always closed it when I left—just in case someone noticed the decreased flow and went investigating. Just like with the power, I needed to do everything I could to keep my safe room off the grid.

As oxygen flowed in, I removed my breather and let the air current from the vent wash over my face. The smell was dusty and electric, but wonderful all the same. Something inside me unclenched. Not the part of us that seizes up in the cold, though the warmth that spread across my shoulders and torso was delicious after the deep chill of the abandoned conduit. No, the relief was from the momentary safety I felt. Solace in the storm, one I created the second those bombs in the refinery and Hyperloop went off. I luxuriated in the air's embrace, allowing myself one full minute of peace. I knew it was exactly one minute, because as much as I wanted to, I couldn't help myself from counting the seconds. I added them to the other seconds I'd been subconsciously ticking off since I'd terminated the call to Earth. But I don't need to explain this to you. You know how my brain works.

I hopped off the bench and checked the screen. No response. There was no choice but to continue to wait, my mind running wild with what might be going on back home. How people were reacting to the news, how the global community was processing the blow I had struck for humanity whether they wanted me to or not. So many sheep, enslaved to a technology that's slowly warping our collective spirit, rotting us from the inside. Turning us into something ugly and thin, devoid of nourishment.

Disaster is an astrological term meaning "bad star," so says the Librarian on the dog-eared page, which I ripped out and shoved into my mouth. My saliva mixed with the ink and paper and created an earthy mush. I moved it to one cheek and sucked the taste out of the wad. Bad star on the ground, indeed, so here I was among the stars to fix it. It was my job, and I thought I did okay. Bumpy here and there, but in line with what we'd mapped out. I'd only know for sure, though, when he called back.

Why wasn't he calling back?

Other than the antiquated communications terminal, which was surrounded by stacks of spiral-bound manuals and a lone clipboard hanging from a peg with a work schedule from sixteen years ago, the room was mostly filled with old handheld tools, a lot of raw tubing, wiring, fiber optic cable, and fasteners—all stuff that the refinery churns out in droves, which is why they never bothered to collect any of it before sealing the conduits. I'd since added a fold-away cot, lanterns, battery-powered space heater, food, and some spare clothes. And of course, the tools of my particular trade. A few 3D-printed weapons, a chemical kit I'd mostly assembled from late-night trips to the refinery and whatever random things I could get Asaad to order from back home and have delivered to the general store, a small cache of homebrewed explosives—my supply now significantly diminished, of course—and an EVA suit I'd recently acquired from the wreckage of the *Victor Hugo*.

I spit the partially dissolved wad of paper on the floor, pulled my knees up to my chest, burritoed myself in a thick blanket like I used to do on our couch, and waited. Exhaustion washed over me as I sat staring at the terminal, waiting, waiting, waiting . . .

————

I HAD A DREAM.

I was in a dark space. My flashlight flickered off, then on, then off again. Bone-chilling darkness swallowed me. There was only the sound of my breathing, huffing in and out and in and out, until . . .

Skittering.

I clicked the flashlight's button repeatedly with my thumb. Slapped it on my palm. Shook it. Finally coaxed out a weak beam that only partially illuminated the area. The ray of light revealed the thing ahead of me, small in the distance, lost once again in the darkness as the beam flickered then vanished. I unscrewed the top of the flashlight then tightened it down again. The plastic creaked and cracked under my death grip, and I slapped it some more.

Another burst of light. The thing was closer. Hairy legs pulling it forward. Mandibles gnashing.

The light went out again.

I tasted copper mixed with bile. Fear shot up my spine as I frantically slapped at the flashlight, then smacked it on the metal floor.

Once more a dim yellow, dying beam, and there it was. Closer still. So close.

The flashlight died and I knew that this time it wouldn't come back again.

Scritch, scritch, scritch . . .

Me alone in the dark with *scritch, scritch, scritch . . .*

Then something binged, and I woke up.

The tangled blanket was the only thing that kept me from falling out of the chair as I flailed my way out of the dream. I ripped it off my shoulders and swiped frantically at my fore-arms to eliminate phantom webs. Moon webs from moon spiders.

The sound came again, the one I'd thought was part of the dream, but I quickly realized it was emanating from my watch. I tapped the face to shut off the alarm and saw that I'd been asleep for hours. I shivered as the creature from my dream receded, took one of my pills from my go-bag, swallowed it dry, then dropped onto the cot.

I started to wonder what I'd do if he never called back. I couldn't just stay in that abandoned conduit, lurking underground forever. Like a spider or an animal in its burrow. A mole or vole or whatever the fuck those things are called that tunnel around under the dirt. I'd eventually run out of food and water. And light. *What about the light*, I thought, staring at the glow from the lanterns, trying to remember which of them, moles or voles or both, are blind. I jumped up from the cot and turned off all but one lantern, suddenly very conscious of the need to conserve light.

My watch binged again, but for a different reason. My heart rate was spiking. I ripped the watch off and pressed my thumb against my wrist, digging it into the hollow between the tendons. You remember how I used to do it.

One, two, three, breathe. Four, five, six, breathe . . .

I counted and counted, waiting for the pill to kick in. A few times I lost count and had to start over, but bit by bit, second by second, lucidity leaked its way back into my brain, and I was able to stop squeezing and counting. I kept breathing, though. You have to keep breathing, dear.

In. Out. In. Out.

He had a plan. I was sure of it.

There *had* to be a plan.

———

THE NEXT TIME the binging started out at the far edges of my mind. As it got more insistent, I pawed at my wrist to try and silence the watch that was no longer there. That's when I realized the sound was coming from across the room.

I rolled off the cot onto the floor, then scrambled over to

the terminal. It had been over ten hours since I'd made contact.

The pop-up window flashed in time with the chiming. A dialogue box said *Incoming Call*.

I tapped the answer button on the screen. Before I could even start, though, he told me to stop.

"They're probably already running a trace," he said, no visual, only his quavering voice coming through the speaker. But I didn't need to see his expression to grasp his urgency. "You need to get to the shipyard," he told me.

"Do they know it was me?" I asked.

He didn't answer, instead he said, "Listen to me—"

"Do they *know*?" I shouted at the terminal, regretting the volume as I glared into the dark corner where air was hissing into the safe room through the vent.

"We don't think so. Not yet." He told me they were evacuating nonessentials, but didn't think it would last very long. I needed to get on one of those trains right away. Then he dropped a bomb on me.

"Get to the shipyard. Our operative will handle the rest," he said.

I was incredulous. Another operative!

"How do I find him?"

"He'll find you," he said.

I started chasing the implications down a rabbit hole, my mind going a mile a second, until he brought me back. He said that as long as the lunar network was restricted, it was nearly impossible for anyone to follow me through my tracker. But my people would know when I got to the shipyard because I'd be in line of sight with Earth, and they'd get a lock on my signal. That's when the operative would make contact.

"Tell me his name at least," I pleaded.

"Fallon," my handler said, after a brief pause. "His name is Fallon."

I had so many more questions, but never got a chance to ask.

"There's a plan, Julia. I promise," he said, then abruptly terminated the call.

Julia, he called me. He'd never used my name in all the years we worked together. There was also an uncharacteristic warmth in his voice, which lifted me up. I could tell he really cared. I had to get home!

I stared at the *Call Ended* notification and elapsed time, which was less than a minute. The encryption key was robust, and given the short communication between us, I thought it would be okay. But I still unplugged the terminal, just in case.

I sorted variables, counted obstacles. All this time I'd thought I was on my own. It would have been nice to have had someone, *anyone*, to talk to. A like-minded companion. But it didn't matter now. They were right to keep me in the dark about Fallon. The organization's safety had to come first.

I needed to get aboard the Hyperloop. If they were evacuating people, it had to be from the Hub. But despite what my handler had said, I figured Municipal had to be looking for me by that point. *You* had to be looking for me. So getting aboard the Hyperloop through the Hub wasn't an option. And of course I'd have to figure out how to hide for the duration of the trip on the train. But there are ways of doing that.

I needed information . . . and fast.

Not far from the safe room, the abandoned section of conduit I was in connected with the portions that were still in use—but from the conversation I'd overheard with station operations when I was hiding behind the atmospherics panel, I knew Municipal had people sweeping all the regular conduits. Too risky. And going back through the maintenance shed and Neighborhood was impossible.

There was really only one choice.

I looked at the vent in the corner—the spider corner—and

listened to the hiss of the air streaming in through the ventilation shaft. I'd examined the vent in the past, and knew the shaft was wide enough. It ran parallel to the abandoned conduit for a few hundred yards, then shot straight upward until it reached the core ventilation system beneath the docks and main concourse. I just needed a way to climb the vertical portion of the shaft.

I started rooting around the old equipment in the room. As I searched, the power indicator on my breather started buzzing. I'd foolishly forgotten to turn it off when I opened the vent, and now it was almost out of juice. I cursed my stupidity as I grabbed it off the cot and powered it down. But as I watched the screen on the device go dark, the answer hit me like a bolt from the blue.

I tossed the breather aside, reached under my cot, and pulled out the *Victor Hugo* EVA suit I'd nicked. The name "Bastien" was emblazoned on the sleeve just above the embedded control panel, which lit up at my touch. I swiped a few times until boot controls appeared. I touched a button, and the suit's boots scooted toward the metal leg of the cot. I adjusted the magnetic settings, and the boots let go.

I looked back to the air vent and put on the EVA suit, running over the plan taking form in my mind.

8

Seeing Things

WATER WASHES over the smooth sand, leaving glossy, iridescent bubbles and froth in its wake. In and out. In and out. Again, again, again. Golden sunlight sparkles and dances in time with the susurration of the waves, gentle, peaceful, calm.

The whisper of water grows progressively louder, more insistent. Tiny then larger waves begin to crash against the shoreline, faster, harder.

The water churns. So much water. It sloshes and burbles and sprays and splashes and—

Thea jolts awake, her bladder on the verge of bursting.

The clock says she's been asleep for nearly twelve hours. She grips her bulging bladder and swings her legs over the side of the bed, wincing as snaps and crackles and pops go off all over her body. Although she needs a bathroom more than she's ever needed anything ever, she forces herself to get up slowly. And when she's finally upright, she's surprised to find that despite some dull aches and pains, she feels almost normal. A little weak—she can't remember the last time she's had anything to eat—but all in all, not too terrible. She makes a mental note to thank the medic who took care of her as she double-times her way to the bathroom.

Once the ocean in her bowels is unleashed, she studies herself in the mirror. The cut under her eye is an angry red. Dried blood is caked in her hair near the blob of liquid bandage holding her scalp together. There's also a yellow-green bruise on her chin at the spot where her mother hit her and knocked her out.

She double-checks her watch then turns on the water, not waiting for it to warm before splashing it on her face. The sharp cold helps to counteract her spiking anxiety as she imagines all that's transpired while she slept. She scrubs at the cut under her eye so that the blood starts to flow, then grabs a tube of ointment from her medicine cabinet and a bandage. She's desperate for a shower and clean clothes, but those will have to wait, she thinks, as she throws on her robe and goes to look for her crew.

Her first stop is the galley, where she finds Lola working on her laptop and Beetle at the stove stirring something in a large pot that smells like heaven. Lola's out of her seat and has her arms wrapped around Thea before Beetle even realizes she's walked in.

"Jesusholyshit," she says, squeezing until Thea lets out a small gasp, at which point Lola finally lets go. She stiff-arms Beetle to protect her captain as he tries to take her in his arms.

Beetle points his sauce-encrusted wooden spoon at the bandage on Thea's cheek and busted scalp. "Are you okay, *ma chère?*"

"A little banged up, but all right," Thea says, then kisses them both on their cheeks. "Where's Rory?"

"Right here," he says before either of them has a chance to answer. Thea turns directly into a gentle bear hug that Lola has no chance of preventing. She lets herself be swallowed in it, happy to disappear into the safety of the big man's arms and chest. Especially happy for that momentary sanctuary when seconds later he steps aside and reveals who's followed him into the galley.

"Sorry, luv," Rory says. "I put them off as long as possible."

"No, it's fine," Thea replies.

Darcey looks uncharacteristically out of sorts, flyaway strands of hair swarming her head like summer mosquitoes, dark circles under her eyes. She seems as if she too wants to embrace Thea, but catches herself.

"Hey," she says, trying to smooth the deep wrinkles criss-crossing the front of her blue Conglomerate jumper. "I'm glad you're okay."

Everyone's eyes dart back and forth between the two women. They know there's history here and are ready to step in and defend their captain, especially after everything she's been through. But Thea squashes any tension before it can take root by stepping forward and grabbing Darcey's hand.

"You too," she says, then walks to the table and sits down, which is everyone's cue to do the same. Except for Beetle, who rushes back over to the stove. A brimming bowl of rich brown stew is in front of Thea seconds later. Beetle then hauls the pot over to the table and ladles out bowls for the rest of them too, including Darcey.

Thea digs in, her hunger getting the best of her. She's midway through the bowl before she realizes no one's talking; they're all patiently waiting for her to speak first.

She wipes a drip of stew off her chin. "So, what've you all been up to?"

"Oy, you keep us in suspense any longer, girlie's gonna explode," Rory says, receiving a smack from Lola, who doesn't deny the accuracy of his statement.

Thea takes a few more bites just to torture them, then sets her spoon down and launches into the story of what happened after the refinery exploded. They sit with rapt attention as she tells them about the chaos in the docks, the unfortunate people who got sucked out of the station through the breach that the boxcar made in the main concourse, her scramble to make it into the Hub, and then coming face to face with the saboteur.

At this point in the story, she pauses. She purposely spoons in an extra-large helping of the stew to buy herself some chewing time. She wants more than anything to tell them the truth but is afraid of what her crew will think. These people have become her entire world, and they've just buried one of their own; their collective sadness is still an open wound. How will they react when they find out that her own *mother* is the one who took Elliott from them?

It'll affect everything, ruin everything they've built. They won't mean to, of course, but they'll trust her less, question things more. It'll *change* things. And Thea can't tolerate any more disruption to her world.

And then there's Darcey. She'll have no choice but to immediately report the information to Allgood, who will use it against Thea, use it to destroy her and finally get his hands on the *Zephyr*.

Thea can't let that happen—won't let her mother's treachery do that to her father's legacy. That woman's done enough already.

She feels she has no choice but to stay silent.

"Then what happened?" Lola says, way past the edge of her seat, practically sitting on the table.

"I followed the person into the conduits," Thea says, unable to make eye contact with any of them, keeping her gaze fixed on the dregs of stew in her bowl. "It's kind of a maze up there. I got spun around, and they found a way to get the jump on me." She points to the bruise on her chin. "Knocked me unconscious. I was out until Municipal found me."

"A friend of mine in Municipal told me about the scene

down in the Neighborhood," Rory says. "You're lucky to get out in one piece."

Pointing to her split head, Thea says, "Almost didn't."

"You'll be happy to know that the admiral took care of the guy who did that," Darcey puts in. "He was immediately relieved of duty and will be sent back as soon as flights out of the shipyard start up again. There's a lot of people who'll be rotating back Earthside once they're cleared."

Beetle sits forward. "Cleared?" he asks. "What does that mean?"

"A plan is being finalized," Darcey says, rubbing pink lines into her forehead then looking at her watch. "I don't know all the details. But we'll all find out soon enough. We should get the summons in the next hour."

Thea seizes the chance to shift the focus off herself. "If Allgood's just gonna *summon* us, then why did he send you here?" she asks.

"I was coming to check on you anyway," Darcey answers, radiating sincerity. "But, yes, the admiral wanted me to show you something before he shares it broadly.

"We have video of the saboteur."

She pulls a handheld device from her pocket and places it on the table in front of Thea. "We had our team scrub security footage from the refinery, looking for anything out of the ordinary," she continues. "This is from two days ago."

Thea waits until the others gather around, then touches the play arrow on the screen.

The video shows a person kneeling next to one of the refinery's automated lifters; a large cylindrical tank is strapped to a pallet that rests on the lift's forks. The person—the elevated camera angle and the figure's nondescript outfit don't make clear whether it's a man or a woman—is shining a light into an open service panel on the side of the machine, and beside them on the floor sits a bucket and a few tools. The person fiddles with something inside the service panel, then closes the door, collects their tools, and places them in the bucket.

"Go back," Rory says.

Thea rewinds the video, and they watch again as the person works on the machine then stands up.

"They took something from the bucket and put it in their pocket," Rory says, tapping the back button so everyone can see it.

"Yes, and you'll see why," Darcey says. She reaches for the device and speeds up the video. They all watch at double speed as the person with the bucket walks to a workbench on the opposite side of the refinery floor, sits down, sets the bucket beside them, and begins doing something unknown, their back turned to the camera.

"This goes on for just over a half hour," Darcey says. "Long enough for the shift to change, which is important, as you'll see in a moment." She taps the screen again to greatly accelerate the video, then resets it to normal speed after thirty-two minutes have elapsed—at which point the person picks up the bucket again and starts walking toward the camera.

Darcey keeps her finger poised over the screen as the person moves away from the bench. After a few strides, Darcey pauses the video and pinch-zooms the still image.

"Whoever it is, they clearly know there are cameras, as they keep their head down," she says. "This is the clearest shot of their face we have."

It may be the clearest shot, but it isn't much. Heavy safety goggles, a turned-up collar, and a chin against a chest combine to leave little of the person's face visible.

"Gait analysis indicates there is an eighty-seven percent probability this person is a woman," Darcey says, then meets Thea's gaze. "Is this the person you chased into the conduits?"

Sweat breaks out all over Thea's body as she stares at the image of her mother. She says nothing, and neither does

Darcey, who waits patiently as if hoping the frozen image will trigger some kind of recognition in Thea.

Little does she realize how much it does.

After a few tense seconds, Thea says, "Yes?" She shrugs. "I mean, I think so."

Darcey studies Thea a few seconds, then when it becomes clear a more definitive answer isn't forthcoming, she turns her attention to the rest of Thea's crew. "Anyone recognize her?"

They pass the handheld around, playing with the fast forward and rewind sliders to see if the motion helps spark recognition, but none of them know the woman in the video. With a sigh, Darcey takes back her device, advances the video to the moment where she'd stopped it to zoom in, puts the device on the table in front of them, and hits play.

Thea's mother walks toward the camera. Then her hand drifts into her pant pocket, the same pocket where she stowed something earlier.

"Keep your eyes on the top left," Darcey says.

The automated lifter starts moving. It picks up speed and slams the cylinder on its forks into a heavy steel column. Steam bursts from a rupture in the cylinder. Seconds later, emergency lights begin to swirl on the walls.

"She installed a remote override, didn't she?" Beetle says.

Darcey nods. "The collision was initially blamed on a brake failure," she says, "but obviously that wasn't the case."

"Wait, this was two days ago?" Lola offers. "So this isn't what caused the explosion?"

"No, that canister was filled with liquid oxygen." Darcey points at the video, which now shows people scrambling. "It was meant as a distraction."

In the video, Thea's mother waits until she's alone, everyone's attention on the canister, then reaches into the bucket and takes something out. She moves quickly to the base of one of the helium-3 processors and reaches underneath. When she pulls her hand back, it's empty.

"You know who was working the refinery floor that day, though," Lola says. "That should help narrow down who it could be."

Rory sits back, arms across his chest. "Yeah, but you know how it goes over there. On busy days, the place is crawling with non-refinery workers. Crews delivering rocks for processing, repair crews, even just the people coming and going to ship-building and fabrication. It's a madhouse."

"We're looking at everything," Darcey says, acknowledging Rory's assessment with a nod. "We're cross-referencing footage from the other cameras, the main concourse, traffic through the Hub that day."

"And this is the same person who hit the Hyperloop?" Beetle asks.

"Without Thea's confirmation, we can't be one hundred percent sure. But we assume so," she says, then turns to Thea. "We found that backpack you told us about. It had a few magnetic charges and a Hyperloop operator's badge. But when we ran the badge, we found that the operator's on extended shore leave in Seattle."

Before Thea can respond, chimes sound from everyone's handhelds. They've all received the same message:

If you are receiving this notification, report to Dock A at fourteen hundred hours.

"That's soon," Beetle says.

They all stare at one another, the gravity of the situation setting in. Thea is the first to move. "I need to get cleaned up," she says, and starts toward her quarters.

Darcey follows, grabbing Thea's elbow before she can disappear.

"Listen, Thea, I know things between us have been terrible, and part of that is my fault," Darcey says. "But I want you to know that you can trust me. Even though I work for the Conglomerate, I'm here for you too. You may not believe that, but it's true."

Thea doesn't know how to respond, and she must take too long deciding, because Darcey takes a step back, resuming a more professional tone.

"Anyway," she says, "I'll let the admiral know you didn't recognize the woman in the video."

As Darcey walks away, Thea feels an overwhelming urge to confess. She wants to just be done with it. Let go of the weight of it, the shame of it. But she also knows that's impossible. She's not brave enough to risk what might happen if she does. Not yet anyway.

Instead she swallows hard, turns quickly to hide the tears streaming down her face, and heads up the *Zephyr*'s main corridor to get ready to face Allgood.

9

Spun Up

THE BEAM from my headlamp illuminated the curved interior of the ventilation shaft, which was only slightly wider than my shoulders due to the extra bulk from the EVA suit. If I could have worn just the boots, I would have, but the suit was all one piece; the only element I was able to leave behind was the helmet. It made for a tight squeeze, and my forearms and chest ached with the repeated movement of pulling myself forward, my knees going almost numb from crawling. But I could feel the air current getting stronger on my face, and that told me I was approaching the ninety-degree vertical main, which kept me going.

When I finally reached it, I flopped onto my back. Once the pounding in my ears subsided and I caught my breath, I was able to detect the low hum of a fan above. That was when my heart dropped. Not just because I knew the fan would be in my way as I climbed up the shaft, but because it was out of sight. The shaft went up farther than I realized.

Sitting up felt good. Standing even better. After letting the blood flow back into my legs, I activated the boots. The heels immediately snapped down against the floor. I could adjust the boots' magnetic force by turning a dial, and I moved it clockwise then counterclockwise a few times until I was comfortable with its sensitivity. I needed to just find the right balance—strong enough to grip the metal inside the shaft so that I could climb, weak enough that I could lift my feet without straining too hard.

It took a few tries to get it right, but soon I was making steady progress. I kept my back pressed against one wall, my feet taking small steps against the other, my outstretched arms relying solely on friction to help boost me upward. Take two small steps, slide my back up. Two more steps, another slide. I had to pause from time to time to rest my arms, each time dialing the boots' strength up and dropping my arms to my sides. My wrists and hands were pins and needles from pushing so hard against the walls of the shaft.

Then I'd be off again.

Step, step, slide.

Step, step, slide.

And just when I was sure I was running out of gas, I looked up and the beam from my headlamp strobed as the blades of the fan cut through it.

These fans were inline boosters, built into the shaft and centrally controlled by the Darkside atmospherics team. But I'd encountered them before and knew that every fan had a manual shutoff directly in the center of the blade hub. I knew shutting the fan down would result in some sort of notification up above, but I hoped everyone was too busy to get spun up about a single fan malfunctioning—and honestly, I didn't have any other choice. I inched closer to the spinning blades, dialed up the strength on my boots so I could be hands-free, and tapped the manual override button.

The fan stopped—that was step one. Step two was getting

the fan out of the way. At the base of each blade is a release that enables you to fold the blades together like one of those traditional bamboo hand fans. Once they're joined together, you can swing the entire assembly upward so that it rests parallel to the shaft wall. A simple hex driver is all you need to do the job, so I got to work with my multitool.

The carbon-fiber blades came together with ease, but the assembly wouldn't swing upward. I thought maybe the servo was shot, but when I examined the joint, I found a cotter pin locking the assembly in place instead. Easy enough, I thought —until I pulled it out and the pin slipped from the teeth of my multitool's pliers. It bounced down the shaft, pinging off the walls as it fell. I was annoyed, but didn't fret too much . . . until I swung the assembly up and realized that I needed that stupid pin to lock the assembly into its upright position.

A goddamn ten-cent piece of steel. It's always the little shit that does you in.

I searched the EVA suit's pockets and came up empty. There was nothing I could use to replace the pin. I'd just have to try to hold the blade assembly out of my way while I shimmied up the shaft, which had been hard enough all by itself, let alone while wrestling a hunk of machinery.

And it was a long way down to the bottom. One slip and I was a goner.

I settled on what I thought was the best line of attack up the shaft. I increased the strength of the boots in order to account for the added weight of the fan assembly, and spun my body around so that my back was opposite the blades. This allowed me to push against the assembly with my hands, but I had to spread my legs to place my feet on either side of it. Add in the added strength in the magnets, and this was not going to be fun. Thank God the damn blades were carbon-fiber, or I'd have been running the risk of the magnets from my boots interfering with my ascent.

I moved even more slowly than before. My thighs spasmed and my knees felt like they were going to come out of my skin as I step-step-slided up the shaft, an inch at a time, holding the blades away from my chest.

It wasn't until I reached the tips of the blades that I recognized my next problem.

With nothing to hold them upright, as soon as I let go, the blades were going to crash back into place across the shaft beneath me. I had no way of letting them down easy.

This was going to be loud.

Maybe if I wasn't so gassed I could have gotten the blade assembly past my hips and then held them below my ass as I shimmied back down the shaft to ease them back into place. But my body already screamed against the strain. My arms and back and thighs were no longer quivering; they were shaking. Even going back down was no longer an option at this point.

I crept up a few inches more until I was confident my body was clear of the blade assembly. I held the tips of the blades below me a second or two longer, then let go.

The assembly came down like a clap of thunder that filled the ventilation shaft. It echoed for a long time. Too long! When it finally faded, I waited, expecting shouts of discovery, voices mobilizing against me now that my position was compromised. But as I counted the seconds, nothing came. I was in the clear.

I breathed a sigh of relief and got back to it.

Step, step, slide.

Step, step, slide.

I kept going up, not thinking, functioning completely on autopilot. And then I saw it. The top of the shaft was in view, the horizontal junction just ahead of me. I'd made it! I pushed forward, but my joy was short-lived. I heard a series of beeps behind me, then air drifting across my head and shoulders. The fan was back on.

As the blades picked up speed, I felt the tug from below. Gentle. Not a sucking by any stretch, so I knew I wasn't in danger of getting pulled down. But the air current was enough to make one thing very clear: if I did fall, I wouldn't have to worry about the drop killing me.

I dialed up the boot strength a bit to compensate for my fatigue and the added airflow, then got moving. My left knee popped as I grabbed the edge where the vertical and horizontal shafts met. I hauled my upper body into the horizontal section, shut down the boots, and fell face-first into the horizontal shaft. The cold metal was like heaven against my cheek. I pulled myself all the way inside, then rolled onto my back, sucking in huge gasps of the dusty air. My knee protested as I brought it to my chest, but I was able to flex it back and forth, so I knew nothing was busted inside. Just an old knee doing young knee things.

I stared at the circle of light reflecting off the metal above my head, the beam from my headlamp concentrated on rivets made in the refinery decades ago, at the very beginning of Darkside Station. I lay there, gathering my strength.

I heard a sound. Barely a ping on my eardrums. I held my breath.

The noise came again. Faint, but there.

The shaft was larger here. I could practically stoop. I clicked off the headlamp and waited for my eyes to adjust to the dark. When they did, I saw a faint glow, far down the shaft.

An exit.

I moved toward the glow, quiet like a mouse. No, like a spider, skittering in the dark. The light was coming from a grate in the top of the shaft, a floor grate if you were standing in the dock. Only a few inches separated me from the people walking around above me.

The noises were clearer now. Voices. As I inched closer to

the grate, I could even make out words. A man was speaking. I wanted to scoot forward enough to look through the grate, but I fought the urge. Instead I went very still, slowed my breathing, and listened to what the man had to say.

10

New Assignments

THEA IS SWARMED as soon as she and her crew arrive. It seems the story of her adventure following the explosions made its way around the people gathered in Dock A. Most of them simply want to clap her on the back or shake her hand, appreciative of her efforts to try and apprehend the saboteur, which makes the guilt burning just under the surface of her skin into a supernova. She feels dizzy from the attention, overwhelmed by her sudden and unwarranted celebrity, which she knows will quickly vanish and turn to cries of derision and fury when these same people discover her secret—when they find out that she's no hero at all, but instead a liar and a fool who protected someone unworthy of any form of sanctuary, undeserving of any mercy for the murder and mayhem wrought on this community. Her colleagues and competitors' praise will make her eventual fall from grace all the worse, make it hurt all the more when it comes. And as Brian Allgood makes his way to the makeshift platform at the front of the gathering, she has a feeling that fall is coming soon . . . very, very soon.

Allgood issues a sharp whistle using his index and pinky fingers, summoning anyone whose attention he doesn't already have, like you might summon a sheepdog from the prairie at the end of the day. Gasira Achebe stands a few paces to his right, chin held up despite the embarrassment about to befall her.

"Listen up!" His voice booms across the space. "We have a lot of work to do, so I'll cut straight to the point. After an emergency meeting of the IAA, the Conglomerate has been placed in charge of Darkside Station."

Allgood is forced to pause amid shouts of surprise and scattered applause, mostly coming from Allgood's subordinates. But not everyone welcomes this news. Captain Saito of the Japanese fleet is the first to speak up.

"Admiral, when will access to the lunar satellite network be restored?"

"We're not there yet," Allgood says.

"I'm sorry. But I need to speak to my government."

"I understand."

"So, when will I have access to the network?"

"Soon," Allgood says. He turns his attention away from the Japanese captain and is about to continue when Saito interrupts him.

"I'm sorry, sir, but you clearly have been able to contact Earth and the IAA. It is imperative that I speak to my leadership. And I'm sure I'm not the only non-Conglomerate captain who feels this way."

"If you'd let me continue . . ."

Undeterred, Saito manages, "Until I do, Admiral—"

Allgood's patience snaps. "Shut up already, will you! We don't have time for your whining, Saito!"

Gasira, who has been silent up until now, takes a step forward before the confrontation can get going. "Captain Saito, I know you and others here will want to talk to your leadership as soon as possible. But for now, access to the lunar network must remain restricted, for all of our safety. We've already detected unusual activity."

"Wait—what does that mean?" another captain asks.

"We don't know, and that's why no one gets on the sat network until we do," Allgood says.

"I ask—" Achebe jumps back in, then catches herself and motions to Allgood, "*we* ask for your patience. The entire astro-mining community needs to unite as one team to restore order to the station and apprehend this saboteur. And for what it's worth, I agree with the Alliance's decision. The best way to do that is to let the Conglomerate call the shots for now."

Allgood and Achebe exchange glances, at which point she steps back to her previous spot.

"Moving on," Allgood says, then smooths back his hair, glowers at the now-silent Japanese captain, and signals to one of his team members. "Video captured by a refinery security camera is being sent to your devices. Take a moment to watch it."

The dock goes quiet as everyone becomes engrossed in their devices. A few people gasp in surprise and some murmuring begins as people watch the saboteur plant the bomb beneath the refinery reactor. Thea doesn't watch the video. She's seen it. Instead, she scans the crowd, looking to see if anyone recognizes her mother, hoping that maybe someone knows her—at least the version of her that exists up here, her alias. She prays that someone will call out and know exactly where to find her, thereby doing the dirty work for her.

As if reading her mind, Allgood asks, "Does anyone recognize this woman?"

A few people confer in hushed tones, but no one speaks up. Thea hears some expressions of surprise at Allgood's assertion that the saboteur is a woman, but it appears the video hasn't sparked recognition among those gathered—which means Thea silently, painfully, remains on the hook.

"Too bad," Allgood says. "Because this is our target. We believe," he says, gesturing to Achebe, "she's a member of a terrorist organization called 'The New Muses,' one of those bullshit humanist factions afraid of technological progress. There's evidence that connects past attacks aimed at the rare earth metals industry by this group to some of the recent incidents up here. Which is why we also believe the woman in this video is the same person responsible for the incident on the *Zephyr*, and the destruction of the *Victor Hugo* and the *Lillehammer*."

Shock ripples through the space. People shout questions at Allgood, who gestures toward Gasira Achebe, literally sidestepping the vitriol being flung at the platform. Achebe, for her part, maintains a stoic stance, peering at the floor as the anger builds. After a minute of this, Allgood steps to the front of the platform once again, hands up to quell the group.

"I cannot speak to the decisions that were made by Municipal or the IAA in the past," he says. "And frankly, it doesn't matter right now. This woman in the video and her radical group continue to threaten not only our livelihoods up here, but our very lives. So it's our job to end this, right now."

Cheers go up. Allgood lets his words sink in, takes the time to lock eyes with everyone assembled before him, hovering the longest on Saito, who stays silent.

"Good," Allgood says, calm, in command. "Let me tell you what we're going to do. Right now, all permanent residents of Darkside are sheltering in place in their homes. This includes refinery workers, maintenance staff, shipbuilding, Hyperloop control, the Hub, general store . . . everyone not on a flight crew. A security team is in the Neighborhood right now ensuring people comply with this order. In addition, the Hub itself and all maintenance conduits have been locked down, so there is no way in or out of the Neighborhood. Anyone not here in this dock, is in their residence."

"What about the people on security?" someone calls out from the back of the crowd. "What if she's one of them?"

"Everyone deployed in the Neighborhood has been cleared by my team," Allgood says. Darcey takes up a spot next to Allgood on the platform and hands him a tablet.

Barely able to contain himself this whole time, Rory decides to jump in. "Oy, and who cleared your team?"

"I did," Allgood says, not glancing up from the tablet.

Rory seems like he's about to retort until Thea rests her hand on his arm. "Easy," she says. He issues a dissatisfied grunt, but bites his tongue.

"The rest of you have been given assignments, which are being sent to your devices now. Repair crew, you are going to follow Miss Achebe over to Dock B where you'll be deployed to either the refinery or main concourse repairs," Allgood continues, gesturing to Gasira then turning back to his tablet. "Sealant foam is holding for now, but we need those breaches fixed as soon as humanly possible."

"Is it safe?" someone shouts. The question is met with nods from others in the crowd; it's the question on everyone's minds.

With a thumbs-up, Allgood reassures the crowd. "The radiation from the reactor was quickly contained. Values are slightly elevated but in the safe range, and the damaged reactor is offline."

"What about the Hyperloop?" someone else asks.

"Inbound suffered significant damage. Outbound is still functional, but we've cut all power to the system, so repairs are not a priority right now."

"You're not evacuating anyone?" Thea says.

At the sound of her voice, Allgood finally glances up from his tablet. "Until we find who's responsible, Captain Watts, no one is going anywhere."

He then swipes across the screen like slicing across an enemy's throat, tosses the tablet to Darcey, and continues. "Systems integrity team, you're going to work out of my ship," he says. "Lieutenant Grey will be leading this effort. When we break, she'll take you up to the *Bellwether* and give you specific instructions. Everyone else, you have been assigned a partner and a Neighborhood residence. You are going to go door-to-door, looking for information on our target. I seriously doubt you'll find the terrorist sitting on a couch reading a book—but who knows, maybe we'll get lucky. If not, show the residents the video of her. Ask questions. Be thorough. See if anyone recognizes her. And most important of all, immediately report all leads you get, or anything that seems at all fishy, to the security team and to me.

"Any questions?" he says, but it's clear to everyone he doesn't mean to actually address any, because he immediately turns his back to the group and says something to Achebe. She tries to say something in response, but he waves her off, steps off the platform, and confers with a small group of his people.

Taking up Allgood's former position on the platform, Achebe says, "Captain Saito, can I speak to you please?"

Everyone watches as Saito moves through the crowd and joins Achebe on the platform. She leans in close to him, her hands clasped together like a penitent. Seconds later, Saito's voice booms out through the dock, a deep guttural burst of Japanese that requires no translation. But it isn't aimed at Achebe, but rather at Allgood and his small cluster of people. Allgood doesn't even bother to look in Saito's direction, doesn't so much as acknowledge his presence or the fact that all eyes are on this one-sided exchange, which ends when Saito eventually stops, bows to Achebe, straightens his coat, then storms off the platform and out of Dock A.

Only then does Allgood turn back to the crowd. "Let's go, people," he says. "Good luck."

Thea turns to her crew as the gathering starts to break up.

"What did everyone get?" she asks.

Beetle and Rory compare screens. "We're both on repair," Beetle says. "But it looks like I've got the concourse and he's got the refinery."

"I used to pull shifts there back in the day, so it makes sense," Rory says, then turns to Lola. "How about you, girlie?"

"Systems," she says, shaking her head. "I don't like this."

Thea pulls them together. "Well of course they want you on the systems team, Lola. You've got to be one of the biggest brains here."

"No, I don't mean my assignment," Lola says. "I mean, I don't like that we're being split up."

"Me neither," Beetle offers, then gives Thea a quizzical look. "What about you?"

Thea checks her handheld again to be sure. "I didn't get an assignment."

"That makes no sense," Rory says. "You have the best chance of figuring out who this person is. You saw her in the flesh, for fuck's sake."

Thea shows her blank notification screen to her crew.

Achebe walks over and breaks up the discussion. "Thea, a word." She takes Thea's elbow and steers her to an unoccupied part of Dock A.

"Are you okay?" Achebe asks. Only then does Thea notices the dark circles under her eyes.

"I'm fine," she says. "How about you?"

This elicits a small chuckle from Achebe. "I've been better. Listen, I want you to know that I'm here for you, despite the new *structure* that we're all operating under. Don't hesitate to come to me. If I can help you, I will."

"Thank you," Thea says. But when Achebe grabs her hand and forces Thea to meet her gaze, she realizes that her offer is more than some sort of platitude.

"Do you understand what I mean?" Achebe says. "I can

still help you . . . regardless of whatever it is. You can trust me."

Thea can feel herself flushing, but there's no way of stopping it. And as the former head of Municipal's eyes flit over her reddening neck and cheeks, it only confirms to Thea that Achebe suspects something. Between the interrogation after the incident and now, she must have picked up on something from Thea that has her on alert. And more than anything, Thea wishes—would give anything at this moment, in fact—to believe that she can trust Achebe with her secret.

But it's too big. Too big and getting bigger with each second that Thea keeps it inside.

"Thanks," she manages, unable to meet Achebe's gaze. "I appreciate that."

Achebe sizes her up a second or two longer, then lets go of Thea's hand. "The admiral wanted me to tell you to find him after seeing your crew off," she says, and points over to where Brian is still meeting with a small group next to the platform.

"Am I about to get the same treatment as Saito?" Thea asks.

"I don't know what it is, but I don't think he's got repair duty in mind for you. Be careful, okay? And remember what I said."

As Achebe leaves, Thea returns to her crew, who waited for her even as almost everyone else has already left for their assignments.

"All good?" Beetle asks.

"She just wanted to make sure I was feeling okay after everything that happened."

"Woman just got royally screwed and still took the time to check on you," Rory says. "Decent of her."

"Yeah, she's a class act," Thea agrees, then gives them each a hug. "You better all get going. Keep me updated on what's going on, okay?"

"You too, Cap," Lola says, then jogs over to Darcey. Darcey gives Thea a wave, which she returns.

"What about you?" Rory asks. "Any idea what you're supposed to do?"

Thea points to Allgood. "Supposed to go see him," she says, then waves him and Beetle off. "Be safe, boys."

"You too, *ma chère*," Beetle says, and pulls a reluctant Rory after him.

Thea watches them go, dreading the sight of her crew scattered, then heads over to Allgood. When he sees her coming, he disengages from his group and meets her halfway, so they are the only ones standing in the center of Dock A.

"Nice speech," Thea says, which gets a nod and grin from Allgood.

"Thanks."

"Miss Achebe said to come see you. I don't have an assignment."

"Sure you do," Allgood says, his grin broadening into a full-blown smile. "You're with me."

11

Problem of Me

I COULDN'T UNDERSTAND why Allgood was showing people a *video* of me. Why not just broadcast my picture? Even if you didn't have one, which I imagined could be the case given the state of our relationship, it wouldn't be impossible to dig one up. True, I'd been off the grid for years and my people had worked hard to erase and confound my digital footprint, so nothing recent existed on the web, but as we all know, disappearing *entirely* is impossible. Any image, even one from twenty years ago, would be better than whatever footage they'd managed to capture of me in the refinery. I knew where those cameras were—I'd scoped them out way in advance and was really careful—and I made sure they didn't get a good shot of me. So why the video?

And that's when I got worried.

As I crouched there in that ventilation shaft and listened to Allgood address the crowd, I thought about the mob in the Neighborhood swarming the truck you were in. The security team having to beat them back to keep them away from you. All that anger and rage pouring off the people. Had those animals *gotten* to you? I was suddenly panicked, and at the same time filled with this weird sense that I'd somehow escaped. I hadn't been discovered yet, but only because you might be seriously injured—or worse. It's hard to describe the dichotomy. The simultaneous fear and hope, both psychological and physiological, almost something you can taste in the back of your throat. A candy-coated poison pill.

Terror twisted in my core while the rest of my body seemed to float. Like drowning, maybe, that moment when you have no choice but to give in to the waters, let yourself go out and away to the sparkles and flashes of light and life before your eyes as your oxygen disappears. It felt like that, too, because I could barely breathe.

But then I heard you—your beautiful voice! Alive and asking Admiral Asshat about the Hyperloop. My baby, there, above me, safe and sound.

Tears sprang to my eyes, and I had to clamp my hands over my mouth to stifle sobs. The wild emotions that poured out of me short-circuited my brain. I think it wasn't until that moment that I really and truly let myself process all that had happened. Coming face to face with you, but still not able to say the things I wanted to say. After all the years and miles between us. After your father, too. Neither of us saying what *needs* to be said. I let it all flow out of me as I lay there in a fetal position. You were alive, and it was going to be okay. That's all that mattered.

But just as I began to collect myself, spent and exhausted, a new thought crashed through my brain.

Why hadn't you told them?

I couldn't imagine what might have transpired in the time since I left you unconscious in that maintenance conduit— what sequence of events could have prevented you from telling them I was the saboteur. Because clearly, given what was happening above me, you hadn't. Did you have some sort of head injury? Were you suffering from memory loss? Or a form of shock-induced denial after finding out I was responsible for everything, including killing your boyfriend?

Had you unknowingly blocked out the whole thing as some sort of defense mechanism?

Or maybe you and Allgood had planned this charade as a sort of interrogation of the community to root out co-conspirators. Were the two of you in cahoots?

I ran through possibility after possibility after possibility, up and down, all the ways, but none of them felt right to me. None made any sense . . . except for one. And as soon as it surfaced, I knew it was right.

You *chose* not to tell them.

You hadn't told them because none of what happened made any sense to you. It must have felt unreal, totally imaginary. How could I be gone from your life and here now? Why was I always *ruining* things, down there and now up here too? And until you could make sense of it, figure out how to square that circle, you weren't going to let anyone in. You were going to solve the problem of me all by yourself. It was the only explanation that made any sense.

Do you remember Maisey Carter? That tall girl with all those freckles. So many, in fact, you thought she was mixed just like you, despite the fact that her hair was orange like a pumpkin. You found out she was cheating off your vocabulary tests, so you purposely filled in wrong answers one day to catch her. Your second-grade teacher, whose name I can't remember for the life of me, called and said he'd asked you about it, but you wouldn't admit to doing it on purpose. But he knew, and so did I. There was no way you'd let someone get over on you like that, so you did what you had to do. Just like you're doing now.

I lay there and listened to the cacophony of noises and voices as Allgood's meeting broke up, thinking maybe I'd catch a few more snippets about the plan to find me, but then realized it didn't matter. By keeping my identity a secret, you had given me an opening, and I was going to seize it.

I had to get to the shipyard. I would meet my contact there, and with his help, I would get off the moon and back to Earth. I knew Allgood had shut down the Hyperloop—thanks, again, to you, or at least to your question a few minutes earlier— which meant there was only one way left to get me where I needed to go.

I had to steal the *Zephyr*.

PART II

Search and Rescue

12

Little Things

THE NEIGHBORHOOD FEELS POST-APOCALYPTIC. Security personnel in riot gear roam empty streets. The day-night-cycle lighting has been abandoned, so instead of a soft, late-afternoon yellow and lengthening shadows crisscrossing the landscape, a harsh white blasts the buildings and cul-de-sacs. Overturned benches and trash bins are scattered around the common area. The back wheel of a maintenance vehicle—the same one used to transport Thea to Municipal after they fished her out of the conduits—is up on a curb, an information kiosk crushed between the truck's front grille and a bent light pole.

"Go ahead and ask. It's okay," Allgood says, gallantly kicking some debris aside for Thea after taking the last step.

"What?" she says, glancing into the bed of the truck at the dried pool of what she assumes is her own blood near the cab. She reflexively touches the bandage on her head and checks her fingers, which come away dry.

"Ask me the question," he says, a boyish smirk on his face. "I know you want to."

Annoyed, she stays quiet and lets him lead the way around

the wreckage of the common area. But he's patient, unhurried. The intensity he displayed earlier while dressing down the Japanese captain is gone. He seems at ease, almost calm, like he's out on a Sunday stroll.

"Fine," Thea says when it becomes clear he's going to force her to play along. "Why did you pick me as a partner?"

He drops back a step, so they're walking side by side. "I think you've experienced a trauma, Thea. Several, in fact. Between losing friends on the *Lillehammer* and then your own man . . . what was his name again?"

Thea glares at him. "Elliott."

"Right, sorry." Allgood gives himself a light whack on the forehead before continuing. "Just think about it. Before you had sufficient time to process losing those folks, not to mention the damage to your father's ship—"

"*My* ship."

"Of course," he says. "After the damage to *your* ship, this mystery woman strikes again. Then you narrowly escape the blowout in the main concourse, only to get coldcocked in the conduits, zapped by security, and knocked for a loop by that asshole kid with the trigger-finger billy club. Honestly, it's a miracle you're not balled up in the fetal position somewhere."

"Thanks for the highlights," Thea says. "But that still doesn't explain why you picked me."

"Well, that's it right there. Despite everything that's happened to you, you keep going. I admire that. Plus, if anyone has a chance of putting together the pieces of this puzzle, it's going to be you. You've been at the center of a lot of this, directly and indirectly. Hells bells, you actually came in contact with this fucker. Who knows, we get some nugget of information about her from one of these residents, and *bam*, it could all suddenly snap into place."

Thea shakes her head. "I get what you're saying. But I told you everything I know."

"I don't think you have."

Thea stops and folds her arms across her chest, not meeting Allgood's gaze. She hopes the gesture comes off as defiant rather than what it really is—an overwhelming sense of guilt and shame.

After a pregnant pause, she manages to say, "You think I'm lying?"

"No, that's not what I mean." He shrinks the gap between them, getting uncomfortably close. "I went back and rewatched the video of our conversation about what happened in that maintenance conduit," he says, then taps her forehead with his index finger, like pushing a button on an elevator. "And I think there's details in there buried underneath all the bad shit that's happened to you. If there's one thing I learned during my time as warden of Angola Prison in the great state of Louisiana, it's that the truth will seek the sun like a sprout from soil. And I want to be there when whatever is stuck in that head of yours pops out into the light of day.

"That's why I picked you as my partner," he adds, clapping his hands together so forcefully it causes Thea to flinch. Then with a chuckle: "Come on. Let's start over at the south end, shall we?"

Thea swallows hard. The air smells metallic, like the heating coils of a hairdryer. She glares up into the piercing white light radiating down from the ceiling, which is apropos because it's at that moment she realizes Allgood's not done interrogating her. Turns out, he's just taken his show on the road.

———

THEY DON'T GET VERY FAR before two Conglomerate men spot Allgood. One of the men glares at Thea as they flank their boss, and it isn't until she takes the hint and drops back a few steps that he begins speaking in a low voice. Thea strains to listen, but just then her handheld buzzes in her pocket.

A message from Rory.

Refinery's fucked. Beetle and the rest of the concourse detail have been brought here. We need all hands.

As she replies, Allgood sees her typing and calls to her. "Who's that?"

She hits send. "One of my crew." She waggles her handheld before sliding it back into her pocket. "He said the refinery's in bad shape."

The man who was speaking to Allgood takes a step toward Thea, his cheeks puffed out like a child who's just discovered someone ate his cookie. At the same moment, his partner says, "They shouldn't be communicating with you at all," then faces his boss and snaps a salute. "Don't worry, I'll take care of this, sir."

Allgood waves it off, patting his man on the shoulder. "It's okay. We'll let this one slide, but let's have our team collect all of the repair crews' devices while they work."

Each man issues an *Aye, Admiral*, glares at Thea, then jogs off.

She imitates Allgood's lackeys by giving him a crooked salute. "What was that all about?"

"Nothing."

"Oh, come on, now. I just told you about my message from Rory, now it's your turn."

He shrugs. "Fair enough. We're partners, after all. Right?"

Thea nods like a car salesman and gives Allgood an okay sign. "You betcha."

Playing along, Allgood says, "Tests confirmed the explosives we recovered from the saboteur's backpack were retooled miner ordnance with a homebrewed remote detonator."

Thea tries to reconcile the image of her mother burning

waffles in their toaster with the kind of person who could reconfigure miner tech into an explosive device. "Why's that important?" she asks.

"Because it means she built the explosives up here," he says. "I figured as much. No way she'd have risked having something shipped from back home. Too easy to trace to the source."

Thea was almost able to smell charred waffle. "She's smart," she says.

"Yeah, but all the smart ones have the same fatal flaw."

"Oh, yeah? What's that, warden?"

He gives her a wide grin. "The smart ones always, always get tripped up by the dumbest things. Body in the trunk while getting pulled over because of a broken taillight. Cigarette butt on the lawn of the house you just robbed. Ransom note written on custom stationery. Shit like that." He continues talking as they walk toward Cul-De-Sac Six, which houses most of the refinery personnel. "Happened to one of the smartest men we ever had in lockup. Big-time bioengineer for a pharma company. I mean, one look at this guy and you knew he had something serious going on upstairs. His eyes looked like they could see right into your soul. Piercingly intelligent peepers."

"What'd he do?" Thea asks.

"Murdered his wife and made it look like a hit and run, only it turns out he was the one behind the wheel."

Allgood pauses, smiling, forcing Thea to drag it out of him.

"So . . ." she says, allowing him his moment of fun. "How'd you catch him?"

Pleased as punch, he goes on.

"Well, this guy had planned his wife's murder for a long time. Years in the making, in fact. He bought this vintage gasoline wreck with cash almost two years before he killed his wife with it. Kept it parked inside an abandoned shed in the woods along the Jersey floodline, way back in the part of the state that used to be miles and miles of blueberry fields before the ocean took over.

"According to everyone who knew her, his wife was a real creature of habit. Fitness nut, too. She ran at the same time every morning along a wooded bike trail near their home. On the morning he killed her, our guy got up, went to his lab in the city, and logged into a three-hour mandatory town hall. Trick was the week before he had recorded hours and hours of himself in front of his computer screen using a tablet device. You know, one of those old jobs with the big screen. Anyway, before he logged into the town hall, he positioned the tablet with the fake footage in front of his computer camera so it looked like he was actually sitting there. Then he threw on a bunch of bulky clothes and a hoodie he had hidden in his desk, jogged a few miles to the local train station, and went out to the flood zone in Jersey, using a one-time ticket he bought with cash, of course. Trying to leave no trace.

"The shed where he stowed the car was only a mile or so from the end of the train line. He drove the murder weapon to the bike trail near his home, waited for his wife, then mowed her down as she came around a bend. Backed up over her body a few times too for good measure before leaving the car on top of her and riding a kid's bike he'd stowed nearby in the woods back to a different train station. Did all this and made it back to work before the town hall ended—the town hall he had, by all accounts, been paying attention to the whole time."

Thea tries to puzzle it out as they walk. Allgood is all smiles as he watches her.

"Fingerprints or DNA in the car?" she asks.

"Nope."

"Someone else was on the trail? Saw him do it?"

A slow head shake. "Nope, they were all alone," he says.

A few seconds later, Thea brightens. "One of his coworkers stopped by his office and saw he wasn't actually there. That's gotta be it."

"Nope," he says again, clearly having a ball.

She thinks it through a bit longer, but is unable to see the hole in the guy's plan. "I give up," she finally concedes. "What'd he do wrong?"

"You're gonna love this," Allgood says. "You ready?"

He holds off continuing until he gets an actual confirmation from Thea that she is, in fact, ready.

"Get this," Allgood says, sounding almost giddy. "While our biopharma genius was waiting for the train to Jersey, he bought a scratch-off from a vending machine. Had some extra cash in his pocket, so he thought, why not. Turns out the ticket was a winner, too."

He pauses there, as if the answer is obvious. It isn't until Thea waves her hand in a "go on" motion that he connects the dots.

"You see, the spouse is always the primary suspect in any murder investigation, so when detectives got footage of him cashing in that winning ticket a few weeks later at his local supermarket, the lottery board was able to tie the ticket back to the vending machine at the train station, which proved he wasn't actually at his lab on the day his wife was murdered. After that, all they needed to do was lean on the guy, and he cracked like an egg. And thanks to capacity issues in the northeast, smarty-pants ultimately ended up in my care."

Allgood's eyes sparkle as he wraps up the story, his fondness for the cautionary tale apparent. "Perfect crime ruined because of a hundred-buck cash prize," he concludes.

"Sounds like you enjoyed your job," Thea says.

Allgood guffaws at her remark and nods his head vigorously. "It had its moments, that's for sure."

"Why'd you leave?"

He thinks about it for a few seconds as they approach the first tenement building in Cul-De-Sac Six. He quick-steps to the building, grabs the handle to open the door for her, then pauses and asks, "Have you ever been to Louisiana?"

"No."

"Beautiful place, but the heat. Boy, there's only so long you can endure that kind of abuse. It beats you down, physically and mentally. Day after day, it's hard to—"

He stops, listening to something, then lets go of the door handle and runs into the cul-de-sac.

Puzzled, Thea chases after him. When she rounds the bend, she finds him walking up to a group of people sitting in a circle in the cul-de-sac's center. No one seems to take much notice of the admiral of the Conglomerate fleet's presence, which combined with the empties scattered around the ground indicates to Thea that these people might require a softer touch than what Allgood is capable of, so she quickens her pace.

"Come again?" Thea hears one of the residents say as she catches up to Allgood.

"You are supposed to be sheltering in place, not congregating," Allgood says, unable or unwilling to hide his contempt at having to repeat himself.

A man in a greasy refinery jumper crushes his beer can on his thigh, then stands. "Listen, Captain, we all just lost folks," he says, indicating the gathering of people all similarly dressed and lubricated. "Had to watch friends and coworkers of ours—"

"Admiral," Allgood says.

The man blinks hard at being cut off. An incredulous look blooms on his face. "Excuse me?"

"I'm an admiral, not a captain," Allgood says. "And I don't give a good goddamn that you're all sad. There will be time to mourn the dead later. Right now, you are going back to your homes, where you will await further instructions. Or you can wait for them in the Municipal lockup. Your call."

Two other people shoot up from their seats, ready to back up their friend, who looks like he's about to make a move of some sort—a wobbly one at that. And as much as Thea would love to watch Allgood get some comeuppance, she knows it will be disastrous for these people.

She puts herself between Allgood and the group, holding up her handheld for everyone to see. "We need your help," she says, tapping the screen to start the video she has queued. "This is the person responsible for killing your friends. I need you to look at it and tell me if you recognize her."

The gambit works, because the group's spokesperson seems to forget all about Allgood's douchery as he takes Thea's handheld and his colleagues huddle around him.

"Sonofabitch," one of them says as the video plays. "I was on the floor when that loader went haywire."

"Go back!" another says.

The man slides his finger back and forth across Thea's screen, manipulating the video. Then the group passes it around so that everyone has a chance to examine it up close. Meanwhile, Allgood seethes at Thea's side. She has to grab his arm at one point and hold him there so he doesn't interrupt their examination of the video. The group confers for a few minutes, throwing out names, testing theories, speculating, pontificating, cursing, spitting, drinking, and swearing retribution against the culprit. But when it's all done, none of them recognizes the person.

Thea takes her handheld back from the first man, whose eyes keep darting between her and Allgood. "All right, well, we're gonna talk to everyone else around here," she says, "so why don't you guys call it a night and head inside?"

Thea turns to Allgood so that no one else can see her thumb back toward the first tenement in this cul-de-sac, where they were going to start in the first place. He glares at the group, who are indeed gathering their things and folding up chairs, and then reluctantly turns with her. But they don't get more than a few steps before one of the women calls after them.

"You're wasting your time," she says.

Allgood snaps around. "Excuse me?"

"I mean, looking here," the woman replies.

"Why?" Thea asks.

The woman spits a looger on the ground and strides over to them, her grimy hand out. "Let me see that again."

Thea hands her device to the woman, who immediately uses her index finger to fast-forward the video. She stops it, then pinch-zooms on the frozen image, blowing up the picture of the Darkside saboteur.

"See her boots?" the woman says, pointing at the screen then handing it back to Thea. Allgood looks at the screen over Thea's shoulder.

"Yeah, what about them?" he says.

"Look at the toes." The woman leans in, the pungent scent of whiskey on her breath. "They're all scuffed up."

"Why's that important?" Thea asks.

The woman makes a circle motion over her head. "This cul-de-sac is all refinery and Hyperloop people. You ain't gonna find that person in these buildings."

Thea can tell Allgood's patience is gone, so she grabs the woman's hand and tries to get her to focus. "Why won't we find this person here?" she says, very calmly.

The woman grabs Thea's other hand, the one holding the device, and stabs at the screen. "Her boots! That's conduit toe if I ever saw it. You get that from crawling around in the maintenance conduits all day."

Allgood puts himself between Thea and the woman and forces her to meet his eyes. "Are you sure?"

"Fifty bucks you're looking for someone in maintenance," she says, then lets out a small-but-acidic belch that makes Allgood flinch. "Most of them live next door in Cul-De-Sac Seven."

Allgood turns to Thea, his bright white grin on display.

"Like I said. It's the little things that get them every time."

13

I Know You

I WAITED until the voices were gone before stealing a glance through the metal floor grate. Looking up, all I could see was ceiling, so I didn't have a great sense of where I was other than knowing I was beneath a space large enough for Allgood to gather a crowd. Not an ideal spot to pop up into the dock, so I was forced to explore the rest of the nearby ventilation shafts for another way out. I considered trying to get all the way over to Dock D underground. It certainly would have been the safer choice. But I'd been down there for so long at that point I felt the walls closing in on me. You'd think being close to the surface would have helped, but it didn't. I needed to get out of that shaft! It's like when you're stuck in traffic and have to pee really bad. It's easy to push the urgency down when you're miles away from your destination. But the second you're in sight of it, the floodgates always threaten to burst open. Like that time we drove back from Amarillo and your father had to pull over and take a leak on Miss Morris's bushes. Do you remember that? We could see our house; it was right there! But he swore there was no way he was gonna make it. My God, I can still picture her standing there on her porch in that fuzzy yellow bathrobe, Texas Big Bird we used to call her, and cursing at your dad, whose head was thrown back in total ecstasy as he unloaded all over her honeysuckle. He mowed her lawn that whole summer to make good on what he'd done. After that, every time we walked by, he'd pretend to go for his zipper.

He was funny, I'll give him that.

Anyway, after navigating a maze of interconnected branches, I rounded a corner and felt vibrations from what turned out to be Dock A's lift. A few turns later, the shaft got larger and a broad beam of light streamed into it through a wide access panel in the side wall. Even though the area sounded quiet, I knew there was a good chance I'd run into someone if I exited there. But I also knew the assignments Allgood had doled out, and figured that if I did, I could simply claim to be part of the refinery repair crew and running an errand for Gasira Achebe, who Allgood had said was coordinating them. Only people who were at Allgood's gathering would have that information, so it was a decent cover story, especially since no one seemed to recognize me from the video he had shared. And then, once I was past Dock B, I figured it would be smooth sailing over to the *Zephyr*. From what I'd heard, those docks seemed to be empty.

But for it to work, I had to shed my EVA suit.

It took forever to peel off that crotch-killer. My base layer was soaked in sweat by the time I finished, and the sudden cold inside the vent felt like heaven. Being rid of the EVA suit and its heavy magnetic boots also helped with the claustrophobia.

I crouched near the access panel and waited until Dock A's lift stopped moving before risking a quick peek around the edge. I didn't see anyone, so I disengaged the access panel's latch. But just as the panel popped open, I heard a voice. Closing the panel would have called attention to it, so I had no choice but to leave it cracked open.

I peered through the slats and saw that girl from your crew, the one with the purple streaks in her hair, calling out to someone named Darcey. Another woman, this one wearing a Conglomerate officer's blue jumper, jogged up to her and said, "Hey, Lola. How's Thea doing?"

Lola. That's perfect. She looks like a Lola.

I couldn't stop myself from humming the song as I watched her tell Officer Darcey she thought you were holding up okay, all things considered. Which made me immediately angry. Despite what Lo-Lo-Lo-Lo-Lola said, I knew there was no way you were okay. You were simply putting on a brave face for your crew. Just like your father, you'd apparently gotten good at hiding your feelings, stuffing them down, swallowing them whole, keeping them secret from the people around you.

And, yeah yeah, I heard it from him a million times before, so don't you start too.

That's what a captain has to do.

It's bullshit and it's not healthy, Thea. You keep all that poison inside and it'll just end up making things all the worse when it finally comes spilling out. Trust me, I know.

"Can you explain to me why we're not all floating around in the dark?" Lola asked. In response, Darcey held up a tablet and told her that engineering had decoupled the helium-3 processors months ago when they suspected a saboteur was on the loose. That way if one or two were to go offline, they wouldn't lose power station-wide. For me, it also explained the low level of radiation emitted after the explosion.

They talked a little more, then Lola left. I was hoping Darcey would follow her, but instead she glanced down the corridor with a puzzled look on her face and started walking toward me. I immediately ducked back behind the edge of the panel, so I wasn't positioned right behind it. I hoped that if she had noticed the panel door was open, she'd assume it was knocked loose during the explosion or something along those lines and simply push it back into place and be on her way.

But that's not what she did.

I had my back flat against the ventilation shaft wall. I heard her footsteps stop just outside the panel, and a second later it swung open. She poked her head inside, using her handheld as a flashlight. We locked eyes for a split second, hers going instantly wide at seeing me huddled there in the dark. But before she could react, I grabbed her by the front of her jumper, pulled her inside the vent with all my might, and slammed her head against the wall opposite the access panel opening. The bang was tremendous. She instantly crumpled. I quickly pulled her the rest of the way into the vent and then closed the panel door. Her handheld light was still glowing, so I shut it off and made sure we were away from the access panel in case anyone came to investigate the noise. Luckily, no one did.

Darcey was unconscious, and her breathing was shallow and hitched. I clicked on her device's light again and examined her forehead. Blood had started to seep around the edges of a baseball-sized bruise that was already beginning to form from where she'd struck the vent wall. I pulled her deeper into the shaft and was about to leave her behind when I realized the gift she'd given me, the cloak of safety that Conglomerate lieutenant Darcey Grey—her last name was stitched over her heart —had provided by poking her head into my business.

Her blue jumper.

I slipped off my damp base layer. My skin broke out in gooseflesh as I knelt over her unconscious body and unzipped her jumper. But the zipper caught midway down her torso. As I tried to free it from the bunched fabric near Darcey's solar plexus, she whimpered and tossed her head to the side. I froze as her eyes fluttered open, the stuck zipper still gripped in my fist. Her eyes met mine and she muttered, "I know you."

She was blinking hard, trying to focus, but I didn't give her that chance. I balled my fist, lifted her slightly off the ground so that her chin fell back, and delivered an uppercut that put her out again. I didn't think she'd be waking anytime soon. But still, I knew I needed to move.

Turns out we're about the same size, so her jumper fit well. But I was worried about having her last name so easily readable on the breast pocket. White stitching on dark blue. My face still had traces of the grease I'd smeared on it earlier, but not enough to obscure her name. So I dabbed my greasy fingers in the beads of blood on Darcey's forehead, then used the dark mixture to black out her last name as best as I could. It wasn't perfect, but it would serve at a distance.

As anxious as I was to get out of that vent, it felt like I was about to leap into the void. I steeled myself against the fear rising in my chest, checked the area outside the access panel again, and then stepped out into the silence of Dock A. I winced against the bright overhead lights and let myself revel for a few seconds in the sensation of being out in the open. Then I clicked the access panel door closed behind me and started toward Dock D.

14

Another Life

THEA HAS to jog to keep up with Allgood as he strides into Cul-De-Sac Seven. She expects him to turn toward the first tenement, but instead he heads across the central courtyard and straight to Tenement Four.

The building hasn't changed since she and Rory came here looking for Bobby Bean, the man who sold Rory the acid-filled case that melted a hole in their ship and killed Elliott. But as she approaches, she's suddenly captivated by the squat gray structure and its brutish surroundings. She can't help but imagine her mother sitting on its stoop, carrying in groceries, taking out the garbage, borrowing a cup of sugar from a neighbor, hanging a holiday wreath on her door—the door to the apartment that contains her secret life, a life that had been taking place right under Thea's nose the entire time she was at Darkside. Her guts twist and she's forced to swallow down a surge of rage. But it's not one sparked by her mother's deception, not this time. Instead, she's infuriated by unwanted and inexplicable feelings of being shut out of her mother's other life. At that moment, not being invited to take part is intolerable. She can't understand the insanity of these emotions, nor can she push them aside. After her mom abandoned her and her father—which feels like a lifetime ago—she'd written the woman off, vowed to shun her for the rest of her days. And now, seeing what has likely been her mother's home here on the moon, she's what, hurt? Bruised by the discovery that maybe her mother felt exactly the same way about her—that she too had to be written off, shed like a bit of dead skin? And if so, why should it matter? Why should she care?

Two guards round the corner of the tenement. They exchange a quick glance then rush over to Allgood and Thea. "Sorry, sir, I thought you and Captain Watts were starting next door in Cul-De-Sac Six," one of the men says.

"Change of plans," Allgood replies.

The guard who spoke thumbs over to the first tenement in the cul-de-sac. "Want me to run over and tell the other team you'll be taking over questioning here?"

"No, I only want to talk to the people in this tenement," Allgood says, then adds, "No one goes in or out of here without my approval, understood?"

"Yes, sir," the guards say in unison.

As the two guards jog away to get in position, Allgood turns to Thea. "You ready?" he asks.

Not willing to meet his gaze lest her face give away the turmoil inside, she says, "Let's go," and takes a few quick steps toward the building. But Allgood jumps in front of her and hurries to the front door. He whisks it open then gives Thea an "after you" wave.

Stepping past him, Thea asks if his action is "a courtesy, or do you just want me to be the first one through in case something bad is waiting on the other side?"

He follows her in. "That hurts, Captain Watts. After all, we're partners."

"Why'd you pick this tenement?" Thea asks, keeping her voice low.

"Call it a hunch."

"Is it because this one has the maintenance shed up top with access to the conduits?"

She isn't at all surprised when he responds with a shit-eating grin and a shrug.

It takes a few knocks for someone to yell an answer from inside the first apartment. Seconds later, the door swings open.

"Inga Vasilyev?" Allgood reads from his handheld, then slides it back into his pocket.

The woman Thea first met only days before takes a sip from her martini glass. "People call me Inky," she says, swiping back her wet, white-blond hair. Her porcelain skin is glistening and she's wearing a fuzzy pink bathrobe.

Thea steps out from behind Allgood. "Oh, you again," the woman says. "Where's the big guy?"

Caught off guard, Allgood says, "You know one another?"

"Sure, last time the captain came by my little slice of heaven, my friend turned up dead."

"Your friend was already dead," Thea says, eyeing the woman as she tosses back the rest of her drink.

"Well, we're in Schrödinger territory now, aren't we," the woman says, tucking the empty glass into a pocket.

Thea waves her handheld like a talisman, hoping its presence will mesmerize the others enough that they can drop the subject of her last visit to this building. "I need you to take a look at something," she says, handing the device to the woman.

But Allgood is undeterred. "What is she talking about?" he asks as Inky begins studying the video.

"You know about the man who was murdered a few days ago in this tenement, right?" Thea says.

Allgood's face reddens. "Of course. But how do *you* know about that?"

"The thing that burned a hole in my ship and killed Elliott . . ." She pauses and steels herself before continuing. "The dead man, whose name was Bobby Bean, sold it and its hidden acid device to Rory. We came looking for answers and found him murdered in his apartment."

Allgood grabs Thea's arm and pulls her a few steps away from Inky. "Gasira told me her team discovered the body," he says quietly, through clenched teeth. "She didn't mention you were there."

"Well, we share the credit on that particular find."

"This is weird," Inky says. She slides down the wall into a sitting position, gathering her robe around her as she leans into the video.

Allgood ignores her, all his focus on Thea. "Anything else I should know about?"

"Nope."

She tries to step away, but Allgood won't let her.

"Did she tell you?" he asks.

"I don't know what you're talking about."

"Bullshit!" he snaps, his voice echoing down the hallway. It barely draws a glance from Inky.

"I don't need to tell you about our conversation," Thea says, wrenching her arm from Allgood's grip. "The rest of the station may have anointed you commandant, but I haven't. To me, you're still the same prick that's been fucking with me and my crew for the better part of a year now."

Allgood lets the insult wash over him.

"When this is done," he says, "I'm going to have that woman sent home in chains to face charges."

"Hold on," Thea says. "Did you really expect Gasira not to provide me with some sort of explanation? Do you think for a *second* I'd have let it go? Of *course* she told me everything. We all nearly died. And one of my crew *did!*"

"Guys," Inky says, slowly rising to her feet.

"Even still—" Allgood snaps, but Thea talks over him.

"The *Victor Hugo*. The *Lillehammer*. My ship. And now the

whole fucking station." She pokes him in the chest. "Maybe if you assholes hadn't kept so many secrets, we wouldn't be in this mess! People might still be alive."

"Guys!" Inky says again, Thea's device thrust toward them. Her eyes are wide and her bottom lip is quivering.

Swiping a tear from her cheek, Thea walks back over to the woman, making a motion with her hands to draw the woman's attention to her open robe. Inky ignores her and stabs a finger at the device's screen, her modesty forgotten.

"This can't be real," she says. "Somebody fucked with this."

"The video is authentic, I promise you," Allgood says, joining Thea, his anger set aside for now.

"Do you recognize the person in the video?" Thea says, breaking out in a sweat.

Inky starts wandering around the hallway, seemingly in a daze. "Nah, I don't believe it," she mutters.

"Ma'am," Allgood says. After a few seconds without a reply, he tries again, this time more forcefully. "Miss Vasilyev. Do you recognize the person in the video?"

"Yeah, I do," she says, shaking her head. "Worked side-by-side with her in maintenance for almost a year and a half." She shoves Thea's device back at her like it's hot. "That's Mae," she says, wiping the hand that had been holding it on her robe, sending a breakaway pink string to the ground.

Thea's mind reels. She tries to process her mother's alias, searching for any bit of significance in the choice of name, but comes up blank.

"Do you know where she lives?" Allgood asks, his eyes darting back and forth between the two women. Thea fears she's turned nearly as white as the stunned albino maintenance worker who's finally chosen to draw her robe tighter around herself as if against a cold draft.

Inky's shaking finger points down the hallway.

15

Fake It to Make It

It wasn't until I was standing outside the access panel that the words of the woman whose jumper I was wearing, Darcey Grey, registered with me.

I know you.

What did she mean? How did she know me?

I kept away from the flight crews at Darkside as much as I could—which had a lot to do with not wanting to run into you—but it was impossible not to interact with some of them in the course of my regular duties. Especially the Conglomerate, who *always* needed something from maintenance. So maybe that was it? I ran through my recent trips to Docks A and B and didn't remember ever coming across Darcey Grey, but I couldn't be one hundred percent certain. It was possible.

The other possibility was the video. No one at Allgood's gathering spoke up when he showed them the footage, but maybe seeing me right in front of her triggered something, some connection to the images captured by the security cameras. That, too, seemed unlikely. We only locked eyes for a second or two, and she'd just suffered a mind-splitting blow to the head when she said it. Who knows what she was thinking or seeing right then? But it was another thing I couldn't rule out. Perhaps Darcey simply realized I was the person everyone was looking for, and in her daze and confusion that's just the way it came out.

But I didn't think so. The way she said it . . . *I know you*. It had to be something else. I kept rolling it over in my mind, half tempted to go back to the ventilation shaft and make her tell me what she meant, but then I heard voices coming toward me.

I froze in my tracks. Fear shot through me as I glanced back toward the access panel. It was too far away. I'd never get back in time to open the panel, slip back inside, and secure the door before they reached me. Plus, time was running out. I had to get to the *Zephyr*. So I went with a different approach—one I knew worked pretty well, in fact, because it had worked on you one time.

I usually worked the graveyard shift. That's when the Hub and Neighborhood are quietest. But one day, my friend Inky woke up with a migraine and asked me to cover her shift. I'd just wrapped up eight solid hours on my back underneath a condenser, so it was a big ask. But Inky begged me, and I did it, which was the only reason I was in the Hub that afternoon. I was so exhausted at the end of those back-to-back shifts that you and your boyfriend were practically on top of me by the time I realized it was you. I turned around and tried to scurry away, but the Hub was packed, and I couldn't see a path that would get me out of your line of sight fast enough. So I did the next best thing to become invisible.

A worker from the general store was behind me when I turned around, this poor young guy, all of twenty years old if he was a day, probably coming off work just like me. He looked dead on his feet, at least until I shoved him and started screaming at him about sleeping with my best friend. *He said I was the only one! Promised me we'd move back home and get married!* All kinds of crazy shit like that. I can't even remember all the dumb clichés I threw at that poor bastard, who was too stunned to say anything in response. But it accomplished the goal. Everyone steered clear of the crazy woman, including you and Elliott. Then the second you were out of sight, I ran back to the Neighborhood, leaving that guy standing there utterly dumbstruck. I found out a few months later that he left Darkside, word of his philandering apparently ruining any chance he had at love on the moon.

Anyway, as the voices got closer, I pulled out Darcey's Conglomerate-issued handheld device and started yelling into it. I said I needed "it" done immediately—"it" being some imaginary thing of great importance—then I threatened the lazy, incompetent, insubordinate idiot I was speaking to with reassignment to the plumbing detail, toilets being the most advanced technology they'd ever again get their hands on. All the while, I stole glances at the people walking past where I was pacing back and forth and screaming into Darcey's device. All three of them were wearing Conglomerate red jumpers, so I knew that my stolen blue one would make me stand out as one of their superiors. They picked up their pace as they heard me ripping into who they must have assumed was someone like them, but then one of them met my gaze and stopped, his two buddies following suit.

"Is everything okay, ma'am?" he said, his eyes scanning the front of my jumper.

I placed Darcey's handheld on my chest, covering her partially blacked-out last name, and yelled toward the ceiling, "For fuck's sake, why am I surrounded by incompetents?" I waved the three crewmen off, saying, "Unless the admiral assigned the three of you to be hall monitors during this inter-stellar fucking crisis, I suggest you get your asses to wherever the fuck it is you're supposed to be right now!" Then I turned and continued berating the imaginary person on the other end of Darcey's silent phone, ramping up the profanity and threats as the seconds ticked by. Which worked, because when I glanced back, the three of them were gone.

And the Oscar goes to . . . Julia Watts!

For good measure, I kept the device to my ear until I was out of the Conglomerate docks, but I didn't come across anyone else. Dock C was completely dead, so I picked up my pace, Darcey's words once again taking center stage in my mind.

I know you.

I know you.

16

Smells Like Home

THE SECURITY TEAM creeps past Thea, little creaks and pops from their carbon-fiber riot gear the only noise in the quiet hallway. They take up positions on either side of the apartment door while a thick officer with a heavy steel battering ram takes aim. All eyes shift to Allgood, who is positioned a few steps further down the hallway and out of any immediate line of fire. With a nod from their boss, the officer swings the forcible entry device and delivers a crushing blow to the door. The slap of metal on metal rings out like a gunshot as the door flies inward and the security team pours into the apartment.

"Mae Green!" they scream, while under her breath, Thea can't help but whisper her mother's real name.

After a few agonizing seconds she can bear the suspense no longer and starts walking toward the door, but is waved off by Allgood, who looks just as anxious as she feels. He shouts "Anything?" to the team inside the apartment.

"Hold!" someone yells in response, which makes him wince.

Thea rocks back and forth while chewing an already ragged

thumbnail, hoping to see her mother emerge from inside the apartment peacefully and compliantly, but at the same time seriously doubting that she's been just sitting in there, waiting to get caught. Sweat beads her brow as she and Allgood trade glances, keeping each other in check while they wait for a signal from the security team. So she's startled when the door next to her cracks open, and an old Indian man's face appears.

"Mae, is that you?" he says, his watery eyes searching Thea's face.

Thea swallows hard, her throat suddenly too parched and tight to utter a sound. Allgood notices the open door and signals that she needs to get the resident back into his apartment. The man meanwhile has pulled on a set of wire-rimmed glasses and sees that she's not her mother.

"Sorry," he says. "You look like someone I know."

She fights off the urge to hide her face from this man's scrutiny, but he's already lost interest in her and instead steals a glance at the commotion happening down the hall.

"What's going on?" he asks, swinging open the door a bit wider. A spicy aroma wafts from the man's apartment, and Thea's stomach growls in response.

"I'm sorry, but you need to stay inside," she says, holding out a hand to prevent him from stepping into the hallway.

Before the old man can speak again, one of the security officers shouts "Clear!" and Allgood springs into the apartment. Thea wants to follow, but the old man reaches out and touches her arm. He has a deeply lined forehead and wispy white hair. His teary eyes have a tenderness to them. He's curled toward Thea as if bearing some invisible weight, and he nods his head, silently pleading for information about his neighbor, a person for whom he clearly holds some affection.

"I'm sorry, sir. But I can't—"

Undeterred, he says, "Please, miss, you must," cupping his

dry, wrinkled hands like he's trying to catch water. "Mae is my friend."

Thea relents, takes his hands in hers, but can't bear to meet his gaze. She's sad and ashamed and embarrassed that he's been so taken in by her mother's lies—something she knows a lot about. After a few tortured seconds, all she can manage is, "She's not who you think she is."

She expects a rebuttal from the old man, perhaps some defense of his friend's honor, but instead his chin begins to bounce up and down and his cheeks quiver. Having seemingly chewed his way to a decision, he says, "Yes, well, that happens a lot up here." Then he nods once more to Thea, takes a step backward into his apartment, and closes the door.

———

THE SCENT of lilacs transports her back.

Their yard was overrun by lilac bushes. She could count on at least two or three bee stings per year while swinging on the swings or building castles in her sandbox. Petals perpetually clogged her dad's mower. But despite her daughter's stings and her husband's annual threats to rip the bushes out by their roots, Thea's mother never flinched from her devotion to those bushes. She would tend them and prune them and replace them with new ones should one happen to die. She'd clip bunches of the violet, pink, and blue flowers and put them in every room in the house, a practice that she's apparently continued even here on the moon, despite the absence of any real lilacs—or gardens, for that matter. Thea runs her fingers through the scented plastic petals bunched in a glass vase at the middle of her mother's coffee table and curses the burst of nostalgia brought on by the fragrance.

A purple memory, like a bruise.

The rest of the apartment is unremarkable. Nondescript

furnishings, minimal kitchenware, no pictures or artwork or keepsakes or knickknacks or tchotchkes or anything that can be described as a *personal item* of any sort. It feels more like a hotel room than a space someone's lived in every day. Even the clothes in her closet and toiletries in her bathroom could belong to anyone.

"I want someone from forensics in here immediately," Allgood says to one of the officers. "The rest of you take up positions on every floor in this tenement. No one moves, understood?"

The security team starts to file out of the apartment. One officer stays behind and gives Allgood a handheld device. "We got this from Mae Green's application for residency."

Allgood studies it for a few seconds, then holds it up for Thea to see. "Is this her?" he asks.

Thea's hand is trembling as she takes the device. She pretends to be carefully considering the picture, even going as far as to pinch and zoom and cover parts of her mother's face with a thumb to simulate the goggles she wore during the attack, but in reality she's trying to control the adrenaline racing through her body. Finally, after a few more manipulations of the screen, she hands the device back to Allgood.

"Yeah, that's her," she says.

"You sure?"

She nods, and Allgood breaks out in a wide smile. "Excellent," he says, handing the device to the officer. "Make sure that image goes out to everyone."

"Yes, sir," the officer says, immediately tapping away at her own device.

"And put someone outside this door until further notice," Allgood adds, then nods for Thea to follow him. "Captain Watts and I are going to the roof to have a look at Mae Green's locker."

Thea has to work hard to keep up as Allgood strides back

down the hallway. Her feet feel like lead. She knows that now they have her mother's picture, it won't take them long to cross-match it and discover her real identity. The truth is about to come out.

"Do you think that was a good idea?" she calls to Allgood.

"What?"

"The image," Thea says. "If she knows we've identified her, she might get desperate."

Allgood glances over his shoulder at her, a bemused look on his face. "She's trapped on the moon and is being hunted by every other human up here," he says. "And you think sending around her picture is what's gonna make her desperate?"

Instead of going directly to the stairs, Allgood stops in front of Inky's door. "Inga Vasilyev!" he shouts, and pounds on the door with his fist. When she doesn't answer, he pounds again and again until she yanks the door open. Her bathrobe has been replaced by tartan boxer shorts and a vintage Soviet Union sickle-and-hammer t-shirt.

"What now?" she says, then takes a swig from the bottle of vodka she's clutching.

"I need you to come with us," Allgood says.

She lets out a cackle. "What? Like this?"

"Yep, let's go."

"Where to?" she asks.

"The maintenance shed," he says, reaching for her arm, which she snatches away from him, a splash of vodka landing on her bare feet.

She looks to Thea. "Do I have to?"

"I'm afraid so," Thea says.

"Right now," Allgood adds.

"All right, all right," she says. "Gimme a second." She turns and heads back into her apartment. When she returns, she's absent the bottle and has slipped on a pair of work boots with the same sort of wear on the toes that Thea's mother's had in the refinery video.

"Lead the way, Captain," she says.

"It's Admiral," Allgood corrects her.

"I wasn't speaking to you, *Admiral*." Inky motions for Thea to lead the charge up the stairs to the maintenance shed.

Thea gives her a smirk, then heads into the stairwell. Allgood brings up the rear, at the ready should the swaying Russian in front of him stumble on the steps.

"Didja find Mae?" Inky asks.

"She wasn't home," Allgood says. "Do you have any idea where she could be?"

"Nope. And I still think someone messed with that video. Mae wouldn't—"

"She did," Allgood says, cutting her off. "Your friend is guilty."

The woman moves closer to Thea. "Captain, what do you think?" she says in a low voice.

"I'm sorry, Inga," Thea says, then slaps the crossbar on the door leading to the roof where the maintenance shed is located. "It's her. I'm positive."

Inky pauses, absorbing the impact of Thea's words. Allgood brushes past her and says, "Believe me now?"

He doesn't wait for a response as he follows Thea to the shed, where they both turn and look back at Inky. She walks over to them slowly, in a daze, as though her whole world has been turned upside down.

"Would you mind?" Allgood says, motioning toward the keypad next to the shed door.

Without a word, Inky places her palm on the pad. The light on the device goes from red to green, and she walks into the shed.

Thea stops Allgood from following. "You didn't need her for that."

"Nope," he says.

"Then why'd you make her come up here?"

"I just wanted a record of her being here with us," he says. "That way, if shit goes sideways once we catch this bitch, we can say that 'Inky' Vasilyev did her part."

Thea can't mask her surprise. "So . . . you did it to *help* her?"

"Is that so surprising?"

"Little bit, yeah," she says.

"When this is all said and done, a lot of people are gonna be thrown to the wolves over what happened up here," he says. "That woman in there has got some issues, no doubt. But other than unknowingly befriending a terrorist and a murderer, she didn't do anything wrong."

"You sure?" Thea asks.

Allgood's expression radiates unequivocal confidence. "She didn't know anything about all this. Trust me, I can tell. I know when someone's hiding something."

Inky is standing in the middle of the room, staring at everything as if for the first time. "We used to hang out in here sometimes, drinking and watching old TV shows on a tablet. Telling stories and gossiping." She swallows before continuing. "I just can't believe that whole time . . ."

Allgood takes out his handheld and nods to the lockers. "Which one is hers?"

"Middle one," Inky says, pointing.

Allgood glances at the number at the top of the locker, then dials someone. When they answer, he says, "I need you to open locker four-dash-three of Cul-De-Sac Seven's maintenance shed."

Second later, there's an audible click and the locker door pops open. Allgood shines his device inside and scans from top to bottom. Then he slides the two spare jumpers on their hangers against the side wall, one at a time, doing a quick pass over the surface of each with his hand, feeling for anything unusual. He picks up each spare boot, checks inside, then finally takes a quick look up at the locker's empty top shelf before turning around to face Thea.

"Nothing. Just like her apartment," he says, brushing off his hands and directing his attention to Inky, who is leaning against the bench, head in her hands. "Miss Vasilyev, can you think of anywhere Mae could be hiding?"

"I already told you—"

"Yes, I know," Allgood says, impatient. "But there must be somewhere besides her apartment and this locker where she kept things. Maybe a different friend's place, or somewhere else in the Neighborhood."

While Allgood interrogates Inky, Thea creeps up to her mother's locker. It smells like her, she thinks, but then corrects herself. No, like her parents' bedroom closet back home. Thea pinches her nose to block the scent and all the unwanted memories it evokes as she glides the fingers of her other hand across the sweat-stained neckline of the first spare jumper. She twists the fabric in her fist and slides the jumper aside to view the next one, which she notices is missing the front zipper. In its place is a silver paperclip, the same fix her mom once used on Thea's puffy pink winter coat when she was a kid. She flicks the dangling paperclip and peers down into her mom's empty boots. As she imagines sliding her feet into them, she runs her hand over the top shelf and feels something uneven. It's just at the tips of her fingers, but the shelf is too high for her to see, so she has to step on the base of the locker and get on tiptoes to peer over the edge. When she does, she discovers a small square piece of paper adhered to the surface. She peels it free.

Allgood's taken notice. "Got something?" he asks.

Thea looks at the note and finds a list of items scratched out in her mother's unmistakable handwriting.

Peanut butter, jerky, gin, toothpaste.

Thea holds the note up for Allgood to see. "Just a shopping list."

He nods and turns his attention back to Inky, who is squeezing lines into her forehead.

Thea flings the note back onto the shelf. But as she steps off the base of the locker to the floor, she notices the back of the locker shift slightly. She shines her handheld inside and steps back onto the base of the locker. The wall shifts again.

Thea reaches inside the locker and yanks out the spare jumpers, tossing them onto the floor. She kicks her mother's spare boots away, wedges herself partially inside the locker, and pounds on the back wall. The metal subtly bends outward, which should be impossible, seeing as these lockers are pressed up against the maintenance shed's wall.

"Thea?" Allgood says, now at her shoulder.

She shines her light along the edges of the back of the locker and sees small clips holding it in place. She pulls one of them free, and the metal wall shifts away from her.

"There's something behind here," she says, pulling out another pin. The wall shifts again.

She removes the final two pins, and the back wall of the locker comes free. She pushes it away from her, slides it into the newly discovered open space behind the locker, and finds herself staring at the rungs of a ladder.

She backs out of the locker so that Allgood can see what she's discovered.

"What is this?" Allgood says to Inky.

The stunned woman edges in past Allgood to have a look. "No way," she says, peering up the ladder. "Thought they got rid of these when they shut down the conduit."

"What conduit?" Allgood asks.

Inky turns on the light on her handheld. "Up there," she says, pointing the light up into the shaft, "is one of the original maintenance conduits. They've been sealed off for years now."

Allgood's eyes go wide. He rips out his own device and after a second or two starts barking a rapid stream of orders at whoever's answered his call.

Thea takes a step toward Inky, dizzy from the sense of dread now coursing through her body.

"Where does that conduit go?"

A flash from Inky's device exposes the chipped paint on the bottom rungs of the ladder. "Before my time," she says as she frames up another shot. "But I'm pretty sure the old system used to stretch all the way over to the docks, maybe even parts of the refinery."

As Inky snaps a few more pictures, stealing peeks at Allgood to make sure he doesn't notice, Thea stumbles away from the lockers, the implications of her discovery short-circuiting her mind. Because in that moment, she knows exactly where to find her mother. In fact, she curses herself for not having seen it sooner. There's only one possible move, one possible *fix* that might work given the limited options available to someone being hunted by everyone and trapped by oxygen and gravity and space and cold. Plus, this move gives her mother the added bonus of seeing through to the end of this entire fucked-up Shakespearean drama she's created.

Allgood is screaming into his device in an attempt to get people to materialize instantaneously, so he doesn't notice as Thea slowly backs out of the maintenance shed. As soon as the door shuts behind her, she tears down the tenement's steps to the ground floor and races across the Neighborhood to get to her ship.

17

Past is Prologue

Do you remember your father's video journal? *Daddy TV*, you used to call it. He actually had a bunch of names for the damned "episodes," as he called them, over the years. *Footprints on the Moon. Great Gig in the Sky. Mining for Dollars.* Stuff like that. I used to keep track of them in this little notebook I kept in the coffee table. My personal favorite was *Blowin' in the Wind.* You'd get so excited when a new episode would show up in the home entertainment menu. And that'd restart the cycle of you watching them over and over again, especially at night when you couldn't sleep. But your favorite part of every video, hands down, was always the ending. He'd conclude each one the same way: "This is Scottie Watts, Texas Spaceman, signing off," followed by a close-up of his nostrils, or a stupid, toothy grin, or something along those lines before he'd cut to black.

Your dad, always the comedian.

In the early days when he was still excited to show us *every-thing*, he'd send us an entry at least once a week. Less and less as time went on. Most videos took place on the *Zephyr*. But occasionally we'd get a shaky walk-and-talk from places like the shipyard observation deck, or inside the Hyperloop station or on a train, or at the Leaderboard so he could show off where he and his crew ranked. And when he wasn't out in the field, there'd always be a parade of guest appearances too. "This is Aunt Kimmie," or "this is Uncle So-and-So." All one big happy space family. His *other* family, the one that got the best parts of him.

By far, though, the video you watched the most was the takeoff video. You'd sit in front of the television, propped up on throw pillows behind that cardboard replica of the ship's control console the two of you made, the one drawn in crayon and with one of my wooden spoons stabbed through the top of the box as a thruster. You'd play that damn video on a loop, repeating each step in the sequence, mimicking all the moves he was making on the screen.

Deactivate lift.

(Tap the red square)

Initiate launch sequence.

(Twist the yellow circle, thumb the green slider)

Release docking clamps.

(Pound the blue rectangle)

Engage thrusters.

(Slowly raise the wooden spoon)

It's burned into my brain!

For weeks and weeks, no matter how hard I tried to get you to do something else, you sat behind that box watching your father and ignoring me. You see, even when he was gone, I couldn't compete with him for your attention, which made me hate those videos. All except for one. The one you never saw because he filmed it just for me.

The episode opened on a shot of your father, standing in front of the *Zephyr*'s lift, wearing a suit and tie. Not one of his own suits, of course, but a "real snazzy one" he borrowed from a friend of his in Municipal just for the occasion. He showed off the fancy cufflinks, then switched the camera to capture the keypad as he typed in his access code. His eyebrows danced up and down mischievously as the lift doors hissed open, and he "took me up" to the ship's cargo bay, where a small candlelit table was set. He leaned the camera against something on the table, lifted a bottle of champagne from the golden tableside ice bucket, popped the cork, and poured himself a glass.

It was our anniversary—the fifth or sixth anniversary in a row he'd missed.

He made some little speech, blew me kisses, and then tipped his glass back.

Scottie Watts, Texas Spaceman.

Can you believe that?

He honestly thought *that* table, *those* candles, *that* champagne would somehow make up for his absences—all his constant, unrelenting absences. He honestly believed—he would later say this during what went down as one of our most epic fights—that his gesture meant that no matter how far apart we were, he was always thinking about home, always thinking about me. When all I remember thinking was "Who did you actually share that champagne with when the camera stopped rolling?" Probably Aunt Kimmie.

You'd think I'd hate that video most of all. But that video was important because it was the ending of one thing, and the beginning of something far more meaningful. For me it was the beginning of the end for our marriage—a catalyst, the most important impetus of my life other than giving birth to you. Because a few months and dozens of arguments later, I found the New Muses and a new purpose.

It turns out, though, that the anniversary video wasn't done changing my life. As I said, your dad pulled out all the stops that day. Nice suit, candles, bubbly. And one more *extra-special* touch, his new access code for the *Zephyr*'s lift . . . the date of our wedding, which he thought I'd love.

And he was right. I do love it—now.

I still had my electromag popper. It certainly would have done the trick. But I was pretty confident your dad didn't bother to change the access code even after our marriage fell apart. He would have viewed it as . . . I don't know, a concession of some sort, which he never made. Not Scottie Watts. I also figured that you hadn't changed it either. You would never abandon your dad's code.

Turns out I was right on both accounts. I keyed in the code, and the lift doors opened.

Thanks, Scottie.

Just as the lift reached the surface, my tracker activated again for a split second. A flash appeared beneath my skin, and a stab of pain radiated across my forearm. I was surprised, especially after hearing Allgood and Gasira Achebe telling the people at that gathering that the lunar network was locked down. But we have some great hackers. Which is ironic, I know, given that we hate technology. You gotta *know your enemy*, right?

When I reached the cargo bay, I walked around with my arm held aloft, hoping that I could catch another blip from my handler, but it never came back on. It didn't matter, because that tiny little moment of connection energized me. I headed toward the bridge knowing that my people were trying to talk to me, to find me despite all the odds.

They hadn't given up on me.

———

AFTER DECADES of living in my mind as a sort of "other woman," I wasn't expecting what I felt when I was finally aboard. I thought I'd feel hatred and disgust. But instead, it was something closer to . . . I don't know, absolution, maybe? A kind of forgiveness for the ship itself. You see, I'd vilified it for so long; it was the thing he chose over me. But as I walked through its corridors, I felt no malice toward it, which caught me off-guard. I can totally understand what you must have felt like the first time you set foot on her. Honestly, it's mesmerizing! Sure, it's just a *thing* like a car or a plane or a refrigerator, but it has a unique magnetism, too, its own gravity. I'm not talking about *real* gravity—of course it has that. I mean something else, something intangible. But make no mistake, even though I was finally able to let my anger and hatred toward the ship go, it didn't for one second change my plans.

I hurried along the main corridor toward the bridge. Despite the urgency I felt, I couldn't resist stopping when I reached the captain's cabin—your cabin. No matter how old your kid gets, every mother still wants to know where they lay their head each night.

If I had walked in blindfolded, I still would have known it was your room. Your scent was everywhere, flannel and butterscotch. That's how you've always smelled to me. And no, Thea, I didn't snoop. I didn't go through your drawers or closet or anything. I just took a moment to take it all in, the tumult that was you—that has always been you. Stray sock, bra in the corner, unmade bed, half-eaten muffin on the nightstand, which I was going to shove in my mouth (I was so hungry) until I saw it had nuts. As I put down the muffin, I noticed the picture on the nightstand of your "first catch," which is what was written in the margin. It's a great picture. You looked so happy, your head resting on Elliott's shoulder, your friends around you.

Seeing it broke my heart.

I'm so sorry he's gone, honey. I never would have done anything on purpose to hurt you. I hope you can one day believe that. I tried, I really did. But despite all my planning and efforts to keep you away from what I had to do up here, something bad still happened. At least now, I get a do-over. Now, I can keep you safe.

That's why after I get where I need to go, I'm going to kill this ship.

18

In Through the Out Door

THEA SPRINTS past pink mounds of rock-hard sealant foam separating her from the deadly vacuum outside the main concourse. She forces her eyes forward as she runs toward the docks, knowing bodies lie scattered across the lunar surface just outside the station walls. Bodies of people who deserve justice, people like the lost crews of the *Victor Hugo* and the *Lillehammer*, and the dead refinery and Hyperloop workers. Innocent people, all of them. People like Elliott. People who should be alive—would be alive—if it weren't for her treacherous, deceitful, murderous mother.

Thea quickens her pace even as the weight of all those bodies bears down on her. She nearly collides with a team of Conglomerate and Municipal security personnel racing in the opposite direction, undoubtedly heading toward Allgood and the newly discovered maintenance conduit above her mother's tenement. They give her sideways glances, but no one slows. Several of them are carrying stun sticks she knows they won't need because they won't find her mother in that conduit. There's only one place her mother could be—only one place that makes any sense at all. And if Thea's right, then this can all be over. All of it, everything . . . it can all be done, she thinks, beginning to face a possibility she's thus far been able to ignore—that this might end things for *her*, too.

She doesn't know how people will react when they find out. The accident of her birth, her shared DNA with a terrorist, could destroy the life she's built for herself up here. Guilt by proxy, even if she's the one who stops her mother. Thea's heart aches at the thought of losing everything—her crew, her ship, the moon, the station, her new home, her newfound purpose—and having to go back to Texas, to that big empty house with no idea what to do next. But she knows she can't control any of that right now. She pushes it down, buries it beneath the adrenaline and anger propelling her along the main concourse. This is all she can do, all that matters. The fallout will certainly come, but right now she needs to get to her ship.

As she crosses into Dock B, she looks up through its transparent roof to where the Conglomerate's flagship is slowly lifting off. *He's making sure* his *ship is out of harm's way*, she thinks, annoyed by Allgood's selfishness while at the same time knowing the only ship that's truly in danger is her own. But at least Lola, who's aboard the *Bellwether*, will be safe. She'll be safe, and so will Darcey.

As Thea watches the retro engines on the *Bellwether* fire, she replays her and Darcey's conversation onboard the *Zephyr*. Darcey promised that she could be trusted, that she would be there for whatever Thea needed. And she'll have her opportunity to prove it, Thea knows, as soon as the news of her mother breaks.

Her device buzzes against her thigh.

She ignores it and keeps running, but the buzzing is persistent, so she fishes it out and answers without breaking stride.

"Captain Watts, where'd you go?"

Thea tries to control her huffing and puffing. "I'll be back soon," she says, unable to muster anything more in her sprint across the station.

"Where *are* you?" Allgood asks, unable to conceal the menace in his voice.

Thea scrambles to come up with something that could hold him off, anything that could explain her vanishing as soon as they found the abandoned conduit.

"Captain?" he tries again.

The entrance to Dock D is a few paces up ahead.

"Answer me, goddammit!" Allgood shrieks, his patience clearly gone.

Thea turns the corner without slowing, sprints toward her lift, and finally says, "Brian, you need to trust me." Then she ends the call.

Her heart is pounding through her chest. She glances up and sees the *Zephyr*'s keel lights are lit, their amber glow illuminating the glass walls of the lift. She was right—her mother is in the ship!

She taps the eight-digit code into the keypad, but the surface remains red. The same thing happens on the second and third attempts, which means her mother has deactivated lift access.

Thea pounds on the glass and screams at the top of her already spent lungs. Her mind reels while above her the *Zephyr*'s keel lights change from amber to bright white. She races back to another lift and keys their intercom. Then she does the same at the second- and third-nearest lifts, praying that someone, anyone will answer. But no one does; every crewmember is currently spread out across Darkside, looking for the person who is now trying to steal Thea's ship.

She's about to try another lift when she notices the door to one of the dock's decompression closets is ajar. She figures some people must have gone for the closet when the explosions began. Her assumption is confirmed when she yanks open the door and finds scattered articles of clothing on the ground and only one emergency suit left inside. But that's all she needs.

The emergency suits are designed to be one-size-fits-all through a series of straps and cinch clips positioned on the arms, legs, and torso. Thea doesn't have time to make significant adjustments, simply tugs a few clips to shorten the arms and legs before snapping the helmet into the neck ring. She then jogs to Dock D's external airlock, the same airlock Elliott and Beetle used when she met them after the *Victor Hugo* went down. She has to choke back a sob at the memory of first laying eyes on the man she'd grow to love, the woolly blond hair she'd twist in her fingers so often and the toffee-colored skin she can still taste in her dreams.

She steps into the airlock, throws the handle to seal the door, and the depressurization cycle begins. She makes a few last tweaks to her suit as she watches the countdown, each second feeling like an eternity. As soon as the panel glows green, Thea twists the handle on the exterior door and steps out onto the lunar surface.

The first thing Rory did when he agreed to become her pilot was conduct an exhaustive, weeks-long, tip-to-tail survey of the *Zephyr*. He pored over every inch of the ship, including their dock. That was the last time Thea was outside the station, shadowing him so that she could learn as much as possible about the ship she'd just inherited. She'd even made him snap a picture of her as she stepped off the ladder that descended from the launch pad to the chalky surface, commemorating her "one small step" moment as she planted her foot in the white-gray lunar dust. She looks for that boot print now as she bounds onto the bottom rungs of the ladder, but it's been erased by months and months of lunar winds. Another happy moment, gone.

Above her, she can tell by the intense glow that the *Zephyr*'s running lights have been turned on. She can't fathom how her mother knows what to do. *Did Dad show her?* she wonders as she climbs the ladder, taking advantage of the moon's low gravity to skip two and three rungs at a time. Even if he did, it would have been during the early days before Thea's mother and father grew distant, so it's unlikely her mom would remember all the steps. But the ship's computer wouldn't let her skip any, so it's also entirely possible her mother is simply fumbling her way through the launch sequence and adjusting as she goes, the computer keeping her on track. Either way, Thea has little time. The untethering and launch process isn't extensive, and she has to get aboard the ship before it pushes off from the dock.

She yanks hard on the top rung and launches herself clear of the ladder. But she's pulled too hard and has to wait for herself to float back down to the landing pad, hoping her mother is too occupied to notice her drifting in space. As soon as her feet touch down, she scrambles toward the ship and away from the view of the bridge.

She's only halfway to the ship when the glowing umbilicus that supplies power from the dock to the vessel detaches. The ship's reactor is online, and her mother is one step closer to taking off.

Thea reaches the *Zephyr* just as red warning lights on the perimeter of the cargo bay doors begin to swirl. The external lift—the one her mother took and Thea was locked out of— detaches from the ship and begins to descend. Seconds later, the top of the lift becomes level with the surface of the landing pad and transforms into the glowing white circle that pilots use as a target when they land.

Thea glances up at the exterior service door. It's not an option. Not only will any access attempt from the outside alert her mother, but the cargo bay will be fully pressurized for launch, so opening it would result in a blowout. The harpoon bay is a better choice.

The ground shudders as the ship's engines come to life. Thea skirts around the aft landing gear and sees the harpoon bay a few meters away. A low vibration begins, then quickly grows in intensity. She overshoots the space directly beneath the harpoon bay and has to backtrack to position herself beneath it as it slowly starts to rise along with the rest of her ship. She crouches in a three-point stance like a reverse super-hero landing, then springs upward. As she reaches for the grab bar affixed to the hull of the ship, she only barely brushes it with the fingers of one hand before drifting back down to the landing pad. The ship, meanwhile, continues its slow rise. She adjusts her angle and launches herself upward again. This time she manages to grab the bar and hold on.

She climbs hand-over-hand up the bar to a keypad located next to the harpoon bay door. Like the cargo bay, these doors will also trigger an indicator on the bridge, but at least the harpoon bay won't be pressurized. Thea can only hope that her mother will be too distracted by the launch to notice the alert, or won't know what it means.

The keypad screen comes to life at her touch. As she taps through the warnings, the ship continues to ascend, and she forces her eyes forward. When she reaches the final screen, which is blinking a red-and-yellow warning, she takes one last quick glance down at the lunar surface, rapidly shrinking below her.

Then she opens the *Zephyr*'s harpoon bay doors.

19

Birds of a Feather

OKAY . . . I think I did this right. While the takeoff sequence is moving right along, I put this file in the ship's main directory, and the good news is it looks like it's recording what I'm saying now too. So I'm just gonna let it run and hope it'll survive. I hope you'll be able to recover it and listen to it someday.

I can't believe what I'm looking at. Of all the things to find!

The last time I saw this, it was on the mantle with the rest of the family pictures. How the hell did it end up here, taped to the console like this?

Boy, just look at you. That smile.

I was making your lunch that morning, and you came downstairs in your pajamas and those ridiculous space alien slippers you wore all the time, the dingy green ones with the springy antennas. You were all yawns and eye rubs and wild bedhead. You shuffled straight over, handed me a crumpled piece of paper, mumbled something about homeroom, then walked over to the cabinet to get Fruity Pebbles. I knew it before I even unfolded it. It was a notice from your teacher— dated the week before, of course—reminding parents about the Thanksgiving parade happening at school *that very day*. And as the note said in big, bold letters, you needed to arrive to school in your group's costume. Teachers would not be responsible for dressing up students (God forbid), and any student not in costume could not participate in the big parade. Dire consequences indeed. But worst of all, when I asked you what your group was supposed to dress up as, you couldn't remember. Of course not! The only thing you had to offer was that your nemesis Maisey was in your group, and that sent you on some rant about how she chewed with her mouth open at lunch and would mix pizza with strawberry milk, which totally grossed you out.

I had half a mind to send you to school without a costume, force you to stand with the teachers and other derelicts. But of course, I didn't. I called Maisey's mom and let her chew my ear off about how she just couldn't understand why you two girls couldn't be friends. You had *so much* in common and had done sleepovers in Girl Scouts, her usual pitch. I had to promise to set up a play date just to get her off the phone, which made you wail and scream that I was the worst mother ever.

I raced around the house, looking for supplies. We had the colored construction paper for the feathers, eyes, and beak, but we didn't have any paper bags. You know how hard it was to come by actual brown paper bags back then, let alone the big ones? I woke up your dad and sent him knocking on doors all up and down the street until Mrs. Morris gave him one. I had all the pieces cut out and ready when he finally came rushing back into the house with the bag, but we had to let the glue set. While we waited, he whipped up a quick costume of his own, took down the big wooden spoon we had hanging on the wall for a prop, and drove you to school just in time for the parade, but not before I took this picture of the two of you.

The hungry pilgrim and his little turkey.

You with your dad, always the hero. And me behind the camera, always the footnote.

When he got back home after the parade, he told me he had to leave the day after Thanksgiving and might not be back in time for Christmas. He had just gotten back a few days before that, so I couldn't believe he was leaving again. Dumping everything on me *again* so he could go off and be a goddamn astronaut. Thea, if you only knew . . .

———

I DON'T EXPECT you to forgive me because of what's captured in this log, but I hope it helps you understand me a little bit, at least. I really wanted to do this differently. But Allgood's changed things now, and I have to go a different way.

I wish I could talk to my handler. He'd know what to do. But even if I could, there's no time.

If I do this, it will be a huge blow. Catastrophic! It'll make up for the bomb in the refinery not crippling the station. It'll fix everything.

And if I'm being honest, the odds of me getting back home were pretty slim anyway. I know that. It wasn't gonna stop me from trying, of course, but still. At least this way, I'll know for certain . . . I'll be certain that you'll be okay, because if I do this there will be no reason for you to be up here.

It's just hard. Harder than I expected.

No.

This is better. It's right. Definitely! Kill two birds with one . . . well with one bird, actually. Both birds die if I do this. Yours and his.

I'm scared, though. But I have to—how could I not. It's *right there*! His damned ship, the holy of holies, is right ahead of me. That's what your system's been warning me against. But it's not a warning. It's a wake-up call, because the beating heart of the Conglomerate's operation is just off the *Zephyr*'s bow, rising from its dock, slow and steady and stupid like one of those obnoxious cruise liners. The *Bellwether*, the very thing me and my people have been fighting against for years and years, it's right in front of me: a big, fat turkey.

Ha, I've got turkeys on the mind!

Ever since I got here, I dreamed of destroying Allgood's baby. But the ship is always too well-guarded when it's in town, which isn't often. It's always out there, setting the pace for the rest of the fleet, accelerating humanity's march to the edge of the cliff. Our souls dying more and more every time she swings back to Darkside, her cargo bay full of the metals fueling the technology that enslaves us and destroys the essence of what it means to human.

Enough!

What am I waiting for?

I'm doing it . . . right now.

I just wish . . . well, I wish a lot of things, I guess. But it's too late. I can't let this opportunity pass. Your father's ship. His mistress. And the *Bellwether*.

Two birds.

Two. Birds.

. . .

. . .

. . .

I'm sorry, honey.

There's no other choice.

Now let's see . . . where's that wooden thruster spoon?

20

Collision Imminent

THEA SWINGS her body through the harpoon bay's exterior door. As she sits with her back against the adjacent wall, catching her breath, the ship lurches forward. Had she not made it to this wall before the ship began to accelerate, she would have been sent back out through the open door. Realizing this, she activates her suit's magnetic boots. Relief floods through her as the boots' heels snap down against the metal decking.

The airlock she needs to pass through connects the harpoon and cargo bays, but it's typically entered from the cargo bay side, so the airlock rests in a pressurized state, to match. That means when Thea reaches the door, she'll be forced to initiate the airlock depressurization cycle before the system will let her enter.

The vibration from the ship's engines radiates up her legs as she makes her way across the harpoon bay. She reaches the airlock and peers through the two sets of glass doors into the cargo bay, anxious to get inside and gain control of her ship from her mother. She enters the necessary codes into the control pad next to the door, and just as she starts the depressurization cycle, the emergency light above the airlock door begins to swirl.

Her suit isn't calibrated to the ship's comms yet, so she spends a few frantic seconds bathed in the emergency light's awful red glow as she establishes the link, then listens to the *Zephyr*'s warning system issue a "proximity alert," followed in a tone far too calm for its next dire declaration: "Collision is imminent."

Collision? With what? The station? Has her mother lost control of the ship? The computer would be giving her some guidance, but she's never flown—

Then a terrible realization takes hold, one that sends fear icing up Thea's spine.

The image of the *Bellwether* rising from Dock A flashes in her mind.

She's going to ram the Bellwether*!*

The terrible-yet-probable possibility settles on Thea's heart like a stone. She screams in frustration, pounds the heavy glass door of the airlock. The airlock is only midway through the depressurization process. It's taking too long! And when she finally gets inside, the airlock will need to repressurize again before she can go into the cargo bay—a delay she can't afford, which is underscored when the computer once again reminds her of their "imminent collision."

Her mind reels as she imagines the two ships colliding. *Her* ship. Her *dad's* ship. Her *crew's* ship. All the people on the *Bellwether*, including Darcey and Lola.

She can't let it end this way. Won't let it end this way.

She has to stop this ship, and there's only one way she can do that now.

Heavy, multicolored hoses are attached to the side of the harpoon cannon next to a control panel with the word "Central" displayed in blocky blue letters. Thea races over, enters her master code into the panel, and swipes through a series of screens until she reaches the cannon's primary controls, which she switches to manual. She's forced to endure a number of pop-ups that warn her against shutting off central harpoon controls. The override's primary function is to serve as a fail-safe in the event that bridge control goes down and you need to release a harpoon line or retract a bolt from a captured asteroid.

But you can also use it to fire a bolt.

Thea dismisses the system's final warning and accesses the manual targeting controls. The display changes to a 3D rendering of what's currently in the harpoon cannon's line of sight. Next to the rendering are dialog boxes with the current target's coordinates, which in this case are constantly changing since the ship is in motion. Below the dialog boxes is a red rectangle labeled *Fire*. She can tell by the rendering of the lunar surface that they're clear of the station and docks, climbing away from the surface.

Thea presses the button.

The hoses on the side of the cannon tense, like serpents about to strike. Vibrations from the floor ripple through her feet and into her legs and hips. Her eyes go wide as her boots begin to jump off the floor. She stabs a finger at the control pad on her suit's sleeve in an attempt to ramp up the boots' magnetic strength, but it's too late. The bolt is jettisoned, and a burst of energy throws Thea away from the cannon. She flies backward into the shot loading system, the back of her head cracking against one of the heavy coils of tungsten line.

Her helmet goes haywire. The information on the screen blinks out. The interior lights strobe for a few seconds before going dark as well.

The room seems to twist and swirl around her, and she has a coppery taste in her mouth. She squeezes her eyes shut to ward off a wave of nausea and wraps her arms around her torso in a tight hug, trying to force her world to settle. She's afraid she might be losing consciousness. But she doesn't feel the black, null sensation she's come to know from other times when she's been knocked out, including recently at the hands of her mother. And when she risks a glance, she finds herself staring at a dented rivet on the ceiling, up close, nothing holding her to the floor now that her boots are deactivated.

She waits a few seconds longer to let her world settle, then pushes off the ceiling and floats down to the top of the cannon. She grabs hold and maneuvers her body so that she's able to look down through the harpoon bay door. The harpoon line is stuck in the moon's surface, quivering wildly, apparently under tremendous strain. Rory or any other pilot would mitigate the tension on the line by backing off the engines. But Thea can tell by the wild gesticulations in the heavy tungsten line that her mother has not eased off the thrust.

She tries to take a deep breath, but the air in her suit feels thin. She instinctively checks her oxygen reading, only to remember that her helmet is dead. She has no way of knowing how much oxygen is left in her suit—but her lungs tell her it's less than she would like, maybe less than she'll need. In her race to get to the *Zephyr*, she hadn't even thought to check the gauges when she first put on the suit.

She swings her body around and kicks off the cannon back toward the airlock leading to the cargo bay. But her adrenaline has gotten the best of her and she's traveling a lot faster than she intended. She barely manages to hold on to the door handle to prevent herself from bouncing off after smashing into the glass. The airlock display informs her that the depressurization cycle is complete, so she heads in, closes the door behind her, and initiates the pressurization process. All the while, she tries to take only small sips of the remaining oxygen in her suit. It's not easy under the circumstances.

As the airlock re-pressurizes, she peers back through the door into the harpoon bay. The line extending from the harpoon barrel is vibrating so fast that it's become a blur, and as she looks on in disbelief, the cannon itself begins to bend, ever so slightly, toward the open bay doors. Then it begins to bend the floor with it.

It's going to rip the bay apart—and potentially the airlock door with it.

She realizes with horror that if the airlock is compromised, she'll have no way of getting into the cargo bay in time. And even if she could somehow override the system and force the interior door, it wouldn't matter because the second it opened, the cargo bay would go vacuum.

The floor behind the cannon continues to not just bend, but tear. The barrel of the cannon is now partway out the harpoon bay door. The airlock shudders violently around Thea.

And the pressurization cycle pauses, the display flashing red.

That's when she knows she must do the thing she's been dreading most since discovering that her mother is Darkside's saboteur.

She reaches for the airlock control panel and hails the bridge.

21

Interrupted

"No, no, no, no, no. What happened?

"Why are we stopped?

"Did I hit the wrong button?

"None of this makes any sense. All these readings!

"Allgood, you fuck! Did you do this?

"I won't let you! You've got to go down, goddammit!

"Stop. Stop!

"Dammit! He's getting away!"

Ba-woop, ba-woop, ba-woop.

"A breach? Where is there a breach?

"Holy shit, did I shoot—"

"Mom?"

. . .

. . .

"Mom, do you hear me?"

"Thea?"

"Mom, if you can hear me, comms controls are on the right arm of the captain's chair. The third button from the—"

"Thea, are you on board the *Zephyr*?"

"Listen to me—"

"What are you doing here? You shouldn't be here!"

"Mom, you need to throttle back."

"How did you stop the ship?"

"I'm in the airlock between the cargo bay and the harpoon bay, my suit's been compromised, and there's a breach. Throttle back!"

Ba-woop, ba-woop, ba-woop.

"You shot a harpoon?"

"Did you hear me? Throttle back *now*, or I'm going to die!"

. . .

. . .

"Mom! Mom, please! I need you!"

"Okay, yes. Yes! I'm here. At the controls. Throttling back now. How far do I go?"

. . .

. . .

"Thea, how far do I pull back?

"Thea, talk to me! What do I do?"

. . .

. . .

"Oh my God. Thea? Are you there?

"Thea?

"Thea!

"I'm coming! Hold on, baby. I'm coming!"

END RECORDING.

22

Turnabout is Fair Play

JULIA WATTS RACES down the *Zephyr*'s main corridor. As she rounds the final corner to the cargo bay, the shipwide announcement warning against a collision with the Conglomerate's flagship begins once again but then cuts off midsentence and changes to "*Proximity alert terminated.*"

Julia howls her frustration. The *Bellwether*, which had been in her grasp, has escaped. Her chance to strike a crushing blow to the international astromining operation is gone. It would have made all the difference, validated all her sacrifice over so many years. Her bosses would have been proud.

There's nothing she can do about it now. It's over.

But she can still save her daughter.

She's breathing hard as she reaches the entrance to the cargo bay and slaps the control panel to open the door. Stacks of crates, bins, and metal hoppers form an obstacle course she needs to traverse to reach the opposite side of the room where the airlock is located. She's moving so fast that she stumbles over the hard metal brushes of a robotic sweeper. As she scrambles back up to her feet and around a pocked and dented metal hopper filled with silver- and copper-colored rubble, she sees the airlock door leading out of the cargo bay is partially open. Curled up on the ground, just inside the cargo bay, is Thea.

Julia screams her daughter's name, but there's no response. She covers the few meters between them in a heartbeat and is just reaching down toward her when Thea swings a heavy wrench at her mother's head, catching her above her left temple.

Julia's eyes go wide for an instant, then the light goes out of them, and she crumples to the cargo bay floor with a stifled murmur of surprise.

———

THEA CROUCHES OVER JULIA, the wrench poised to deliver another blow if necessary. She rears back, shaking with rage, ready to do it, wanting to do it, but her mother doesn't stir. She lowers the wrench and pokes her mother's shoulder, but the woman remains unconscious, her breathing ragged but regular.

Thea lets out a choked burst of held air and stares at her mother, takes in her face. New crow's feet at the corners of her eyes. The faded line of an unfamiliar scar on her cheek. Same thin nose, unlike Thea's. Same chin, one they share.

Thea tosses the wrench aside and finally, finally releases some of the misery and anger she's been holding on to for days and months and years and years. She digs her fists into her eyes as the flood comes, her shoulders hitching under the unbidden and unwanted sobs that rack her whole body. She falls to the side and lies on her back, crying like she hasn't cried ever before, even when her father died, even when Elliott died. She's totally and completely overwhelmed by the emotions crashing through her mind and body—

Until the ship-wide proximity alert returns, including the

ominous coda "Collision imminent." It's a warning you never want to hear, let alone twice in the span of minutes.

Thea rises to her feet in disbelief.

She takes a few steps toward the bridge, skids to a halt, then spins around and looks down on her mother. She can't leave her like this. If she wakes up, she could create problems.

Thea grabs her ankles and drags her toward the airlock. The same airlock Thea herself nearly died in. Only when her mother reduced the ship's throttle, reducing the pressures on the harpoon bay, and by extension the airlock, did the re-pressurization cycle resume, allowing her to escape into the cargo bay. Her collapse to the floor had been real. Only once she was there did she see the opportunity to leverage that position.

Her mother's head bounces off the metal decking as Thea hastily moves her, but she doesn't slow and her mother doesn't awaken. Once her mother's stowed inside, Thea steps back into the cargo bay. She closes the airlock door and locks it so that her mother is trapped inside, then races to once again save her ship.

———

As soon as she reaches the bridge, she knows what's happening. Her mother throttled back too far and now the ship is falling toward the moon's surface like a kite when the wind suddenly dies.

"*Proximity alert. Collision imminent,*" the system announces as Thea jumps into Rory's pilot's seat. She takes in the console readings and her heart drops. The ship's too close to the surface! She fires the starboard thrusters and pushes them to their maximum to try and send the ship in the opposite direction, but the ship already has too much downward momentum, is too close to the surface; the thrusters are slowing the ship's descent, but they won't have time to reverse it.

Thea curses her mother and braces for impact.

She's nearly jettisoned from the pilot's chair by a sudden jolt. Metal crunches and seams burst. Pops and hisses and alarms deafen and confuse her as the pilot's control panel crashes in a good old-fashioned blue screen of death.

But it wasn't the impact she expected. It was milder—much milder. For one thing, the ship is still in one piece. After what feels like an eternity, the noise decreases a few decibels and Thea can see through the front viewscreen that the *Zephyr*'s now moving in the opposite direction, aided by her starboard thrusters.

A filtered voice comes over the comms system. "*Zephyr*, do you read?"

Her console is dead, and she has to scramble to find one that's still operational, all the while listening as someone repeatedly and urgently hails her ship. She discovers that Lola's console is the one still functioning, because of course it is. It's Lola's.

"This is Captain Watts. Who is this?"

"This is the Conglomerate ship *Bellwether*, two thousand meters off your bow," the voice says. A man's voice. "Adjust your thrusters, Captain. Your ship is vectoring, and we won't be able to fire another harpoon bolt to stop you from colliding with the surface."

Thea's fingers tap out a frantic rhythm on Lola's console as she adjusts the starboard thrusters, then fires her port ones to counteract her momentum. Now stable above the surface, Thea looks through her front viewscreen and can see the *Bellwether* off in the distance, the metronymic flashing of its ground lights reflecting off the harpoon line extending from its bow to right off her starboard side. They'd managed to not only place their harpoon line in the path of her falling ship, but the pilot also created enough slack in the line so that the tungsten cable caught the ship rather than simply slice into it. The ship that has been her tormentor for months now, it seems, is suddenly her savior.

"Great shot," she says to the Conglomerate pilot. "Thanks for the assist."

"Do you have her?"

"Sorry, say again?" Thea replies, stalling. She heard the question fine.

"Do you have Mae Green?" the man asks again.

Thea hesitates, but not out of reluctance to turn her mother in. She's over that, for sure. She hesitates simply because uttering the words means she needs to face what's next. She remembers feeling the exact same emotions after her father's funeral, the same sort of sinking dread that comes from taking that first fraught step forward into the unknown. But when the Conglomerate officer repeats his question for a third time, Thea bears down and answers him in an unwavering, solid voice.

"Yes, I have her."

Then, after a beat, "And her name's not Mae Green."

PART III

Mother, May I?

23

For the Record

ON THE WALL SCREEN, the adjudicator pounds her gavel and
pleads for order. The individuals around her at the Hague heed
her commands no more than do those gathered here in a
chamber on the moon, watching the adjudicator—and the
general chaos of the Hague—from a quarter million miles
away. But finally, after what can only be described as vigorous
hammering, the International Astromining Alliances' presiding
officer once again gains a moment of control of the session.
She warns delegates in both locations that further outbursts of
any sort will not be tolerated, even though the last few hours
have been characterized by a constant stream of proclama-
tions, declarations, condemnations, and the grossest abject
grandstanding by nearly every IAA member nation's represen-
tative, save the few members who refused to attend the
proceedings and are actively protesting the emergency tribunal
on procedural grounds, contending that proper petitions of
office and subsequent elections must be held before taking the
unprecedented action of naming an international space crimes
adjudicator—a stance the woman with the gavel and swollen
wrist is coming around to as the afternoon wears on.

With a heavy sigh, the adjudicator turns her attention back to the camera—and to the witness currently seated in the chamber on the moon. "Please, sir, continue," she says.

"Apologies, *ma chère*," Beetle replies, "but can you remind me of the question."

His patience spent, Allgood jumps up from his chair near the witness stand and points at the screen. "She asked what your captain told you about the woman who attacked her in the maintenance conduit on the day of the explosions!" he yells.

Turning to Allgood, Beetle says, "Nothing."

"I'm sorry?" Allgood says, taken aback.

"Nothing . . . *sir*," Beetle offers in a weak acknowledgment of Allgood's rank, which gets chuckles from several of the fleet's captains in the audience.

He waves off the unnecessary honorific. "Are you saying Thea Watts didn't tell you *anything* about her encounter in the conduits?"

"No sir, that's not what I'm saying." Beetle glances to where Rory and Lola are sitting at the back of the room. "*Captain* Watts told us everything that happened when she tried to catch the saboteur. But you asked me what the captain told us about *her*, sir, and she told me nothing of the woman herself. In fact at that point, my captain, like everyone else up here, didn't even know that we were dealing with a female terrorist."

"Admiral, please," the adjudicator says, cutting in in an effort to prevent Allgood from hijacking the examination.

"Apologies, ma'am," Allgood says. "Just trying to move us along."

"That is not your role in these proceedings, Admiral."

"Well, it ought to be somebody's," Allgood replies.

At his insult, the adjudicator's calm breaks. She slams her gavel so hard it rebounds out of her grasp and off screen.

Lacking the ability to get physically in Allgood's space, she resorts to waggling a finger at the camera.

"Be it here in these chambers in the Netherlands or there on the moon, the next person who disrupts these proceedings will be escorted out," she says. "I'll also remind you, Admiral, that the authority granted to you and the Conglomerate by the IAA is temporary. Now that the perpetrator has been apprehended, if I need things to *move along*, as you say, I will cede questioning to the head of Municipal, Miss Achebe, who actually has some authority as it relates to this tribunal. Unlike you. Is that clear, sir?"

"Yes."

Not satisfied with Allgood's terse response, the adjudicator asks again if her rules are clear.

"Crystal," Allgood says, though his sneer would indicate otherwise.

The adjudicator's admonition of Allgood manages to keep everyone in check for the remainder of Beetle's questioning, during which he echoes the testimony of his colleagues, Rory and Lola. In fact, the people at the Hague and on the moon remain on their best behavior as the adjudicator interviews Julia Watts's neighbors, Inky and Asaad, and a few others from the Darkside maintenance staff. No one, it seems, wants to test the adjudicator's resolve or delay any further getting to what is undeniably the main event, which begins when the last of the witnesses is dismissed and Thea Watts is led into the room.

———

THEA RESTS her left hand on the outstretched tablet, raises her right, and swears her oath. Formalities done and judicial tradition honored, the adjudicator begins.

"Captain Watts, the members of this tribunal have had the

opportunity to review the video footage of your interview with Admiral Allgood and Miss Achebe on the day of the explosions. In that testimony, you said you didn't recognize the person you chased into the maintenance conduits, couldn't determine their gender, and that no words had been exchanged between the two of you. Now that we know—"

"I'm sorry to interrupt, Madam Adjudicator," a man says to the side of where the adjudicator is sitting. When the camera swings over to the speaker, Thea's overcome by the image of her dad's lawyer, Billy, rising to his feet to address the tribunal.

"Who are you, sir?" the adjudicator asks.

"Legal counsel for Ms. Watts," he says.

"Which?"

Billy swipes a handkerchief across his sweaty brow, then tucks it back into his crumpled jacket pocket. "Sorry, ma'am?"

"Which Ms. Watts are you representing," she clarifies.

"Thea Watts, ma'am."

The adjudicator impatiently waves her hand, indicating that Billy should continue.

"What happened that day was not testimony," he says. "It's important to note that Thea Watts was not under any sort of oath at the time of that filming, and any information she provided should be treated as a firsthand eyewitness account, at best."

The adjudicator's exasperation couldn't be mistaken even if the distance between the two rooms in which the proceeding is taking place was tripled. "Gasira, is this true?" she asks into the camera.

Achebe gets to her feet. "Yes, ma'am."

"Ah, for Christ's sake, Gasira," Allgood begins, but gets no further before Achebe reasserts her position in the Darkside Station hierarchy.

"Her lawyer is right, Brian. It wasn't official testimony.

We may wish it had been, but it was not." She lets her statement hang for a few seconds, then smooths her jacket and turns to face Thea. "I recommend this tribunal ignore that video in its entirety and properly interrogate the witness about that day's events," she says. "Let's get it right, for the record."

Walking into this room, Thea counted Achebe as an ally. But as she watches the woman take her seat, all business once again, she's not so sure. She scans the crowd for her crew and finds them toward the back. She and Lola lock eyes for a split second before Lola joins Rory and Beetle in staring at the floor.

The adjudicator mutes the line and confers with Thea's lawyer and other offscreen members of the tribunal. After three, maybe four minutes, the adjudicator unmutes.

"Thank you for your patience," she says, her hands steepled before her. "Until we can get an official ruling on the nature of the existing interview, we will ignore the witness's previous statements on this matter and proceed with our questioning."

Allgood slaps the table in front of him, but to Thea's surprise, he stays silent.

"Captain Watts," the adjudicator continues, "I will start by reminding you of the oath you just swore before this tribunal. While this body cannot pass final judgment on you as an American citizen, its findings hold significant weight in every nation's courts. Do you understand?"

"Yes, ma'am," Thea says without hesitation.

The adjudicator nods, then makes a statement that sends ripples through both rooms.

"It's also important for you to know that the suspect, Julia Watts, your mother, has pled guilty to all charges, including attacks on the *Victor Hugo*, *Lillehammer*, and your own ship. Her guilt is not in question. The sole purpose of this inquiry is to ascertain your knowledge of your mother's identity during the course of the search efforts led by Admiral Allgood of the Conglomerate fleet."

The adjudicator pauses to let the murmurs die down and allow the gravity of the situation to settle in, then she asks Thea if she's willing to continue, to which Thea responds in the affirmative.

The adjudicator asks her first question. "Captain Watts. After escaping the calamity in the main concourse, you found yourself in the Hub, face to face with the person you believed to be responsible for the bombings. Is that correct?"

"Yes," Thea says.

"And at that moment, did you recognize the person?"

"No, I did not."

"Could you tell, at that moment, the person's gender?"

"No. Given their attire, I could not."

"When did you find out the saboteur was a woman?"

"When Darcey—Lieutenant Gray—came to my ship and showed me and my crew the video from the refinery. You can ask her."

Allgood jumps in. "She's still recovering from what your mother did to her, so we'll just have to take your word for it."

Thea feels a swell of heat rise from her core. She'd love to scream at Allgood for his smugness, but knows it would only play right into his hand. So instead she stays silent while the adjudicator scolds him.

After issuing another "final" warning to Allgood, the adjudicator brings them all back to task.

"Captain Watts, at the moment in the Hub when you came face to face with the saboteur, was she carrying anything?"

"Yes. A backpack, which she dropped."

"Did she have any weapons?"

"Not that I could tell."

"Did she say anything?"

Thea pauses, looks down at her trembling hands, tries to speak, but her throat constricts.

"Captain Watts?" the adjudicator presses.

Thea's voice is soft, barely a whisper. "Yes," she says.

After a beat filled with gasps in both the Earth- and moon-bound rooms, the adjudicator bangs her gavel. "I'm sorry, will you repeat that, Captain Watts?"

This time Thea answers with more conviction. "Yes, she spoke to me."

Allgood is out of his seat in a heartbeat. "You lied to me!" he shouts. Then remembering himself—and maybe seeing the look on the adjudicator's face—he motions to Achebe and amends his claim to, "You lied to both of us!"

"I didn't lie," Thea says. "I just didn't remember, that's all."

"Didn't *remember*?" Allgood says, not hiding his skepticism.

"You'll recall, I had a pretty serious head injury," Thea says.

"That's convenient!" someone shouts from the side of the room, which draws instant rebukes from most of the other people assembled.

"Captain Watts," the adjudicator says, her loud voice crackling the speakers in the Municipal chamber, "can you please elaborate? At that moment, facing the person you suspected to be responsible for these bombings, what did she say to you?"

"You have to remember, she was wearing a facemask, so her voice—"

Achebe cuts her off. "Just tell us what she said, Captain."

Thea's eyes fill at the coldness in Achebe's voice. "She said she was glad." Thea lets out a deep sob. "She was glad I was okay."

Achebe's lips tighten into a thin line as she slowly shakes her head.

Unlike Achebe, Allgood is incensed to the point that he

apparently no longer even cares about the adjudicator's threat to have him removed. "And you expect us to believe that you *still* didn't know it was your mother?" he snaps, looking meaningfully at the shocked faces around him, certain he's asking the question on everyone's mind.

"I hadn't seen or talked to her in years," Thea answers. "She abandoned my father and me when he got sick. She didn't even come to his funeral. And on top of that, she had never been politically motivated, and didn't have any causes she followed, or so I thought. So why in the world would I expect that she'd be the saboteur?"

Thea turns away from Allgood and faces the adjudicator's image on the screen. "My mother led a life I never knew. Learning she's a member of a humanist terrorist organization and finding her on the moon living under an alias . . . to me, that's the equivalent of finding little green men up here. Even if I *had* recognized her voice, there is no way I would have let myself believe it. How could I? She was dead to me!"

Her words hang in the air, no one quite knowing how to proceed until someone offscreen behind the adjudicator asks something.

The adjudicator repeats the question for everyone. "When *did* you realize it was her?"

"When Admiral Allgood and I discovered her alias," Thea says. "When I saw the picture of the person known to everyone else as Mae Green. That's when I knew."

"And what did you do then?"

"Initially, I think I was in shock and just trying to process the whole thing. As soon as we found the abandoned conduit behind her locker, I guessed where she'd be going. My ship was the only thing that made any sense, so I just ran."

"Hold on," Allgood says. "Your mother had just attacked the refinery and the Hyperloop. She'd sabotaged several other ships in the months leading up to this recent assault. Killed a bunch of people, including your boyfriend." Thea flinches at that last remark, and others murmur; Allgood utters a quick apology that seems less for Thea and more for decorum's sake before asking his question. "After all that damage, that violence, why would your ship be the only thing that made sense?"

Thea faces Allgood, resolute. "Because it was my dad's. And now it's mine. It was the last thing of ours for her to destroy. That's why. And I couldn't let that happen." Then in a bit of turnabout, she adds, "And it's a good thing I trusted my instincts, Admiral, because if I hadn't, the moon would have a brand-new crater filled with the twisted heap of metal that was once *your* ship."

Thea expects Allgood to explode, to get himself hauled from the room, spitting curses and threats. Instead of vitriol, however, he unleashes only his dazzling white smile accompanied by a few nods, game recognizing game. She's seen it too many times before to be thrown off by it. She shakes her head dismissively in response, stands, and addresses everyone.

"I know it's hard to believe. I would be suspicious too if I were in your positions. But the second I knew my mother was behind this, I acted. The Conglomerate's flagship, this station, our livelihoods, and the future of our planet are all intact because I stopped her."

She fixes her eyes on her crew, who are finally meeting her gaze. "I know you may have your doubts about me," she says, "but please consider everything that happened since this all started. That's all I can ask."

Thea takes her seat amid silence.

After a quick moment during which the adjudicator once again confers with those gathered around her, she unmutes the line.

"Thank you, Captain Watts," she says. "We are going to weigh all the testimony given here today before rendering our verdict. In the meantime, you are confined to the *Zephyr*."

With a swift crack of her gavel, the tribunal adjourns.

As everyone begins shuffling out of the room, Thea catches Rory's eye. He stares at her, no warmth in his gaze, chewing on the inside of his cheek. She expects a nod, expects some sort of acknowledgment, but she gets neither. He simply turns his back on her.

She collapses back into her chair, knowing now, for certain, that she is well and truly alone.

24

Bitter Truth

THE SCUFFLE, scrape, buzz, and thwap of people trying to put the Hub and their lives back together echoes up the stairwell as Thea and three security officers make their way down from Municipal. Once word of the saboteur's capture reached the Neighborhood, the task of holding everyone there became impossible, so the stationwide shelter-in-place order was lifted. Free from their forced confinement, the residents of Darkside Station emerged to survey the aftermath of the attack, trade stories of where they were and who they were with when it all went down, and share sorrow and rage at the crimes perpetrated against them. They're a community united by a collective catastrophe, all of them, everyone wanting the same thing: justice.

Thea and the officers are almost at the bottom of the stairs when she has to stop, suddenly queasy at the thought of facing so many people.

"Just . . . gimme a second, okay?" she says, then closes her eyes and sucks in a few ragged breaths. The stairwell is too warm, and the air smells like sweat, which does nothing to help her nerves.

Finally, after a fraught minute, the officer in charge decides it's time to move them along. "Come on, let's get this done," he says, and the procession continues.

Thea's dread grows with each step. She wonders how people have been processing the news about her mother, but she doesn't have to wonder very long. The second Thea steps out of the stairwell and into the Hub, the moment she sees the looks on everyone's faces, she has her answer.

The buzz in the Hub dwindles and dies as Thea begins to move through the crowd. The air feels charged like right before a thunderstorm. She's dizzied under the weight of everyone's gaze. She wants to race through the parting onlookers, be free of their judgment. But she's forced to keep stride with her escorts, who squeeze stun sticks beneath white knuckles.

She tries to make eye contact with friends and other acquaintances, but no one will meet her gaze. No one except Molly, that is, who gives her a small wave from inside her booth below the Leaderboard, which is now dark and hanging askew.

That tiny gesture nourishes Thea, and she tries to wave back, but one of the officers grabs her elbow, not in a rough way, but as a warning. He gently pulls her toward the entrance to the main concourse. She expects to see anger or impatience written on the young man's face, but instead she sees that his eyes are bloodshot and ringed in a purple-blue that indicates a lack of rest. Sweat beads on his brow as he scans the crowd. Without making eye contact, he mouths "please" to her, and Thea lets him lead her out of the Hub.

Relief floods through her as she steps across the threshold into the main concourse. Two of her escorts stay behind to secure the entrance and make sure no one tries to follow. She and the young man who coaxed her from the Hub continue on toward the docks, walking a bit easier now.

Up ahead, workers are carving away a section of the hardened foam that sealed the breach in the concourse wall.

"What are they doing?" she asks the young officer, just as a chunk of the life-saving foam falls to the ground.

"They inflated a blister," he says, pointing toward a different portion of the concourse wall freed from the pink foam. And maybe because she didn't put up a fight when he urged her to leave the Hub, he acquiesces when she asks to take a quick look.

Thea peers through the opening but can barely see the yellowish membrane now attached to the outside of the station wall. She moves farther down and is able to step on part of a bulkhead to get a higher view of the structure, which does indeed resemble a bubble on the wall's surface. The officer explains that with the blister in place, they can repair the concourse wall from the inside and won't have to work in the vacuum of space. Plus, it'll prevent them from having to seal off this section of the station.

"We're still gonna restrict movement through the area until it's done, but it should only take a few days," he says.

She steps off the bulkhead and starts walking toward the docks again with the officer at her side. "Thanks for letting me check it out," she says. Then adds, "And for back there, too."

The young man nods. "It's the least I could do. You ask me, I think people should be thanking you. After all, you're the one who caught her."

"It doesn't bother you that she's my mom?"

"Nah."

Surprised, Thea asks, "Why not?"

"We're not our parents, Captain. And thank god for it too. You should meet *my* mother."

She chokes up, trying to hold back the torrent of emotions, knowing that this tiny moment of kindness from such an unlikely source at this improbable moment will stick with her for the rest of her life.

"Come on," he says to her. "Let's get you home."

As soon as Thea steps off the lift into the *Zephyr*'s cargo bay, her eyes begin to water. She can almost taste the aerosolized metal on the pungent air. Her mouth tingles like she's sucking on a penny. She pulls her shirt up over her nose and beelines for the environmental control panel. A *Fume Event* indicator flashes red on the screen, but when she tries to initiate the recirculation system, an error code pops up.

"Oy, won't work," Rory says, startling her. He walks over and hands her a breather similar to the one he's wearing. Beetle is behind him, carrying a plasma welder.

Thea fits the breather over her face. "What's wrong?"

"Stern scrubbers are fucked," he says. "Seems like the intake system got pinched by the *Bellwether*'s harpoon line when . . . well, you know."

The three of them stare at each other, trying to figure out where to begin. Finally breaking the awkward silence, Beetle points to the harpoon bay with the nose of his welder.

"The hull's in pretty bad shape, but we should be able to fix the cannon," he says. "We need to cut her free and get her in here to be sure."

"Where's Lola?" Thea asks.

"Girlie's on the bridge. With your friend Darcey out of commission, a lot of the station's comms system work fell to her. She's been going at it pretty hard."

"I bet," Thea says, hating the distance she feels between them, made all the worse by the breathers and the bad air, which is already filled with so much tension she fears it might combust. Unable to bear it any longer, she takes Rory's and Beetle's hands. "Can we go talk?" she asks. "I have a lot to tell you."

The three of them head toward the bridge.

As soon as they're out of the cargo bay, they take off their breathers. Rory and Beetle give her a status report on the ship. Both reiterate how lucky they are that the person sitting in the *Bellwether*'s pilot's chair was so skilled, otherwise the *Zephyr* would have suffered much worse damage from their harpoon or even have crashed into the surface. As it stands, Rory thinks they should be able to get the ship flying in a matter of weeks.

"Not that anyone is going anywhere anytime soon," Beetle adds. "Rory and I are still assigned to refinery repairs, and I don't see us being able to restore the place to full operation for months."

Rory seconds Beetle's assessment and adds, "She sure knew how to hit where it hurts."

Thea looks at his reddening face. "Trust me, I know."

On the bridge, Lola is hunched over her station, fingers flying over her screen and keyboard, the lights on her earbuds pulsing in time with whatever music she's piping directly into her brain. When Rory taps her shoulder, she nearly flies out of her chair.

"Rory, what the—" Then she sees Thea. "Oh, hey."

"Hey," Thea says.

She takes in the three of them, their slumped shoulders, darting eyes, weird new tics. Rory rocking on his heels, Beetle chewing a thumbnail, Lola tucking her legs under her, then thinking better of it before crossing and uncrossing them. They look confused and anxious. But more than anything, they look hurt, which is almost too much for Thea to bear.

"Listen, the first thing I need you guys to know—" Thea manages before Lola lets her have it.

"You lied to us," the girl says, knees to her chest and arms wrapped around her shins.

"I know," Thea says.

"You could have told us."

Thea can only nod.

"We would have . . . I don't know," Lola continues, frustration etched across her wrinkled brow. She gets more animated, and strands of purple and black hair fly around her head as she barrels on. "I don't know what we would have done! But we could have done it together. Like we always do. *Did*, anyway. But you didn't give us that chance. You kept it from us. From *us*!"

Then with a shudder, she finishes in a small voice, "You shouldn't have done that."

"I know," Thea says, her voice cracking.

Beetle doesn't seem ready for apologies yet and picks up the questioning. "Is what you said to the tribunal true?"

"What part?" Thea asks.

"That you didn't know it was her," Beetle says, then spits out a piece of thumbnail. "That you didn't realize it was your mother until you saw the picture of her alias."

Thea shakes her head reluctantly, then musters the courage to finally, *finally* tell the truth. "No," she says. "I knew it sooner than that."

"When?"

"I think deep down I knew it was her as soon as I heard her voice in the Hub," Thea says. "But I knew for sure not that long after, when I actually saw her face. Right before she knocked me out."

"Wait, you saw her face *then*?" Beetle says. "In the conduit?"

Thea nods silently and lets this news sink in. After a few seconds, she fills in the details she knows they're looking for. "We fought in the conduit, and I managed to pin her down. I yanked off her facemask, saw it was her, and completely froze. That's when she clocked me."

"So you didn't just lie to us. You lied to *everyone*," Lola says.

"Yes." It's all Thea can say, and the brief relief from uttering that simple word is gone as the shame of it floods in.

The silence stretches out.

And out.

Rory, who has refrained from asking anything this whole time, finally breaks the silence by posing the only question that really matters.

"Why?"

Thea lets out a perverse chuckle, swipes the back of her hand across her nose, palms away a stream of tears that have started to flow down her face, and says out loud what she's barely been able to admit to herself.

"I don't know. I really wish I had something better than that. I truly do. You guys deserve a better explanation than that. But it's the truth. I don't know why I did it."

Beetle hands her a greasy handkerchief from his back pocket, which makes her heart shatter.

"There were so many times I wanted to tell you guys, but I couldn't do it," she continues. "I was in denial, and hurt, and angry. I was afraid that people would blame me—was afraid of *this*, right here. Afraid that I'd lose everything I care about, and after Ell died, I couldn't let that happen."

Unmoved, Rory says, "She killed him, Thea. Elliott's dead because of *her*."

"I know." Thea's glad he said it. Glad that Rory's calling her to account, wanting to own it. "And I know that somehow that makes it *my* fault too."

Beetle and Lola both jump to refute that claim, but she cuts them off. "I know, I know what you're going to say. But you see . . . this is what kept me silent. The guilt. Whether I earned it or not, I knew that *I* would be the one to bear the guilt of what she did. That's also why *I* had to be the one to catch her. Why I had to be the one to bring her to justice. So that all of you, in time, would maybe forgive me for being the daughter of the person who took so much from us."

She meets their eyes, each person in turn. "I'm sorry. I

really, really am. I should have told you. I should have *trusted* you."

No one says a word. Which is good, because Thea isn't done.

"I'm doing now what I should have done before. I'm trusting you. All of you. You can tell them what I just told you. Or not. It's up to you."

And with that Thea rushes off her bridge, wondering if standing on it will ever feel the way it used to, and whether the three people in the world she loves the most will still be a part of her life after today.

25

Back at It

DARCEY WAKES WITH A START. Harsh white light blasts down from above, like hot needles piercing her eyeballs straight through to her cottony brain. She tries to turn her head away from the glare, and a jolt of pain sears down her neck and across her shoulders. Her sharp cry draws the attention of one of the nurses.

"Easy there, Lieutenant," the man says, rushing over and placing his hands on either side of Darcey's head. They're cool and soft. "You need to keep your head still."

Darcey's eyes flutter as she peers up at his smiling face. He's handsome, salt-and-pepper hair, smells like lemons. She winces at the halo of light around his head, which triggers him to reach across her body and touch a control pad on the side of her medical pod. The lights dim, then shut off. "There you are, ma'am. That should be better."

"Thanks," she croaks, and she's startled by the sound of her voice. She touches her throat and feels a metal collar. Her fingers trace the device to the back of her neck, where a square plate is attached to the base of her skull, cold to the touch.

She tries to remain calm, be analytical, put the pieces

together—the bright room with this smiling nurse, the bed, the weird collar. She doesn't know how she ended up here or where *here* even is or what's wrong with her neck, which feels heavy and numb. She flexes her fingers and wiggles her toes. Bounces her knees on the bed and reaches out to the man, who gently takes her hand and eases it back down to the sheets, nodding to her and telling her she's okay, that she's perfectly fine. But she needs more than placating words and smiling assurances. She needs answers.

"Where am I?" she whispers, a wave of nausea washing over her as she coaxes out the words.

The nurse turns around, and she hears the sound of something being poured into a cup. "You're in the infirmary," he says as he turns back to her and angles a straw in her direction.

She sucks at the straw greedily, the water magnificent, a miracle.

"You have small fractures of C4 and C5, and a concussion," he says. "That's why you're wearing a craniosurgical collar. It's been in place about thirty-six hours, but we should be able to remove it by morning, and you'll be good to go."

The tension leeches from her body, leaving her empty. She reaches for her blanket, which he helps pull up over her chest. "I've been out that long?" she asks.

"Longer," he says, tapping at the medical pod's control panel again. Beneath her, the bed begins to warm. "We don't know how long you were unconscious in that air vent before the search team found you."

Another puzzle piece falls into place. Something odd was going on with the door to one of Dock A's ventilation shafts. She struggles to surface more, but her mind instead catches on something he said.

"Search team?"

"They were looking for you," he says, radiating calm as he

scans her eyes with a penlight. "When they caught her, she was wearing your jumper."

Her.

The saboteur.

The nurse pockets his penlight then fiddles with Darcey's collar, which gives off a soft beep in response. "Any of this ring a bell?" he asks.

She remembers the woman, crouched inside the dark vent. The woman from the video of the refinery. The same woman she'd seen long ago, in the picture Thea had taped to her dresser mirror in her Cambridge dorm room.

Darcey shivers harder despite the heat radiating from the bed. The awful truth obliterates the last bits of fogginess in her mind. "How'd they catch her?" she asks.

"Maniac tried to steal the *Zephyr*, but the ship's captain— Thea Watts—stopped her," the nurse says. "And it turns out that the woman is the captain's mother. Her *mother!* Can you believe that?"

Yes, in fact, Darcey can.

She tries to summon every conversation she and Thea ever had about her mother, hoping for something to spark, anything that could help make sense of this insanity.

"People are wondering if they're both somehow involved in what's been going on up here," the nurse says. "Word is, they're grilling Captain Watts up in Municipal right now."

"She didn't have anything to do with it!" Darcey snaps. She wants to vigorously defend her friend, certain of Thea's innocence, but she's overcome by a wave of dizziness, the blood pulsing so hard in her temples she's afraid it's going to burst out of her skull.

Her medical pod emits a series of beeps. "Easy, Lieutenant Grey," the nurse says.

Darcey feels pressure in the base of her neck. "What's happening?"

"Your collar is designed to keep your brain activity in check while it's repairing your spine. You're getting a little too excited, so it just administered a sedative." His voice sounds far away. "Everything's going to be fine. You rest now . . ."

She stares up at his naïve, gentle, oblivious face and lets out a small chuckle. "Sure it will," she says, slipping, floating, nearly gone. "Sure. Everything's gonna be fiiiinnne."

———

"How is she?" her father asks.

"Healing nicely," the doctor says. "In fact, better than I expected. Take a look here—"

The crinkly paper crinkles under Darcey's thighs as she scooches forward on the table. "When can I play again?" she asks the doctor, who is across the room and busy pointing out something on the x-ray. Neither of the men look at her.

"That's good," her father says. "Her team needs her back as soon as possible."

"Well, she's going to need to take it slow for a little while."

Her father seems to tense. "How slow?" he asks.

The doctor shrugs. "If she pushes too hard too fast, she could reinjure the area. That could require additional therapy."

"Hellooo?" Darcey says, waving her arm in the air like she's flagging down a taxi. "Did you guys hear me?"

Her father crosses his arms like he does on the showroom floor when he's negotiating with a customer. *Putting up the wall,* he calls it. He uses the same tactic on her when she's done something wrong and he's about to dole out punishment.

"Understood, Doc," he says. "I'll be sure she's careful. But to be clear, she *can* get back at it, right?"

The doctor capitulates under her dad's intense glare. "Sure,

sure. In fact, I'll tell you what. How about if I come by the house and check on her in a few days. How's that sound?"

"I'm right here!" Darcey says. "Right. Here!"

"That'll work fine," her father says, slapping his palm into the doctor's and giving him a hearty double-pump shake.

"Please, someone talk to me!" Darcey screams, tears rolling down her cheeks.

Finally, her dad responds. He turns toward her as if surprised to find that she's in the room.

"It's okay," he says. "You're okay."

"Are you sure? I don't feel okay."

"You're going to be fine, Lieutenant. Just fine."

Darcey's eyes snap open.

She turns her head toward Allgood's voice, able to do so this time without any pain. He's sitting cross-legged in a bedside chair, reading glasses perched at the end of his nose and a tablet in hand.

"Sorry, Admiral," she says, struggling to conceal her confusion. "Weird dream."

"I bet. You've been through a lot," he says. "Good news, though. Few more tests and they're gonna release you later today."

Darcey touches her throat and finds the metal collar gone. She turns her head side to side, then sits up higher in the bed. Her neck is stiff, and her shoulder muscles spasm as she moves, but otherwise she feels pretty good.

"That's great," she says, shaking off the last vestiges of the dream. "I hate hospitals."

He rests his glasses atop his head and scoots the chair closer. "I'm glad you're on the mend," he says, resting his hand atop hers.

"It's good of you to come, sir. But I'm sure you're needed elsewhere."

He waves the notion away. "Things are well in hand. Have you heard?"

"Bits and pieces," she says.

"Ah, well then, let me fill you in," he says, hands steepled together, gathering himself. "In fact, I'd love your take on the whole matter."

———

DARCEY IS ENTHRALLED by Allgood's story of tracking down their main suspect, Mae Green, only to discover that it was actually Julia Watts's alias and that she's the one responsible for the attacks on the *Victor Hugo*, *Lillehammer*, and the recent bombings, among other incidents at Darkside over nearly two years, to which she's confessed. When he tells her about how he and Thea found the ladder behind the maintenance lockers, and then how Thea vanished without leave, she can feel his demeanor change. She's worked for Allgood long enough to know when he's agitated, and that agitation grows as he wraps up the story of the near-collision between the *Zephyr* and the *Bellwether*.

"So as you can see, while your friend *is* the one who ultimately got our man and saved the day, there are still a *lot* of questions about what she knew and when she knew it," he says, sitting back in his chair. "That's what the tribunal is trying to get to the bottom of."

Darcey lets the tale settle, weighing how to wade into things with her boss, who she figures is here to be supportive but also to dig for information, given her history with Thea. Calculated sincerity.

"Where's her mother now?" she asks.

"A few doors down." He thumbs over his shoulder. "Heavily guarded, of course."

"Why is she here?"

Allgood cracks a wry smile. "Whatever Captain Watts lacks in veracity, she made up for in retribution."

Darcey's puzzled look leads him to clarify, which was probably his intent all along. "She nearly took her mother's head off with a pipe wrench."

Darcey lets out an *ahh*, followed by, "I bet that felt good," to which both she and Allgood nod with a touch of envy.

"Other than confessing, has she said anything?" Darcey asks, to which Allgood simply juts out his lower lip and shakes his head.

She circles back to the main subject. "Thea and I have had our differences, but, sir, I can't believe that Thea has *anything* to do with whatever her mother or this organization—"

"The New Muses," he says.

"Yes, sir. I can't believe Thea's a part of any of that."

"What makes you so sure?" he asks. "After all, it's her mother we're talking about here."

Darcey doesn't hesitate. "Her mother abandoned her," she says. "She left Thea to singlehandedly care for and then ultimately bury her father. That woman's a selfish coward, and it nearly ruined Thea's life. And now it sure seems to me—and sure as shit it will to Thea, as well—that the woman's trying to do it again."

Darcey throws the covers off and swings her legs over the side of the bed so that she's facing Allgood. "When she first came up here and decided to restart Watts Astromining, I thought she was crazy. Frankly, I thought she was going to get herself and her crew killed, and I told her so. Which didn't go over all that well with her, as you can imagine. But she proved me wrong. You have to admit, sir, she proved all of us wrong."

He nods, less reluctantly than Darcey expects.

"I don't know why I doubted her," she continues. "She's always been smarter than me, and that's saying something because I'm fucking as bright as they come, sir."

This has the intended effect on Allgood—he smiles. "You'll get no argument from me, Lieutenant. But that's why some of what happened is hard to swallow. I mean, the woman spoke to her. I get that they hadn't seen each other in years, but you always know your mother's voice, right?"

Darcey decides this fire needs no additional fuel, so she says nothing about how she herself recognized Julia Watts in the ventilation shaft.

She shrugs. "Maybe some part of Thea knew the truth, but she was just unable to process it given all the bullshit and baggage that comes along with her mother—and by the way, that baggage now includes killing the man she loved. If you're asking for my opinion, that's what I think probably happened. And honestly, sir, I'd hope that we all can forgive Thea any momentary lapse of clarity or reason and instead focus on the fact that when given the opportunity, it was she who brought her mom to justice."

He seems to consider what Darcey's laid out, then with a steady gaze, he says, "Do you trust her?"

"Yes, sir, I do," she replies without hesitation.

Allgood helps Darcey off the edge of the bed. Her legs wobble a bit as she stands, and he's there to support her. She expects him to let go once she's gained her footing, but instead he holds on tighter.

"I'm very happy that you're okay, Darcey," he says, breaking protocol by using her first name, which grabs her attention. "There are big changes coming, and you're going to be a critical part of what happens." A wicked smile breaks out across his face; it raises the hairs on Darcey's newly healed neck.

"What changes, sir?" she asks.

But Allgood simply turns and waves on his way out, saying as he leaves, "Don't worry, Lieutenant. You and everyone else will find out soon enough."

26

Pillow Talk

DARCEY GIGGLES as the same handsome nurse who tended to her yesterday, the man who certainly has an actual name but not one she cares to remember because it would get in the way of using the nickname she's proudly come up with for him—Nurse Lemon Pepper—holds her toes as he peels the adhesive sensor off the top of her foot.

"Sorry, again," she says, having had to apologize only moments ago for the other foot. "Just a little ticklish."

He smiles up at her. "No problem, Lieutenant."

She pulls on her socks as he taps away at a handheld device. She's been antsy for hours now.

"What's the verdict?" she asks.

He exaggerates a few final taps, then tucks the device into his back pocket. "Nerve signaling to your extremities looks perfectly normal, and the last scan of your neck came back negative. I just sent everything to the attending physician, who should be by shortly to sign your release."

He extends a fist in her direction, and she bumps it with her own. "That's great," she says. "No offense, but I can't wait to get out—"

A loud chime followed by an announcement cuts her off.

"*Code blue, code blue. All staff report to emergency seven. I repeat, report to emergency seven. This is an* all-staff *event.*"

Lemon Pepper immediately heads for the door. "Sorry, Lieutenant, it might be a bit longer."

"What's code blue?" she calls to him.

"Exposure to vacuum." He gives her a short wave. "I gotta go. Good luck!"

She follows him to the door and watches as medical staff rush past her room. After a minute or so, the flow of people heading to the emergency rooms ceases and the hallway is quiet once more.

She lets the door to her room swing closed and finds herself staring at the medical pod where she's spent the last few days. All she wants is to be back on the *Bellwether*, and the thought of sitting around and waiting for God knows how long to be officially released is suddenly too much to bear.

She opens the closet and takes out the new jumper Allgood brought when he visited. Her old one is probably sitting in the Municipal evidence lockup, if they truly discovered it on Julia Watts. She tosses her hospital gown on the floor, pulls on the starched blue jumper and boots, and leaves the room behind.

The unsettling stillness of the hallway is punctuated by the sharp scent of bleach. Darcey pinches her burning nostrils as she heads directly for the exit. She's been here long enough as it is, and if the doctors think she's ready to be released, she's not going to wait around just for a signature. But she doesn't get very far before something Allgood told her rears up in her mind. A unique opportunity is within her reach. And as much as she wants to get back to her ship, it's just too tantalizing to ignore.

Because Julia Watts is only a few doors away.

She assumes it'll be easy to find the room, because it will be the only door guarded by Municipal security. But she doesn't see any officers as she walks up and down a few of the nearby corridors. They must have been called away to help with the emergency—which makes this opportunity all the more undeniable.

She goes back to her own room and restarts her search, this time working in a more methodical fashion, peeking through every door window as she explores the first hallway. When she reaches a door where a nurse is blocking her view of the patient, she simply notes the room number so she can circle back later. She's just moved to the next hallway over when the emergency announcement returns.

"*Code blue, code blue. All staff please report to emergency seven. This is an* all-staff *event.*"

An *all-staff* event . . .

Bitter adrenaline hits the back of her throat as she thinks about the guards' absence—and the single nurse who'd blocked her view. Shouldn't that nurse be with the rest of the medical staff, dealing with the emergency?

Darcey races back to the room in question, her boots squeaking on the heavily waxed floor. She bursts into the room to find the nurse kneeling over the patient. The nurse's back and shoulders are tense, arms thrust downward, and the patient's feet are kicking beneath her at the bottom of the bed.

"What are you doing?" Darcey cries.

The nurse whips around to face Darcey. Her face is red and streaked with tears, and she's holding a pillow in her hands.

"Go away!" the nurse screams. "I have to do this!"

The woman slams the pillow down again and lets out a howl of rage. Darcey rushes over to stop her, but the nurse catches her with a backhanded swipe of her fist, hitting Darcey right on the bridge of her nose. Darcey stumbles backward, blood spurting from her injured nose.

Head still ringing, Darcey rushes back in, and this time Darcey manages to grab hold of the nurse's arm. She pulls the enraged woman toward her with all her might, but the nurse grabs hold of the metal grab bar on the opposite side of the medical pod and is able to resist getting yanked off. As they struggle, the patient thrashes, her shouts muffled by the pillow still resting over her face. But she can't do much to save herself because her hands are cuffed to the grab bars on either side of the pod.

"Stop!" Darcey yells.

The nurse shrieks, "She killed him!" and twists her hips around so she can kneel on the pillow covering the patient's face.

Darcey braces her foot on the side of the pod and pulls harder at the nurse's arm. With the added leverage, she's able to pull the shrieking woman off the bed. The two of them land in a heap on the floor, and the nurse immediately starts pummeling Darcey.

"It's not fair! Why does *she* get to live?" the woman screeches as she rains blows down on Darcey's head and shoulders.

Darcey tries to cover up, but the woman is a windmill of fury. The beating stops only when the nurse rolls off Darcey and tries to scramble back to the medical pod. Darcey manages to snag her ankle and trip her. The woman's face smacks on the ground as she falls, which only serves to enrage her further. She twists and deals a savage kick to Darcey's side. Stars explode in Darcey's vision, and she curls into a fetal position, the wind kicked out of her.

"You're not the only one who wants justice," she manages as she gulps air.

The murderous nurse staggers to the bedside table and rips the metal drawer right out of it, dumping its scant contents at her feet.

"I don't care," she says, licking blood off her quivering top lip. "She's going to die for what she did."

The patient must sense what's coming, because her muffled shouts get louder.

Darcey scrabbles across the floor toward her.

The woman takes the drawer in both hands and raises it over the patient's head, its sharp metal edges suddenly looking like they were designed to kill.

"Stop!" Darcey screams.

The woman's eyes look past Darcey and suddenly go wide. "No, I have to—" is all she manages before the Municipal guard who's burst into the room stabs his stun stick directly into her chest.

The metal drawer lands harmlessly on the floor. The nurse collapses as well, her head cracking the tile almost as loud as the drawer did, and twitches as the last jolts of electricity ripple through her body.

"Holy shit," the guard says, looking down on the nurse, stun stick still in hand. Then he rushes to Darcey's side.

"Are you okay, ma'am?" he says, then notes her Conglomerate jumper, which intensifies the tortured look on his face. "The doctor *made* me go with him," he says, defensively. "I had no choice! He said I had to go help with the code blue. We didn't know how many people were hurt, and it would be okay to leave my post. He said I could come back once they assessed what was going on, ma'am. I'm so sorry."

"It's okay." Darcey waves off the rest. "Just get this nurse out of here."

"Of course. I'll call this in right away." He stows his stun stick in his belt holster, then grabs the unconscious nurse under her arms and starts hauling her to the door.

As he leaves, Darcey goes to the bed and takes the pillow off the patient's face. Given what's just happened, she isn't the least bit surprised to see it's the face of Julia Watts. She has a purple-red bruise on the left side of her head and cheek, which is severely swollen. Her left eye is only a slit.

"Thank you," Julia says.

Darcey wipes a sleeve across her nose, which comes away bloody. "I didn't do it for you," she says, then spits a glob of bloody phlegm onto the floor.

Julia gets a quizzical look on her face, then brightens. "I know you."

"What?"

"That's what you told me in the air vent, right? You said you know me," Julia says. "What did you mean by that?"

Despite the damage to Julia's face, Darcey can see the family resemblance. The curiosity that drove her to find Julia's room in the first place, the prospect of being able to meet this terrorist face to face, to confront her after what she did to her —what she did to all of them up here and who knows how many others—that desire disappears as she marvels at the small but distinct echoes of Thea she finds in this evil person's visage. She wishes she could erase them for her friend's sake, so Thea would never have to see pieces of herself reflected in this person ever again.

"Fuck you," Darcey says, then turns to go.

"How is she?"

Julia's ploy works. Darcey stops.

"Everyone has so many questions. But I told them that I won't talk unless I can see my daughter. Can you tell her that I want to talk to her?"

Darcey swings around. "Why would she ever want to talk to you?"

"She will," Julia says with certainty. "Just tell her. Please."

Darcey stares at the pillow the nurse was using as a murder weapon, wondering if maybe she's made a mistake. Thea would have been spared all of this had Darcey just let the nurse end it.

"I know what you did to her," Darcey says. "And to her dad."

Julia's face wrinkles at the mention of her husband. "You don't know anything."

"You're going to pay for what you've done."

Julia nods dismissively as if the consequences of her actions at Darkside Station are meaningless. "Will you tell her I need to see her?" she asks again.

"No." Darcey heads once more for the door, determined to leave this time. But as she opens it, Julia yells to her, "I'm the only one who can give her what she needs!"

Darcey pauses, hand on the door handle. "And what's that?"

"Closure. If she's your friend, then don't deny her that."

Darcey steps out into the hallway and lets the door swing closed behind her. She knows she should have her face, ribs, and neck checked out after the fight with the nurse. But she feels an urgency rise up in her that makes everything else seem unimportant.

She has to talk to Thea.

27

Decisions, Decisions

Rest is hard to come by despite her bone-deep exhaustion. Moments from the tribunal and the awful conversation with her crew haunt her, both events replaying over and over again in her weary mind. Thea flips onto her stomach and buries her face in Elliott's pillow, inhales deeply, snuffles around the edges, flips it around, desperate for some trace of him deep in the fibers, but there's nothing. His scent is gone. He's gone, and it's because of her mother. All of it, everything because of her.

Her body feels zapped, devoid of some critical stuff, some essential Thea-ness. She hugs the pillow close and cocoons herself in blankets, thinking of him, remembering his touch, his smile, his taste. Eventually, she feels herself beginning to go. She relaxes into the sensation, lets it swallow her whole, and just as she starts to drift off, her handheld chimes.

She waits, hoping it'll go away, sleep still within reach, but it chimes again.

"Sorry to wake you, Cap," Rory says, "but Lieutenant Grey wants to see you. Says it's urgent."

Darcey!

Thea throws off the covers and stands up so fast she has to

steady herself against the nightstand. A stale, half-eaten muffin falls to the ground.

"She's here?" Thea asks, kicking the muffin away and making a silent vow to clean the place up. "Where?"

"She's waiting down at the lift."

Thea can't understand why Darcey isn't in the infirmary. "Let her up," she says, already heading for the door, then doubling back for her boots. She's wanted to see Darcey ever since she found out what happened, still in disbelief that her mother got to her, too. The woman's poisonous reach is incredible. But Thea couldn't muster the courage to so much as enter the infirmary, because that's also where they're keeping her mother. She's just not ready, can't fathom the idea of being in that woman's vicinity, barely able to tolerate her presence on the moon, let alone be in the same building as her.

She picks up her pace and makes it to the cargo bay just as the lift arrives. As soon as the doors open, Thea rushes in and throws her arms around Darcey, truly embracing her friend for the first time in a very long time.

"Oh my God, are you okay?" she says. "What are you doing here?"

"I'm all right," Darcey says.

Thea lifts Darcey's chin and examines her purpling nose, one nostril rimmed in dried blood. But before she can ask the question, Darcey anticipates it.

"Yeah, there's been some developments," she says, then glances over at Rory, who steps out of the airlock that leads to the harpoon bay. By way of hello, he waves a greasy spanner. She waves back and gives Thea a questioning look.

"It's okay," Thea says. "Rory should hear this too."

Darcey eases herself down onto a crate.

"Oy, you need anything?" Rory asks at seeing her discomfort.

"I'm fine," Darcey says. "Where are Lola and Beetle?"

"Beetle made girlie take a break and go over to the Hub for a drink. First thing they got back up and running over there was the bar, of course. I hear there's quite a crowd."

"My team told me she's been instrumental in getting the power grid stabilized," Darcey says. "She's really something, huh?"

They both nod, proud.

"Look, I'll cut to the chase," Darcey says. "Your mother wants to talk to you."

Thea takes a step back, incredulous. She crosses her arms and starts to shake her head, slowly at first and then with more resolve. Until something occurs to her that shocks her even more than her mother's request.

"Wait—did you speak to her?"

Darcey looks like she's suddenly on guard. "Yes, just now." She holds up a hand to forestall Thea's imminent outburst. "This wasn't her," she says, pointing to her bloodied face. "There's no way I'd let her get the jump on me twice."

"Then who did?" Rory asks.

"Someone looking for revenge. And they almost got it."

As Darcey tells them the story, Thea paces back and forth, agitated. She keeps flexing her fingers and shaking out her hands like she's trying to get blood flowing to frozen extremities. She lets out deep sighs and stares at the ceiling, doing everything she can to hold it together.

"I don't know exactly why I went to her room," Darcey concludes. "I guess I just wanted to see her again after what she did to me."

Thea stops pacing. "What do you mean, *again*?"

Darcey quickly edits her statement. "Sorry, I mean *actually* see her. It was only a split second the first time, sort of like a hit and run."

Thea feels lightheaded and has to sit down. She hugs her

knees to her chest and tries to process the idea that someone just tried to kill her mother. She realizes she ought to be feeling a sense of relief or at least gratitude for Darcey's bravery, but instead she's struggling with an overwhelming sense of disappointment—disappointment that the crazy nurse didn't succeed, which sends a shiver up her spine. She wants her mother to pay for what she's done, but does she really want her mother *dead*?

She can't believe how this has become her life now. She'd learned to live with the bitterness and anger after her mother abandoned their family, but how will she ever learn to live with *these* feelings, this new turmoil in her soul?

Rory and Darcey shoot glances at each other, both waiting for Thea's response. After a lengthy pause, Thea finally takes notice, blinking at them as if seeing them for the first time. "Who is she?"

"Sorry?" Darcey says.

"The nurse," Thea says. "Why did she do it?"

"Apparently she was engaged to one of the *Lillehammer* crewmen who died," Darcey says. "In fact, it was the guy you brought in. The one you found floating near the wreckage of their ship."

Thea's head falls, along with another in a long line of dominoes leading back to her mother. "Jakob," she says. "His name was Jakob."

Rory closes the gap with Thea so he's right at her side. "Fucking hell," he says. "Poor thing."

"What that nurse did . . . it wasn't premeditated," Darcey says after giving Thea a minute to process the news. "I mean, how could it be? There's no way this woman could have ever suspected she'd be close enough to try something like this. It wouldn't have happened if it weren't for the code blue and the guard getting pulled away."

Rory rests his hand on Thea's rising and falling shoulder. As she tries to collect herself, he takes the opportunity to ask Darcey about the emergency. Having worked with the refinery repair crew, he's gotten to know a lot of the men and women there.

"Everyone's okay, as far I've heard," she says. "They'd blistered part of the refinery's north wall, but it ruptured. Two people got partially sucked out, but the rest of the crew managed to get them back. They're gonna be fine."

Thea puts her hand on Rory's, gives it a squeeze. "I won't do it," she says.

Rory's confused by the sudden topic change. "Do what?" he asks.

"I won't talk to her."

Darcey slowly gets to her feet. "I understand. I can't imagine what this is doing to you."

Darcey's and Rory's support steadies Thea, strengthens her resolve. "I'm not going to give her what she wants," she says. "She doesn't deserve it."

"What about what *you* want?" Darcey asks.

Thea lets out a small chuckle as she stands and gently touches Darcey's bruised face. "I want that bitch gone. That's what I want."

"Sure, I get that," Darcey says. "What I mean is, don't you want to know why?"

"Of *course* I want to know why!" Thea snaps. "I want to know everything there is to know about the New Muses and how she got connected to those assholes, and why she chose them over my dad and me. I want to know if my dad knew anything about any of this. Was this the *real* reason they got divorced? And I want to know why she's up here. I mean, why her? Why was *she* the one chosen to do all these awful, unimaginable things! Or did she *volunteer* because she knew it would hurt me? I want to know all of it, every single bit of it! And then I want to punch her in the face and make her tell me everything again.

"But I also *don't* want to hear anything. Does that make sense? I don't want to give her a chance to try and explain away what she did. As much as I want answers, I don't want to listen to her . . . *rationale*. You don't know how she is; she'll make it all seem like the most obvious thing in the world, something totally logical. And I can't stomach that.

"Am I crazy? I feel like I'm going crazy," she says, and gets immediate, empathic head shakes from both of them.

"And worst of all," she adds, chuckling wryly, incredulous that she's even able to use that phrase as it relates to her mother, "just when I think I've got the tally of people whose lives she's ruined straight, another one gets added to the list— this nurse. How many more are there?"

They all hear the sound of the lift starting to rise to the cargo bay. "They're back early," Rory says.

"I won't do it," Thea repeats.

Darcey takes Thea's hands in hers. "Are you sure?" she says. "There's no telling what might happen once they send her back home to face trial. I'm not even sure *where* they're gonna send her. Jurisdiction in this matter is murky at best. This could be your only chance for a long time."

But Thea is unwavering. "I'm sure."

The lift doors open. Beetle and Lola are clearly surprised to see everyone in the cargo bay. Lola is about to say something, then sees Darcey's bruised face.

"Shit, are you okay?" she asks.

"Long story," Darcey says. "Good to see you."

Lola nods. "Did you tell them?" she asks. Then when it's clear Darcey isn't following, she adds, "About the tribunal?"

"What's happened?" Thea says.

"They have a verdict," Beetle explains.

Darcey and Rory exchange nervous glances. "That was fast," Darcey says.

Thea's handheld chimes. Then everyone else's does too.

She glances down at the notification from Municipal, summoning her and everyone else to the Hub. She tries to put on a brave face for her crew. "Before we go over, I need to tell you guys something."

"Do you need me to leave?" Darcey offers.

"No. It's better that you're here. I want you to hear this too. I sent instructions to my lawyer, Billy. The one who defended me in the tribunal. He's managed all of Watts Astromining's affairs since day one. I told him that if things go bad for me, he's to transfer port rights and ownership of the *Zephyr* to the three of you."

Rory, Beetle, and Lola are stunned.

"Thea, no," Rory says. His head shakes slowly and his lip quivers; he's clearly struggling to keep his emotions in check. "It's too much."

But Thea won't suffer any sort of objection, pulling the three of them in front of her. "Listen to me: I need this. You guys, and our ship, are all that matters. I can handle everything that's coming my way. But not the *Zephyr* being grounded. That would break me. If our ship is still out there doing what it's supposed to do—if you guys are doing what you're meant to be doing—then my mother won't have won. My dad's dream —*our* dream—will still be alive."

She swallows down a sob, trying to stay strong. "Can you do that for me?"

They look to each other, then to Thea. Each nods to her, and she takes them in her arms in turn.

Thea faces Darcey. "You're a witness, in case anyone puts up a fuss."

"You got it," Darcey says.

Thea looks around the cargo hold, soaks up every detail. Same with her crew, feeling a sense of calm come over her.

"All right," she says, and means it. "Guess it's time."

"We're with you no matter what," Rory says, and they all agree, including Darcey, who slides her hand into her friend's.

Thea squeezes it and smiles.

"Let's go."

28

All for One, One for All

THE HUB IS PACKED, the crowd abuzz with anticipation like a concert before the main act takes the stage. The heat and humidity from all the bodies combines with the tumult of voices to make the air feel oppressive, almost substantial, like a membrane you need to push through to move.

No one notices Thea and her crew at first. But as they make their way through the crush of bodies, the decibel level steadily falls until the Hub is mostly silent. Municipal guards move to clear a path, but it's unnecessary, because the crowd slowly parts so that Thea can navigate toward the center of the Hub, where ropes section off part of the area beneath the Leaderboard, which has been righted and displays the International Astromining Alliance logo. Waiting for her in the designated section are Brian Allgood and Gasira Achebe.

"Thea, please join us," Achebe says, signaling to one of the guards to let Thea into the roped area.

"Don't worry, Captain," Allgood adds as she takes her place between them. "This will all be over soon."

A glow paints the faces in the front rows as everyone looks up toward the Leaderboard. Thea looks over her shoulder and sees above her that the rotating IAA logo has been replaced by the image of the adjudicator who's been chairing the tribunal. She takes a step to get a better view, but Achebe grabs her arm and holds her in place.

"I'm sorry, Thea," she says.

"I was just trying to get a better angle at the screen."

"No, I don't mean—" Achebe starts, then turns to Thea, seemingly reluctant to look her in the eye. When she finally does, instead of finishing her thought, she simply mouths "Sorry," anguish in her eyes, and then faces away from her again.

"Thank you all for joining," the adjudicator says. "Before I begin, let me express the entire IAA's deepest condolences, as well as my own, for the losses you have experienced. And let me also reiterate our continued admiration for your collective perseverance. The work of the astromining community at Darkside Station is helping to ensure the future of humanity, and we vow that these recent acts of terrorism will not deter us from our noble pursuits."

A small round of applause goes up from the crowd.

The adjudicator continues. "The presiding members of the International Astromining Alliance and I have decided that every resident at Darkside *deserves* to learn the findings of our recent, unprecedented tribunal, along with the other news I am about to share. That's why we've summoned you all here today.

"In the coming days, Julia Watts, the perpetrator of these recent atrocities, will be transferred to Earth to answer for her and her organization's crimes against humanity. She will be tried in an international war crimes–style court not seen since the Middle East and Russian trials during the 2040s and 2050s. Rest assured: justice will prevail."

Thea can't see the crowd behind her, but can feel everyone's attention on her. She stands firm, emotionless, letting the news about her mother wash over her. Friends will ask her later how she was able to remain stony-eyed during the adjudicator's pronouncement, and she'll tell them the truth: she didn't care what happened to her mother. Not at that point, anyway.

"As to the matter of Captain Thea Watts," the adjudicator continues, "the tribunal has come to a unanimous decision."

Thea's heart leaps to her throat.

"We find Thea Watts innocent of any wrongdoing in these matters," the adjudicator says.

She's forced to pause as a cheer goes up around the Hub. It's not universal, but what it lacks in totality, it makes up for in enthusiasm.

Lola high-fives Darcey, then everyone else around her.

Rory crushes Beetle against his barrel of a chest.

Thea tries and fails to hold back tears.

As the crowd's jubilation subsides, the adjudicator once again continues. "Given the gravity of recent events, however, a significant change is being enacted that will impact everyone."

Silence falls over the crowd, sticky and thick.

Thea looks over to Achebe, hoping for some indication of what's about to come, but the head of Municipal is stoic.

"The spirit of fair and open competition has fueled our industry since its earliest days and in short order ended the rare earths crisis that swept the globe. Only the fleet's dedication and hard work prevented the hoarding of these precious metals, the rampant profiteering, and the potential for a resource war unseen in our history. Humanity was on a perilous path, but things were set right due in great measure to the work that you, *all* of you, do each and every day. Everyone listening should be proud of the role you've played in our collective success.

"Recent events, however, have proven that our hard-earned progress could have been swept away in a heartbeat—and it's our duty to ensure that never happens. Too much is at stake."

Here the adjudicator pauses, gathers herself, then gazes directly into whatever camera is capturing this moment—a moment that will be remembered for generations.

"The IAA convened an emergency congress of all active national astromining operations. This included the nations currently represented by the Conglomerate and those nations who are not part of the Conglomerate but who participate in the rare earths fair exchange compact. Details of those talks will be made available to the public immediately after this broadcast. In addition, we will be relaxing restrictions on the lunar satellite network in the next hour so you can confer with your governments and home bases of operation."

They all brace for what's about to come, but none are ready.

"I am happy to announce that after a series of negotiations, all national operations at Darkside Station have agreed to join the Conglomerate—creating a single, unified, global astromining effort."

Gasps echo around the space.

"In addition," the adjudicator continues before the crowd can get away from her, "eminent domain has been declared by the IAA for Darkside Station, the Hyperloop, and the shipyard. As a result, all non-Conglomerate operations must cease, effective immediately. The days of independent astromining are over."

What was just moments ago a wave of joy at Thea's exoneration becomes a wail of disbelief. People are in shock. Independent crews, which have been growing in number, many sparked by the *Zephyr*'s success, are incredulous at this sudden reversal of fortune. They push toward the roped-off section where Allgood stands, arms crossed in victory. Everyone is held at a distance by Municipal guards, though Thea suspects none have any interest in engaging in violence. Saddened and upset as they might be, they've had their fill of that in recent days.

A volley of questions fly at Allgood and Achebe, who simply acknowledge the crowd's inquiries without offering any sort of explanation. Above them, on the screen, the adjudicator is continuing to speak, but her words are drowned out by the commotion in the Hub. After a few futile attempts to regain everyone's attention, she simply signs off, the IAA logo once again front and center on the Leaderboard screen.

Thea and her crew push through the crowd toward the massive windows facing the docks, dragging Darcey along with them. As they elbow their way past angry, crying, cursing astro-miners, Thea tries to process what's just happened. In a matter of seconds, she went from being prepared to lose everything, to gaining it all back again, to having it snatched away. Her mind reels, her stomach churns with acid. She feels like she might pass out, and only Rory's snowplowing through the crowd is keeping her moving, preventing her from falling to the floor and curling into a ball.

They break free from the fray and are able to huddle near a window—the same window, Thea realizes, she sat by as she watched Beetle and Elliot try to save the *Victor Hugo* so long ago.

"Did you know about this?" Rory asks Darcey.

"I had no idea," she says. "I came to see you right after what happened in the infirmary. But I think *he* knew all along."

"Who?" Thea asks.

"The admiral," Darcey says. "He came to see me when I was recovering. Said *big changes* were coming."

Rory pounds the thick window. "Why didn't you say anything?"

"How was I supposed to know what he meant by that?" Darcey shoots back. "You know how he is. Plus it kind of got swept aside by, oh I don't know, me stopping a murder!"

Beetle drops into a chair. "*C'est fini,*" he says.

"Can they do this?" Lola asks. "I mean, just like that? Can

they really just decide that this whole thing is now theirs and we gotta go home?"

"It's like an airport," Beetle says. "They get to decide who can fly."

Darcey nods. "Remember, this whole place was financed by governments from all over the world. And those governments created the IAA to oversee it. Independent operators like you guys are technically renters."

"Yeah, and the landlords just padlocked the doors and evicted us," Lola grumbles, slumping down on the edge of the chair Beetle is in and throwing an arm around his shoulders.

"Oh, for fuck's sake," says Rory, angling his chin toward Brian Allgood, who's now making his way toward Thea's group, still fending off questions from the crowd.

Rory takes a few steps toward Allgood, looking like he has every intention of heading him off before he can reach them, but Thea jumps in front of him.

"Rory, no," she says, pushing him back.

"Give me one good reason I shouldn't knock his head off," he says.

"Because you'll end up in jail!"

Rory's face is nearly purple with rage. "Who cares? I've got nothing to go back to anyway. Might as well end up somewhere I'll at least get three squares a day."

Allgood slows his approach as he eyes Rory. He raises his hands in surrender, then calls to Darcey. "Lieutenant Grey, please report to Dock A immediately."

"Sir, if it's all the same to you—" she tries before he waves her off, making clear that it's not.

"We'll talk soon," Darcey says to Thea, then walks past Allgood toward the exit.

"Big day for you, huh?" Thea says to Allgood.

He smiles, feigning sheepishness, which is an emotion she's

sure he's never approached in his life. "It's a big day for us all," he says.

"What are we supposed to do now?" Lola asks.

"Go back to your ship," he replies. "You'll receive instructions from Municipal soon."

He turns to go, but Thea closes the gap and grabs his arm.

"Listen to me," she says, keeping her voice low. "You win. That's fine. I'll be out of your life soon enough. But my crew are the best, and you know that. Please consider postings for them. Don't do it for me, do it because you need good people, and they deserve to stay."

He stares down at her hand until she releases her grip on his arm. "I've known all sorts of liars throughout my life," he says, eyes scanning her face. "And I've gotta tell you, you're really bad at it, Thea."

Allgood then leans in closer, teeth bared as if to take a bite, and whispers, "I know you realized it was your mother all along."

Thea's taken aback.

"But it's okay," he adds, making sure to look toward her crew as he says it. "None of that matters anymore."

"Brian, please," she says.

"It's over, Captain." And with a wink, Allgood turns and walks away.

PART IV

Winds of Change

29

Dregs

THEA's desperate to get back to the *Zephyr* but is swarmed the minute she and her crew make a move toward the exit.

Congratulations, shock, gratitude, and resignation.

Sympathy, anger, disgust.

Too bad, so unfair, really sorry, what a shame.

Everyone has emotions they need to unload, and she's somehow become the designated sounding board for a station grappling with its recent tragic past and uncertain future. Several times during the course of what ends up dragging on for hours, she considers just walking away, faking a summons, sickness, or some urgent appointment to escape the endless parade of needy souls. But each time she's about to pull the trigger, she stops herself, knowing deep down that it's the least she can do for these lost and grieving people whose lives have been turned upside down in no small part because of her. Exonerated or not, this is a debt she owes, so she stays there and listens.

Her crew sticks with her for a while, far longer than they should, but eventually Thea signals to them that they should go. She watches them walk away, and when she loses sight of them in the crowd, a crushing sense of loneliness settles over her, something akin to how she felt right after her father died. During those dark days, she wondered what life had in store for her, and she can't help but ponder that same question now as the man she's been listening to for ten minutes finally wraps up his lecture with a firm, *Whaddaya think?*

"I really don't know," she says, which draws a nasal burst of dissatisfaction from the man, who scratches at his ear then turns away so the next person can step in.

Hours later, emptied out and exhausted, she watches the last few people trickle away, and she's finally alone. Her knees crack and her back protests as she stands up from the chair she's been trapped in for too long. She slowly makes her way toward the exit, rubbing the small of her back with a clenched fist, trying to work out the riot of knots that have taken up residence there. When she reaches the Leaderboard, she can't help but glance up at the IAA logo, bright red on a black screen, painting the area in a bloody hue. She stares at the animation, a tiny astromining rig circling the letters on an endless loop, and feels a sudden surge of anger. Casting around for something heavy, she settles for a metal pitcher someone left on a nearby table. She dumps the dregs of beer on the floor and flings the pitcher at the screen, which sends a spike of pain through her already tender back. It hits dead in the middle of the Leaderboard but careens off without leaving a mark. Again and again, she hurls the pitcher at the IAA logo, but the little ship remains undeterred in its orbit around the glowing red letters. When something in her shoulder pops and her back can bear no more abuse, she finally gives up.

She glares at the logo. "You win," she says, then leaves the Hub behind.

———

THE CONGLOMERATE DOCKS are filled with staff and crew, all of whom seem to be processing the news of the IAA's decision. Some are exuberant, laughing and backslapping, while others show signs of frustration or outright anger over the fact that their ranks have just been tripled. Nothing screws up a pecking order worse than an influx of new birds into the coop.

After what she's just gone through in the Hub, the last thing Thea wants is to get caught up in another soup of emotions, so she keeps her head down and quickens her pace —until a man in a wrinkled, Conglomerate-red jumper steps in front of her.

"This is your fault," he says. The last part comes out as *yer fawt*. She can smell the alcohol on his breath as she tries to step around him.

He throws out his arms like a basketball guard and won't let her pass. "What're you gonna do now, huh, big shot?" he says, then spits a loogy a few inches in front of her boot. "I say they put you and your terrorist bitch mother together in a cell and let you rot for what you did up here."

Thea's about to drop the stumbling idiot when one of his colleagues senses what's coming and pulls him out of harm's way. All eyes are locked on Thea as she stands there, fists balled and knuckles white. She feels naked, overexamined, and desperately in need of solitude after days under the magnifying glass. Off to the side, despite his friends' efforts to calm him down, the drunk is still motioning toward Thea and yelling obscenities.

Not trusting herself to stay calm, Thea hurries out of the Conglomerate dock.

As she crosses into Dock C, she expects to feel a sense of relief, but she experiences something entirely different instead. The tension in the air is palpable. Municipal and Conglomerate security are everywhere. Newly conscripted Conglomerate crew members are standing in a haphazard line that occupies much of the space. Thea tries to find the front of the line but can't see past the edges of the crowd. Other than a few conversations in hushed, clipped tones, the dock is mostly silent.

As she stays close to the wall in an effort to skirt around the anxious crowd, she's surprised to run into the tired young guard who escorted her back to the *Zephyr* at the end of her tribunal hearing. She didn't think he could look any wearier than he did that day, and yet as she approaches him, his eyes are even darker than before, and the exhaustion seems to have traveled to the rest of his face, which looks gray in the dock's bright overhead lights.

"Congratulations," he says. "And sorry, too."

"Thanks." She points over at the slow-moving line. "What's going on?"

"Uniforms," he says.

"Wow, Conglomerate's not wasting any time integrating the national crews, huh?"

"No, and not everyone *has* a uniform waiting for them," he says. "That's why me and the rest of security are here."

"You mean, this is how people are finding out?"

He nods just as a pair of men in Russian jumpers brush past, the older of the two softly crying, his face bright red and twisted in frustration. The man stops and turns, looking as though he's about to shout something back toward the front of the line, but his comrade silences him and steers him away, shooting glances toward Thea and the young guard.

"What the adjudicator neglected to mention was that the Conglomerate would be eliminating redundancies across the fleet," the guard says as he watches the angry Russian fade into the crowd. "Pretty cutthroat, the way they're handling the whole thing. A lot of people are gonna be shipping out of here."

His sallow cheeks flush a dim pink as it clearly dawns on him that his statement applies to Thea too.

"It's all right," she says, to ease his embarrassment.

Ahead, there's a quick burst of angry voices. A pair of Conglomerate security detach from the wall and jog toward the sound.

Thea nods toward where the outburst came from. "Be safe," she says to the guard. "And get some sleep. You look worse than I feel right now."

He smiles at her, but instead of joining his colleagues, he takes her by the hand and blazes a trail through the crowd so that she can get through unmolested. When there's a clear line of sight to the exit, he says, "Good luck, *Captain*"—placing extra emphasis on her former title—before jogging back to his post.

Captain, she thinks, watching the kind young man. *I'm gonna miss that.*

As Thea steps into Dock D, she's surprised to find another line of people. This one is shorter, though, and there are no guards around to police whatever's happening. She walks along the edge of the line, exchanging nods with other former independent operators, who all have pained expressions on their faces. When she reaches the front of the line, she understands why.

"We meet again, Ms. Watts," says Peter Mazur, head of Conglomerate Acquisitions, the man who tried to buy the *Zephyr* from her when she first arrived at Darkside.

The woman at the head of the queue seems annoyed by Thea's interruption, but Mazur holds up his hand to silence her protest before it can begin.

"What's this?" Thea says, looking at the table he's set at the top of Dock D and the stacks of papers arrayed before him.

"I'm throwing these poor people a lifeline," Mazur says,

waving toward the line of out-of-work astrominers like a wizard casting a spell.

"More like highway robbery, I'm sure," Thea says. "Like you tried with me."

"We're offering very fair prices, in fact—especially considering we're the only buyer for this particular product," he says. "It's not like these folks have the option of taking their ships back to wherever they came from. It's either sell them to us, or it's back to the shipbuilders for scrap. We could be taking advantage of that, but under the circumstances, we choose to be generous." He gives her a used-car-salesman smile before turning back to his waiting customer. "At any rate, Ms. Watts, I'm sure we'll discuss this further when your time comes."

"It's *Captain* Watts," Thea says.

His eyes twinkle brighter than the dock's fluorescents as he tilts his head down slightly, looks over the top rim of his glasses, and says, "Not anymore."

———

SHE FINDS her crew on the bridge.

Beetle is using his thumbnail to try and locate the edge of the foil wrapping the neck of a bottle, its empty twin on the console next to him. Rory and Lola wait patiently nearby, Lola with a shot glass, Rory with a tumbler.

"Hey, it's Thea! Hi, Thea," Lola says, tossing her shot glass to Thea, who barely has time to react before it smashes on the wall next to her.

"Oops. Sorry, boss," Lola says, giggling. "I mean, old boss. Not old . . . former. That's it. Former boss."

"Hey guys," Thea says as Lola hunts around for another glass and Rory snatches the bottle away from Beetle, who mutters something in French, then reaches over to the seat next to him and underhands a glass to Thea.

"We started without ya," Rory says, gnawing at the foil and peeling off a long strip.

"I can see that." She leans back against the console and holds out her glass. Rory obliges by tipping out a few fingers of something dark.

"Did you see what's going on down there?" Beetle says. "It's a terrible, terrible thing, *ma chère*."

Thea nods and throws back her drink, delighting in the fire racing its way down her throat to her stomach.

"Fucking buzzards," Rory says. "So, we figured we'd send the old gal off right and proper."

"Hear, hear," Lola says, before dropping into her chair with a "Whoopsie."

Beetle starts to tell them about a friend of his on the Chinese crew who was just let go, and how she's been up here for nearly ten years and doesn't have any idea what she's going to do next. As Thea listens to the story, she suddenly feels like she's about to have a panic attack. She takes deep breaths, in through her nose and out through her mouth, trying to calm the buzzing that's taking over her body. She reaches out, snags the bottle, tips it back, and takes a few long swallows, but it doesn't help. Sweat breaks out across her back, and she can taste metal in the back of her throat.

Rory notices what's going on and tells Beetle to hush.

"I'm sorry, Captain," Beetle says. "So stupid of me, going on and on like that. I wasn't thinking."

And that's when Thea realizes that it isn't panic she's feeling. It's rage.

She hurls the bottle at the forward screen, which spiderwebs as the heavy glass shatters and rum rains down on everything.

"Of course I can break *this* one!" she shouts, then starts pacing around the bridge.

She rages about the chickenshit nations knuckling under to

the IAA and the Conglomerate. She screams about the independent operators being strip-mined down below, their livelihoods being sold for pennies on the dollar. She completely loses her mind when she thinks of her father's ship flying under a Conglomerate flag. She won't let that happen. She'd rather see it get vivisected at the shipbuilders' than become a part of Allgood's fleet.

And then she gets to her mother.

Her throat seizes. She can't get air. She stomps the ground like she did in elementary school when she didn't want to take the bus, slaps her palms against her forehead, and understands for the first time in her life the notion of *seeing red*, because the whole room is rimmed in it. She's positively incandescent with fury—

Until she notices their faces . . .

And the bottom drops out of her world.

Rory is the first one there. He reaches for her slowly, cautiously, like he's anticipating she'll be hot to the touch. At the first brush of his fingertips, she crumples, and he moves swiftly to catch her. He has to hold her upright, all the strength going out of her legs. Then Beetle is there, and Lola too. And by the end, they're holding each other up, as they've done so many times before.

———

THEY OPEN and finish a new bottle of the really good stuff, then sit on the bridge of their ship and try to imagine what comes next.

Beetle says he might go back to France to reconnect with his old troupe. He might not be able to perform, but he knows the circus life and feels he might still have something to give. Rory intends to stay on the moon, the prospect of having to work a heavy loader again better, he claims, than any prospects he might have waiting for him on Earth. Neither man, though, will consider flying for the Conglomerate. That is out of the question, they claim.

The intense rush of blood to Thea's head from earlier, mixed with the dark rum she's guzzled since, has her buzzing all over, but this time in a good way. She talks about going back to Cambridge and finishing her doctorate. It seems preposterous at first, but the more she talks about it, the more the idea solidifies.

But Lola is quiet all through the conversation. Thea watches her pick at the arm of her chair, eyes in her lap.

"What's the matter?" Thea asks her.

Lola looks like she's been caught stealing. "Nothing," she says, then adds, "Just too much to drink, I guess."

"That's not it," Rory says. "Spill it, girlie."

Lola tries a few more times to profess that nothing is wrong, but they all know her too well to buy what she's selling. Finally, after some literal prodding from Beetle, his lightning-quick fingers impossible to stop before they poke her in the side and head, she confesses to considering a job offer.

"From who?" Rory asks.

"Whom."

"What?"

"It's whom, Gramps," Lola says.

"Who, whom, whatever," Rory says. "Whom be after ye, girlie?"

"Someone I worked with on Darcey's team," she says. "Turns out he's on the *Segundo*, and they have an opening. He said he'd recommend me for it if I wanted."

"Do you?" Thea asks.

Lola gets really small in her chair. She's such a huge personality, so confident and competent, that it's easy to forget how young she still is. "I might."

Thea kneels in front of her. "You should," she says. "They'd be lucky to have you."

"I feel bad, though." Lola struggles to look at Thea. "Like a traitor or something. I mean, you're the one who took a chance on me. How could I just go . . . you know, with them."

Thea grabs her hand and squeezes it. "Because that's what you're supposed to do. Life opens up in front of us all the time. We just need to be brave enough and smart enough to see it."

Then to her whole crew, she says, "That's what I did when I came up here after my dad died, and that's what you all did when you came along for the ride. Now it's time for the next ride."

The console in front of Lola bings.

They all giggle at the timing, because it sounds like the perfect end note, a fitting coda to Thea's uncharacteristic philosophizing. And because they're all a bit tipsy, too.

Lola leans forward and taps the console. "It's a notice from Municipal," she says. "Letting us know that our docking slip is being reassigned to the Conglomerate, effective immediately."

Beetle jumps up and starts to unbutton his pants.

"What the hell are you doing, man?" Rory says.

But it's too late, because Beetle's pants are around his ankles. "If this dock is now Conglomerate property, I think I'll just go down and christen it with a mighty shit."

He kicks off his pants and makes his way to the door amid raucous guffaws from Thea and Rory. Lola doesn't join in, however, because she's found something strange on her console's desktop.

"Thea, there's something here," she says, but not firmly enough to cut through the laughter. She tries again, this time spinning around and yelling to them all.

"What's the matter?" Thea says, her sides aching.

"This is weird. Come see."

Thea, Rory, and Beetle walk over and stare at the audio file on Lola's screen.

Its title is a single word.

Daughter.

Thea's mind sharpens instantly, her insides turning to ash.

She reaches out a trembling finger and taps the file.

Her mother's voice fills the bridge.

I'M *sure you're wondering why* I *did it.*

Why I *attacked the station and those ships. How* I *could do that to all those* innocent *people.*

You want to know how I *got here . . .*

30

Keep It Weird

THEA'S IN A DAZE, her mother's words swimming through her brain, pooling together, coalescing into a leviathan, one that she suspects will occupy the deep, dark places inside her for years to come. She listened to the recording with her crew until they could bear no more and drifted away one by one. Then she listened to it alone for the rest of the night and into the next morning, playing the audio file on a loop, over and over for hours, mesmerized not only by what her mother was saying, but also by the way she was saying it. She found herself captivated by the sound of her mom's voice, its timbre and inflection, enthralled by the tone the woman used as she told her story in that slight Texas drawl of hers.

They say you can tell the difference between a stone-cold killer and a dilettante by the sound of their voice. Someone who's committed a crime of passion will express themselves differently from a serial killer. It comes down to a matter of conviction.

And that's what Thea senses in her mother's voice. Conviction. Total belief in what's she's done and why she's done it.

Thea walks through the main concourse, passing people

who still crave her attention or just want to yell at her, but she's so caught up in her own thoughts she barely notices them until a shrill screech snaps her out of her reverie. She sprints toward the noise, and as she crosses the threshold into the Hub, she finds Molly, hands on hips, red-faced and screaming at two maintenance workers on ladders.

"What's going on?" Thea says, running over.

But before Molly can answer, the Leaderboard comes crashing to the ground.

"That!" Molly says with a stomp of her foot and a swipe of her hand toward what remains of not only her job but the astromining community's singular rallying point for decades. "I'm in charge of the board, and no one even told me. I mean, how can they do that? It's my responsibility, and they just took it away from me without even talking to me about it!"

"That's awful," Thea says, staring at the bent and broken screen on the ground.

Molly turns away from the sight, her voice cracking. "It's not fair. What am I supposed to do now?"

Thea leads the girl away from the scene. "It's gonna be okay," she says, but silently adds Molly to her mother's tally of casualties.

"I don't want to go back," Molly says. "There's just no way I can handle that."

"Where would *that* be?" Thea asks.

"Connecticut."

"What's wrong with Connecticut?"

Molly stops, drawing Thea's attention to her all-black wardrobe, tattoos, and piercings. "Do I look like I fit in in fucking Connecticut?" she says, wiggling her chipped black fingernails up and down in front of her like a scanner.

Thea chuckles and concedes the point. "I'm sorry about all this," she says.

Molly relaxes a bit. "How about you?" she asks. "Where are you heading?"

"I don't know," Thea says, throwing her arm around Molly's shoulder as they cross the Hub together. "I'm not sure where I fit in anymore either."

Molly rests her head on Thea's shoulder. "Hey, remember when you first got up here? I dissed your dock pretty hard, but you came right back at me even harder, which was cool. I deserved it, too. Remember that?"

"Of course," Thea says. "I'll never forget that day."

Molly shoves her hands into her pockets, struggles to meet Thea's eyes, but then, with effort, does. "Yeah, me too," she says. She gives Thea a quick embrace, then bounds down the steps to the Neighborhood.

Thea watches her go, and with a deep breath to settle her nerves, she takes the steps up to Municipal.

———

USUALLY A HIVE OF ACTIVITY, the lobby is surprisingly empty when Thea arrives. "Hello?" she says, softly at first, and when she gets no response, louder.

From the open office door across the lobby, she hears, "Come on in, Thea," and finds Gasira Achebe behind a stack of plastic crates near her desk.

Even at her worst, Achebe always looked ready for prime time, so it takes Thea a second or two to register that the woman in tight pink leggings, a black tank top, and sneakers is the same woman she's always known.

"Thanks for coming over," Achebe says, tucking a flyaway behind her ear. "Thought this would be easier in person."

"What's going on?" Thea asks, staring at the containers.

"Just getting my personals together."

"You're leaving?"

Achebe drops a file into an open bin and waves Thea toward the couch. "I have to. You of all people know that."

Thea takes a seat across from Achebe, feeling all the strength go out of her legs at the thought of yet another massive change at the station. She's not sure why it hits her so hard; after all, she'll be gone too.

Achebe grabs a bottle from the collection at the center of the table and tips whiskey into two glasses. She hands one to Thea and holds hers out so they can clink them.

"If you go, no one will stand in his way," Thea says.

Achebe shrugs. "You're probably right," she says. "But it could never be me. Not after what happened. My time up here ended the day the IAA granted him temporary control."

"But they gave it back."

Achebe wrinkles her nose. "Yes, they did. Once the hard stuff was out of the way, they decided I could be trusted again." She tosses back her whiskey. "That doesn't work for me."

Thea nods in understanding, then drains her glass.

Achebe moves on to the business at hand. "Let's talk about the audio file," she says.

"Did you find him?" Thea asks.

"You mean the other operative?"

"Yeah. The one supposedly at the shipyard."

"No one there goes by the name Fallon," Achebe says. "But we've stopped all routine traffic to and from Earth, including railgun deliveries, and we're monitoring all communications until we can clear everyone. If he's there, we'll find him."

"What about the mole in the IAA? The one who got ahold of the station schematics?"

Achebe nods. "That little tidbit already bore some fruit. Those files require a certain level of clearance, so all we needed to do was find out who accessed station schematics in the last few years. It turns out the guy's been inside the IAA for almost a decade. A security team picked him up about an hour ago."

"Finally, some good news," Thea says.

"I suppose. He claims he's just some low-level operative. Apparently everything is handled through a drop location. He said he hasn't met with anyone inside the Muses for years."

"Do you buy that?"

Achebe picks up the bottle and ignores Thea's protest as she pours another finger or two into each of their glasses. "He's got a tracker in his left arm like your mother's, so we think there's more to the story. If so, the adjudicator will get it out of him."

"And what about *her* tracker?" Thea asks. "Anything there?"

Achebe shakes her head. "Device seems to be inert." She takes a sip and settles back in her seat. "So, how are *you* doing?"

Thea chuckles and raises her glass. "Oh, just great," she says. "Who could ask for more?"

Achebe levels her gaze. "Have you decided?"

Thea isn't sure what to say. She's been considering Achebe's offer for hours. "Does it have to happen now?" she asks.

"We're leaving here in about ninety minutes," Achebe says, pointing to the crates. "My last official act will be to accompany the prisoner back to Earth."

Thea stands and moves over to the windows looking down on the docks. The fleet is still grounded, so every pad is full.

"You going to miss it?" she asks, squinting her eyes so that the illumination from the ships below looks like Christmas tree lights after too much eggnog.

"Parts of it, yes," Achebe says. "Not the food, though. Feels like I haven't had a decent slice in years."

"Deep dish or thin crust?"

"Please." Achebe gets up from her seat and goes back to filling the crates. "We all know deep dish is a quiche, not pizza."

"See, this is why we get along." Thea takes a sip of her drink, delighting in the exquisite burn as the liquor glides down her throat.

"Listen, the choice is yours," Achebe says after a moment. "But let me just say this, not in my official capacity—and come to think of it, I actually can't say *anything* anymore in that capacity, since I quit my job—so . . . let me say this to you as a friend."

Thea turns and gazes into Achebe's intelligent, glimmering eyes.

"Things left unsaid are the most toxic sort of things," Achebe continues. "We keep them quiet, thinking that's for the best, but all it ends up doing is making whatever we're not saying worse. In here," she adds, tapping her temple. "And the longer we let things go unsaid, the louder they get in our lives."

"Sounds like you have some experience with this sort of thing," Thea says.

The look in Achebe's eyes gives Thea her answer.

Achebe opens the center drawer of her desk and takes out a folder. "Trust me," she says, handing the folder to Thea. "Say the things you need to say."

Thea's reluctant to open the folder. "What's this?"

"We found it in the EVA suit left beside Lieutenant Grey."

It takes only a glance inside for her resolve to crack.

Memories of the family trip to Austin flood in as she stares at the picture inside the folder. She used to wear that t-shirt with Austin's famous motto all the time, and she's sure it's still somewhere in the house in Texas. She could never part with it; it had become a talisman of sorts, a piece of magical nostalgia for a time when her family was happy and together and it seemed like it would be that way forever. And judging by the faded picture in her hands and its sheer existence up here, maybe that trip means something special to her mother, too.

There's only one way to find out.

Thea stares at the glass of whiskey that she now wants more than anything else. She drinks off the rest of it in a single go, enjoying Achebe's raised eyebrows as she does, then tosses her friend the empty glass.

With a husky, scotchy voice, she makes a decision that will change her life.

"Okay, let's go."

31

I See You

JULIA WATTS IS LYING on the metal bench on her side, facing the cell wall, wearing a white-and-black-striped jumper that calls to mind the ones criminals wore in old prison movies. She's cradling her head in the crook of her arm, the other one resting on her hip, just like in the days when Thea would find her sleeping on their couch—the exact same position, right down to the one bare foot dangling off the edge. But this time there's a metal ankle ring connecting that foot to the leg of the bench, which is bolted to the floor.

She'd been dead set against seeing her mother, but now that she's here, she's captivated by the sight of the woman, the sound of her tiny snores, the rise and fall of her side, her dry and cracked heel.

The door clicks closed behind Thea, and her mother still doesn't wake, doesn't turn around. Until . . .

"Mom."

Her mother jolts around and lets out a strangled cry when the ankle bracelet digs into her flesh. After some maneuvering, she pushes herself into a sitting position and stares across the room at Thea.

"I'm glad you came," she says, rubbing her ankle.

The moment of ensorcellment is gone, and Thea can't bring herself to look her mother in the eye. She crosses her arms and studies the tiles on the floor.

The silence stretches.

"Are you okay?" her mother asks.

Thea doesn't respond. Doesn't know the answer. Doesn't trust herself to speak if she did.

"That was smart, what you did. Drawing me off the bridge like that. And with the harpoon too. I wish you hadn't, though. I would have loved to see that Conglomerate ship go down."

Still Thea remains silent. Suddenly, speaking to her own mother is the most impossible thing in the world.

"Did you find what I left you?" her mother asks. "Did you listen to it?"

Thea seems to coil tighter with each of her mother's questions. She's not sure why she came. And now that she's here, she's not sure why she doesn't leave. But she doesn't. Even if she never says a word, she needs to be here.

Her mother also goes quiet for a while, then she takes a different tack.

"Do you remember that time you came home from summer camp with lice? God, what a disaster. We tried mayonnaise, petroleum jelly, shower caps, even that really smelly shampoo from the drugstore, but nothing worked. Little bastards were there for the long haul. So there was only one choice left."

Thea finally glances up from the tile, looks at her mother, who's running her hands over the remains of her chopped-off hair.

"I realize now what that must have been like for you," her mother says. "Sorry about that."

Thea is incredulous, and the bomb she'd been trying to

defuse inside her explodes. "That?" she screams. "*That's* what you're sorry for."

Her mom's smile is a sharp contrast to the tears suddenly sheeting down her face. "It's a start," she says.

Thea pushes her back against the wall opposite her mother, needing to be as far away from her as the space allows.

"Yes, I found the file," she says. "I gave it to Municipal. Right now, they're using it to root out your people. They already took care of the IAA mole, and they'll have this other operative at the shipyard, this *Fallon*, in custody soon."

Thea hopes for some sort of pained reaction from her mother. But all she gets are nods, placating nods, the same sort of annoying, dismissive nods her mother used to give when Thea was a girl and trying to convince her parents to let her sleep over at Ginny's or Sasha's on a weeknight. It infuriates Thea even more.

"Are you even *listening* to me?" she says. "It's over! They're going to lean on these people to get at the rest of your fucking terrorist organization and bring the whole thing down! And it'll be *your* fault. After all this time, decades, *you're* going to be the one who destroys the New Muses."

More nods from her mother. Then, after a beat, she says: "What about the rest of it?"

"What?"

"Everything else I said in those recordings?"

Thea wants to hurt her, wound her, say things that will cut deep. And not just as retribution for what her mother did up here, but for all that she did and didn't do back home, too. Everything, all of it, years and years of anger piled on anger. She wants to let it all come pouring out in a great flood of words and spit and cursing. But she's just so tired. In mind and body. And spirit. So very, very tired of it all.

In the end, all she can muster is, "What about it, Mom?"

"What I said . . . Does any of it help?"

"With what?"

"I don't know," her mother says, searching for a way to break through. "I was hoping you might understand—"

Thea cuts her off. "No. It didn't help me *understand* anything, and I don't care," she snaps. "The courts will decide what happens next. Not me."

Her mother tries to move closer, but the leash at her ankle is short. "I don't expect you to forgive me. I just want you to understand that some of the things that happened weren't my fault," she says. "Like what happened to Elliott—"

Thea's exhaustion is blasted away at the mention of his name. "Don't you dare!"

"Honey, you have to believe me, I would never have done anything to intentionally hurt you."

"But you did, Mom. You did! And I don't care what excuse you give me. It doesn't change the fact that he's dead and it's because of you. A lot of people are."

Her mother tries to continue, but Thea waves off whatever she's about to say, and the two women silently stare at each other across the room. Thea seethes, trying to collect herself. As she does, her mother settles back against the cell wall, once again resorting to nodding her head, but this time as if she's trying to encourage Thea to do what she's come here to do. To get on with it, whatever it might be. Which makes things worse, because Thea doesn't want or need permission from her mother for anything. In fact, she considers walking away. But she can't, not yet. Because there is *one* thing she wants.

After calming herself down and gathering her strength, Thea finally asks for it.

"I want to know why, Mom," she says. "Why did you give up your whole life for this? For these people and their cause."

"I believe in it."

"Bullshit," Thea says.

"We all have our part to play in this vast and mysterious game," her mother replies.

Amazed, Thea shouts, "What kind of philosophical bullshit is that? Game? You think this is a *game*?"

Her mother smirks and sounds for a brief moment like the person Thea once knew so well. "Honestly, honey, don't be obtuse. You know what I mean."

Thea can't help but chuckle at her mother's all-too-familiar retort. She waves it off and takes a few steps toward the door. "Fine. If you're going to do that, then this is a waste of my time," she says, her hand on the knob.

"Wait!" her mother says.

Thea turns and sees the previous smugness in her mother's eyes replaced with a look of desperation. But it does nothing to soften Thea's resolve. If anything, it hardens it, further tempts her to leave the room without giving her mother a chance to answer the question. As much as she wants to know why her mother chose the path she did, the thought of this woman having to suffer days and weeks and months and years with the knowledge that she missed her one shot at explaining herself . . . to Thea, that cruel prospect is suddenly very tempting. It might even make not knowing why her mother did what she did acceptable, at least for a while. She's about to do it, too, but then her mother starts talking.

"I didn't do it for them," she says. "I did it for me."

Thea doesn't understand. She closes the gap between them, furious. "No way!" she shouts in her mother's face. "I don't believe you! You never gave enough of a shit about *anything* to get me to believe that you suddenly became some fucking humanist. No way! You've never had enough conviction to stick to a book club, let alone plant yourself on the fucking moon. Because of what? Some belief in the evils of technology?"

"You're right," her mother says. "None of that ever really mattered to me."

That catches Thea off-guard.

"Then why? Tell me why!"

Her mother meets her searching eyes—eyes filled with rage and longing and sadness—then tears out her heart.

"I did it because it made me happy."

Thea's head snaps back as if she were slapped. Before she can recover, her mother presses on.

"We moved to Texas so your dad could do this *thing*, and then he was always gone. But it was okay because I had you. But then you started getting older and needing me less and less. It's not your fault; that's what's supposed to happen. Kids grow up. But I was so lonely, Thea. I'd dedicated my whole life to our family and suddenly it was gone.

"I was angry at him, and at you too. So I decided I needed something for me. Just for *me*," she says, pounding her chest. "And that's when I found the New Muses, and with them a purpose again. Something that made me feel like I was doing something important with my time and not just floating through my days, just . . . going through the motions."

Thea flashes back to her dad's funeral and the overriding feeling of that day. The priest. The mourners. Even herself, going through the motions. That terrible, hollow feeling, in part, is what led her here.

"Maybe it doesn't make sense," her mother says, running her fingertips over the metal cuff on her ankle, "but that's why I did it. I wanted to matter again. And with the Muses, I did."

As she's speaking, Thea studies her closely—and knows she's telling the truth. But there's also more she's not saying. Thea can feel it.

"Okay, you were lonely and sad," Thea says. "But come on, Mom, do you really expect me to believe that you thought your best shot at finding a new 'life's purpose' was by joining an *international terrorist organization* and *murdering people*? You could have done anything. Taken classes, volunteered, got a job, got a fucking puppy, for Christ's sake! There's got to be more to it."

A knock on the door interrupts them. Thea walks over and peers through the glass at Achebe, who holds up two fingers, indicating that Thea has only two minutes left.

"They've come to take you away," she says, turning back to her mother. "Last chance."

"I just told you the truth."

"Not all of it," Thea says.

Her mother goes still, quiet. Thea watches her, takes in every twitch, every small detail of the moment, enjoying watching this woman squirm.

And when the time feels right, Thea says, "Okay then," and turns to go.

"Wait!"

Thea turns back. *Last chance*, she thinks.

Her mother digs her nails into the back of her hand, drawing forth little half-moons of blood, wrestling with something unseen, something painful trying to burst out. She grits her teeth, her entire body tense.

Thea presses, sensing the rest is right there under the surface. "Why did you do it, Mom? Why did you become this person?" She leans forward. "Tell me, or I'm gone and you'll never see me again."

Her mother's neck striates as she screams, foam exploding from her lips. "So he would see me!" she screeches. "I did it so he'd finally *see* me!"

She wipes her mouth with the back of her bloody hand, leaving a pink smear across her lips. "But then he went and got sick and ruined everything. And I couldn't stay, and do what? Take care of him? No. There was nothing to stay for, so I left."

Thea should be enraged by her mother's admission. She should be incensed by the woman's utter selfishness, her absurd justification for her actions, her psychotic rationale for what amounts to a marriage under stress, a midlife crisis. She should run over and slap her mother across the face. No one would blame her; she'd face no repercussions. But instead, an entirely different emotion swells through her, washes over her body like surf. Cool, bubbly, effervescent.

Thea's happy.

She's happy, because in her mother's admission, she's found the one thing she can use against her. A perfect reckoning for the *Victor Hugo*, the *Lillehammer*, the refinery, the station, the entire astromining community. For her dad. For Elliott. The perfect retribution, one she knows will stick with her mother, something that will fester as she whiles away the rest of her days in a prison cell. God, Achebe was right! It was all worth it for this one moment.

She takes a few steps closer to her mom. A gentle knocking comes from the door behind her as she leans over and looks her mother in the eyes.

"What about me, Mom?" she says. "You could have stayed for me."

Her mother's rage-filled face suddenly blanches. Her lip quivers.

"All you did was transfer your loneliness to me," Thea concludes as two guards step into the room. "And I'll never forgive you for that."

"No," her mother says as the guards move toward her. "Thea, please!"

Thea ignores her mother's cries, steps out of the room to where Achebe is waiting for her in the hallway. Behind her, her mother howls.

"How'd it go?" Achebe asks, glancing over Thea's shoulder into the cell.

"You were right," Thea says.

"Got what you needed?"

"Yes, for now." Thea shakes Achebe's hand. "Good luck, Gasira. And thank you."

"You too, Captain."

Thea strides down the hallway toward the exit while behind her, her mother screams her name. But Thea doesn't care . . .

. . . and doesn't look back.

32

Connection. Terminated

THIS USED to be her secret getaway, solace from the storm of her job and the demands of the fleet, freedom from the claustrophobia of the Neighborhood and the tumult of the Hub, an escape from the incessant capitulations and indignities that come with being the head administrator, sheriff, parent, and mother to what at the end of the day amounts to a frontier town on the edge of space. She'd retreat to this quiet place when it all got to be too much, sit on this train, earbuds screwed in and Nina Simone singing her truths, and she'd watch the lunar landscape slip past her window. Five hours out from Darkside, and five hours back. Ten glorious hours of rejuvenating solitude away from it all, the moon and stars her only company.

And now she's taking her final trip, leaving it all behind.

She's not sad, necessarily, though she wishes it could have ended on different terms. While the decision to leave was hers, the circumstances surrounding the Conglomerate's newfound control made her departure a foregone conclusion. Still, after decades of service to the astromining community and a planet that she's seldom visited in all those long, arduous years, Gasira

Achebe is excited to be going home to terra firma—a new home on a new continent where no one knows her, a place she can start over.

She adjusts the volume one click, but the music is suddenly cut off by an incoming call from Municipal. Her old job, it seems, isn't quite done with her yet.

"Hello?"

"I was hoping to see you off," Allgood says, the way a doctor promises a kid that a needle won't hurt.

"Yes, too bad," Achebe replies. "I wanted to say goodbye to you as well and wish you luck."

"I know we didn't always see eye to eye, Gasira, but I always respected you. I did a version of your job when I was warden at Angola. Different clientele, shall we say, but similar pressures. We all owe you a debt."

"Thank you, Brian."

"I also wanted to let you know that the team at the ship-yard concluded the interviews," he says. "No one has heard of this guy Fallon."

"You think Julia Watts made him up?"

"I don't know anything for sure," Allgood says, sounding as if he's already lost interest in their conversation. "But I wouldn't put it past her to try to make her organization sound more dangerous, knowing eventually we'd hear the recording."

"I don't think that's it," Achebe says. "She sounded genuinely excited on those recordings at finding out there was another Muse operative up here. You're the expert on crimi-nals. When you talked to her, did she seem like the type who'd be that elaborate with her lies?"

Her strategic praise catches his attention, as intended. "Not really, no," he admits.

"Then we have to assume that it wasn't some sort of misdi-rection for our benefit," Achebe says. "And you've proven there's no Fallon there now. The only conclusion is, the Muses lied to her."

She glances out the window just as they crest a rise in the landscape. The lights from the shipyard glow in the distance, but they pale in comparison to the bluish tint across everything cast by the Earthrise.

"Maybe they were just trying to motivate her to get to the shipyard as quickly as possible, knowing we'd be dropping the net on the whole place," Allgood says.

Achebe shakes her head, though Allgood can't see it. He's reaching, grasping at an explanation that doesn't fit. There's got to be another reason.

Before she can respond, the door separating her train car from the one with Julia Watts slides open, and a security officer rushes in, fear on his face.

"The prisoner," he says. "Something's wrong with her."

"What did he say?" Allgood says, but Achebe's already ripped out her earbuds and is rushing down the length of the train. When she crosses into the forward car, she finds Julia Watts convulsing on the floor, two other officers on either side of her, holding her down by her arms.

"Grab her legs," she says to the officer who came to get her.

Achebe grabs either side of the woman's thrashing head and finds foam bubbling from the corners of her mouth. But she's conscious.

"Julia, what's happening?" Achebe asks her.

"Please . . . please tell her," Julia says, pain contorting her face. Her eyes are wild. "Tell Thea . . . sorry. I'm sorry."

The security officers are using all their strength to keep the prisoner pinned down. Her left arm yanks free, and she whips it at Achebe's face, missing by the barest of margins.

"Get hold of her!" Achebe screams, gripping Julia's flailing arm before the officer seizes it again, roughly. It's then that she notices a glow emanating from Julia's forearm.

"What the hell?" She pushes up the woman's sleeve. The glow is coming from beneath her skin, and even as Achebe looks on, it intensifies, going from a light pink to an angry red.

Julia's body begins to jump off the train floor, and her head whips from side to side. A howl of pain escapes from her jaws, and her tongue is thrashing like a fish in a bucket.

Suddenly, the glow in her forearm disappears.

Julia's head falls back . . .

And she goes still.

Achebe puts her ear to Julia's mouth. The woman isn't breathing. She pushes the officers aside, straddles Julia's body, and starts doing chest compressions. One of the officers takes up position to give Julia mouth-to-mouth.

Achebe calls out the beats, and the officer blows air into their prisoner's mouth. They strike a steady rhythm, sweat beading on their brows. Another officer is on his handheld, relaying what is happening.

After a minute or two, everyone knows it's a lost cause.

Achebe slumps next to Julia Watts's corpse and tries to catch her breath. She looks into Julia's dead gaze, then reaches out and closes her eyelids.

"Ma'am, it's Admiral Allgood," says the officer with the handheld, handing her his device.

She gets to her feet, knees wobbly. Even before she puts the man's handheld to her ear, she can hear Allgood demanding to know what happened.

"She's dead," she says, squeezing her temples with thumb and middle finger.

"How the fuck—" Allgood starts, but Achebe cuts him off.

"It was that tracker in her arm. Somehow it activated. We should have removed . . ."

Her voice trails off as she lowers her hand from her

temples and stares out the train window at the blue glow radiating from Earth. The realization hits her like a thunderclap.

Allgood's terse voice snaps her back. "Say again? I lost you."

"Line of sight," she says. "*That's* why they did it."

"What?" Allgood says.

"They couldn't get to her through the satellites. They needed her *here*. They needed line of sight to her from Earth." She shakes her head to clear it. "We have to trace the transmission!"

"Gasira—"

"Just trace it, Brian!" she screams. "Do it now, before we lose them!"

33

The Game

HE WATCHES the International Astromining Alliance trace program zigzag its way across the global network like a bloodhound, getting closer with each passing second. He created an intricate web of relay points and double- and triple-backs in the hopes they'd lose the scent, but whoever they've got following his trail has skills.

His boss looks over his shoulder at the screen. "It had to come to this," she says. "You know that, right?"

"We all have our part to play in this vast and mysterious game," he replies, clicking off the monitor and pushing back from his desk.

"Despite her obvious flaws, Julia was a loyal operative," the woman says as she walks away and waves for him to follow her. He just nods as they head toward the exit of what was until recently the New Muses base of operations, now just an empty shell apart from his lone terminal.

"What will we do now?" he asks.

"A boat is waiting to take us to New Caldonia. Then it's off to Jakarta to meet with our main investor, who isn't particularly happy at the moment."

"Ma'am—" he starts, but is forced to pause as a young woman runs up to their boss and hands her a tablet. She studies the information on the screen, places her palm against the glass, which flashes between white and green at her touch, then hands the tablet back.

She turns back to him. "Sorry, you were saying?"

"What was that about?" he asks, pointing at the retreating figure, who bursts through the double doors, letting in a blast of sunlight.

"Just some final business," she says, helicoptering her index finger in the air and looking around the space. "This site is officially offline."

He musters as much contrition as possible for a man who rarely feels at fault, then says to his superior, "Once again, ma'am, I'm very sorry for the way things turned out. I pushed for Julia Watts to be left in place at Darkside, and I take full responsibility for this failure. I'll do whatever it takes to make amends."

She gives him a wry smile. "Yes, you will."

They step outside. The sun feels apocalyptic after the darkness inside their shuttered headquarters. He winces against the glare, wishing he had his sunglasses, the sun already baking his bald dome. A sleek electric cutter is silently idling at the dock adjacent to the building. As soon as they step aboard, the young woman who had given their boss the tablet throws the lines, and they set off. Once clear of the dock, the boat tacks north, heading out to the Tasman Sea. He watches the dock shrink in the distance, then follows his boss into the main cabin.

She sits down in a lounger and motions for him to take the matching one across a small table from her. In the center of the table is an accordion file. He eyes it curiously as he takes his seat.

She removes her jacket, drawing an e-cigarette from one of

its inner pockets before tossing the jacket onto the nearby couch. Her taut arms are decorated with elaborate tattoos of winding vines, flowers sprouting from the twists and turns near her biceps and wrists. She puffs out a cloud that smells like hazelnut and vanilla and stares past the accordion file at him.

He reaches for the file. "I assume this will describe the nature of my penance once we reach Jakarta?"

"You won't be joining me in Jakarta," she says.

He unwinds the string from the circular clasp, opens the flap, and looks inside the file, which contains a handheld device.

"What happened at Darkside Station was nothing short of a calamity," she says. "What should have been a catastrophic event for the astromining industry turned out to be no more than a speed bump. Our best guess is that the refinery will be fully operational in just a few months, with mining operations once again underway in a matter of weeks. And to make matters worse, we're now dealing with a united international front. The consolidation of power with the Conglomerate and the end of independent operations will make infiltrating the system incredibly hard."

He's not sure at first why she pauses, not picking up on the cue right away. But then he catches her glancing down at the dark device in his hands, and he places his index finger in the center of the glass to activate it. When prompted, he holds the device in front of his face. A green beam of light scans it from forehead to chin.

Access granted, his screen fills with information, including a boarding pass.

"We need to take advantage of this brief window to get another operative in place while the Conglomerate is getting settled and the indie operators are being made to pack it in," she says, then delivers the punch line. "That operative will be you."

Before he can respond, his attention is drawn to one of the cabin windows. A bloom of fire is followed a second or two later by the sound of an explosion. Black smoke billows from what was once their headquarters. He watches the dark cloud fill the sky over the lush green of the New Zealand coast until his boss calls his attention back to the matter at hand.

"Everything you need is on there," she says, pointing to the device. "Including comprehensive files on Angola State Penitentiary."

He looks at her quizzically.

"You'll be posing as a former prison guard," she explains. "You and Allgood won't have crossed paths, but he'll be keen to populate his new Municipal security team with like-minded individuals, which a background check on you will confirm you are."

He thumbs through a few of the files, then deactivates the device and puts it in his pocket.

"There's one more thing," she says, sliding open a drawer on a side table and taking out a blue pouch. She unrolls the pouch, revealing medical instruments inside, and lifts out a scalpel. "After what just happened, they'll be scanning everyone."

He doesn't hesitate to hold out his arm, which she positions over the table between them. He hopes his immediate compliance serves as a sign of loyalty, though he can't help but notice the absence of anesthetic.

He stifles a cry as his boss expertly slices into his forearm. With the swift motion of popping a zit, she squeezes either side of the wound. His tracker pops to the surface, and she drops it into the pool of blood collecting on the table before taking a roll of gauze and a surgical skin stapler from the pouch.

He stares at the stapler in confusion, dizzy from the pain radiating from his forearm. "No stitches or glue?"

"This will help with the alias," she says. "If it ever comes up, you'll say you were injured during an incident at the prison. The rougher the scar looks, the better."

She grips her e-cigarette between her teeth as she examines his wound. "A seaplane will take you from New Caledonia to Samoa, then Hawaii. From there, it's off to California and Houston, from where you'll depart in two weeks."

She pinches his skin together and sets a few staples to close the wound, adding one or two more for good measure. When she's finished, she leaves him to wrap the wound in gauze, washes her hands, pours him a healthy amount of vodka, and hands it to him along with a brown bottle of pills.

"Anything else, ma'am?" he says, shaking out a few pills and washing them down with the vodka.

She shakes her head and takes another aromatic puff on her e-cigarette. "That's all."

"Thank you for this opportunity. I won't let you down, ma'am."

"Good luck, Fallon," she says.

34

Way of Life

"THIS IS the best we can do," the man from the shipbuilders' office says, turning his tablet around so Thea can see the screen.

Thea looks at the offer, then at the man, whose face is pinched as if he's bracing for a blow.

"We'd be basically buying it for some of the parts," he explains once again. "Your reactor is solid, the harpoon cannon would make a good backup for some of the smaller trawlers, and there's some decent bits and pieces on the bridge, but even those would only be of interest to some of the older pilots up here. You know, people who like a retro flair."

Thea does some quick math. She'd hoped to get enough money from the sale to give herself a buffer while she figured out what to do next. But the measly sum the shipbuilders are offering isn't going to buy her a lot of time once she gets back home.

"Can I ask," the man says, "have you spoken to Conglomerate Acquisitions?"

"I'm not interested," she says.

He looks around the room, even though he and Thea are

the only ones in the shipbuilders' new offices, then leans in conspiratorially. "They could certainly do better than what we're offering." He waves dismissively at the figure displayed on his tablet's screen.

"I can't bring her home with me, and there's no way I could live with someone else flying her," Thea explains.

"I can respect that. I really wish there was more I could do."

Thea glances at the screen again, lets out a deep sigh, then signs on the dotted line. "When do I have to be out?"

"We're at a standstill until the refinery reopens," he says. "Flights out of town are booked up for the next few days, too. So take your time. No rush."

She shakes his outstretched hand, then heads back to the ship she just sold for parts.

———

LIKE THE REST of the station, the Hub is being transformed. In addition to the Leaderboard, the vendor stalls are all but gone, and the few still remaining are in the process of being deconstructed. Darkside is no longer an open market, and all vendor residencies have been terminated. The general store will continue operations, though with a reduced selection consisting of only those items authorized by the Conglomerate. Down below, the Neighborhood is filled with people packing up their lives. Allgood's team has been handing out "golden tickets" to the residents who are being offered continued employment, but that still leaves a large number of people deemed redundant by the new management, or who are going to be replaced by Conglomerate-approved staff from back home. Municipal and maintenance are the hardest hit by these changes, Allgood deciding that a fresh start is called for after recent events.

As she walks through the Hub, watching an entire way of

life being taken apart and placed into boxes and crates, Thea can't help but feel guilty. She and her crew are victims too, but that's certainly cold comfort to all the people who have to figure out where they go from here.

She steps around a stack of crates stamped with Canadian shipping labels and sees Captain Saito walking toward her.

"Captain," he says.

"What are you doing here?" she asks. Japan capitulated and joined the Conglomerate along with all the other national astromining operations. The news that Saito had been relieved of his duty as captain of the Japanese crew came as a surprise to no one who bore witness to the exchange between him and Allgood on the day that the video of her mother surfaced.

"I am leaving shortly," he says. "But I wanted to see you first."

Thea and Saito have always been friendly, mostly due to their shared disregard for Brian Allgood. But this catches her by surprise.

"I'm glad," she says. "It gives me a chance to say goodbye."

"Maybe not," he says. "I'm joining Stilgar Matsson's *Red Venture* project. He sees what's happening up here as an opportunity to grab the best talent who might help advance his Mars project, and he asked me for recommendations."

"Really?" she says, struggling to maintain her composure. She studied some of Matsson's nuclear propulsion designs in graduate school.

"I told him about you and your engineer, Lola," Saito says. "He wants to meet you both."

Thea's heart, which is firmly in her throat, sinks. "What about Beetle and Rory?" she asks. "They're both unbelievable."

Saito nods enthusiastically. "There is no doubt about their talents. And when the time is right, maybe we could find roles for them both. But right now, the project needs certain skill sets, and you and Lola have those."

Thea has been dreading the moment that she and her crew are forced to part ways. But if this works out, at least she and Lola can still be together. Assuming, of course, Lola would be interested in leaving Darkside and living in Australia at Matsson's compound.

"What do you think?" Saito asks after letting his news sink in.

"Well, first off, thank you for recommending me," Thea says. "I'm honored, truly."

"Captain Watts—"

"Thea," she says, interrupting him. "Please, call me Thea."

He smiles widely and is about to continue when there's a commotion behind them. They turn to find Gasira Achebe flanked by two security officers striding across the Hub, heading straight for them.

"Wow, you too?" Thea says, puzzled as Achebe closes on them. "I thought you'd be gone."

But she can tell by the look on Achebe's face that she's not in a joking mood.

"Thea, it's your mother. She's dead."

35

What's Mine Is Yours

THEY OFFER Thea the opportunity to see her mother's body, but she declines. She knows some people need that in order to gain a sense of closure, but there can be no closure for her. She lost her real mom years ago.

The shipyard infirmary dug the device from her mother's arm and determined that it released a synthetic DNA decoupler that transmuted the resulting unwound chromosomes into a lethal neurotoxin. Julia Watts never had a chance. The trace on the signal that activated the deadly device, however, was successful. The IAA and New Zealand Homeland Security discovered the New Muses' base—or at least what was left of it —while it was still burning. When the conflagration was put out and investigators were able to comb through the wreckage, they found nothing but ash. So even after apprehending one of their key operatives and discovering their base of operations, the IAA was no closer to stopping the New Muses.

In the end, Gasira Achebe fulfilled her final duty as head of Darkside Municipal and escorted Julia Watts's body back to Earth, where she would deliver it to Thea's family lawyer to handle the burial arrangements.

Rory, Lola, and Beetle are waiting for her when she arrives back at the station.

"What are you guys doing here?" she asks.

"We wanted to be there with you at the shipyard, but they wouldn't let us on the train," Lola says. "Rory almost got himself arrested."

"I did not."

"He basically tried to commandeer one of the Hyperloop trains," Lola continues. "Beetle had to bribe the guy with some rare scotch—"

"Bourbon," Beetle corrects her.

Lola waves off the irrelevant detail. "Fine, bourbon then. If it wasn't for Beetle, Rory'd probably be locked up."

"We wanted to be there to support you, luv," Rory says. "I'm sorry we couldn't be."

"How'd it go?" Beetle asks as they start to make their way back to their ship.

"It was crazy. Thankfully Gasira was there, or who the hell knows what might have gone down."

As she tells them the details of her mother's death, what the team in New Zealand found, and her decision to not attend her mother's burial, their concern for her is written all over their faces. But Thea doesn't want to spend whatever time they have left together reliving the events of the last few days, so she makes a show of shrugging it all off.

"Anyway, it's over now," she says. "Time to move on."

Dock D is once again a ghost town, like it was when Thea first arrived at Darkside. The other independent operators are gone. Their ships, however, remain parked at the dock, moth-balled, property of the Conglomerate.

"Well, *ma chère*, I have a delicious dinner planned for you, with plenty of nice wine, which we must drink all of because we cannot afford to ship it home, obviously," Beetle says as they board the *Zephyr*'s lift.

"Just what the doctor ordered," Thea says.

Rory pats the side of the lift. "When do they want us out?"

"We have a little time," Thea says as the lift doors open and they step into the cargo bay. "But we need to talk about our options. There are a few interesting possibilities that have popped up."

"Well then, let me add one more," Allgood says.

They are stunned to find him sitting on a crate in the middle of their cargo bay. He's drinking one of their afore-mentioned fine wines directly from the bottle.

"What are you doing here?" Thea asks.

Before he can answer, Rory piles on. "And how in the fuck did you get in here? I change the access codes every few days."

"Come now, Mr. Abernathy," Allgood says after a long swallow. "This station is mine now. I have access to everything."

"Well, this is still *my* ship, and I want you off her right now," Thea says, snatching the bottle from his hand.

"*Was* your ship," he says.

"Excuse me?"

His satisfaction is crystal clear in each syllable. "Was. Your. Ship."

Allgood hops off the crate and straightens his jacket, wobbling from the wine. "Like I said, this is mine now," he says, arms wide. "All of it, including anything recently acquired by the shipbuilders."

Rory catches Thea as she lunges for Allgood. "You bastard!" she screams. "That's not fair. You can't have her!"

Allgood trails his fingers along a bulkhead as he strolls around the cargo bay. "You think I care at all about this ship?" he says. He wrinkles his nose at the residue on his fingertips. "I don't want the *Zephyr*."

Ever the peacekeeper, Beetle steps between his crew and Allgood. "What are you talking about, Admiral?"

"I want *you*," Allgood says. "All of you."

"We've been through this," Thea says.

Allgood can't conceal his exasperation. "This isn't a competition anymore. It's more important than that. The only way we're going to keep things going back home is by working up here as one team, with one mission. To do that, I need the best people flying for me—and that's all of you, in this ship."

"Nice try," Thea says. "But the answer is still no."

Allgood lets out a sigh. "Okay, let's look at your options." He points first to Beetle. "Frenchy goes back to being a vagabond circus freak, but he's been out of the game so long the best he can hope for is an understudy role." He turns his gaze to Rory. "Mr. Abernathy, I'm sorry to say all lift operator roles at the shipyard and station have been filled. You'll have to seek employment at one of the lovely quarries back on Earth, which shouldn't be too hard to find for such a seasoned shit shoveler." Finally he looks at Lola. "And you, madam. We were all very impressed by your work during the crisis. Unfortunately, someone with more experience has been posted to the open role on the *Segundo*."

He lets his words settle in as he moves to stand directly in front of Thea.

"Yes, I heard all about Matsson's interest in you and Lola joining his weird little island of misfit toys. You think *I'm* bad? Wait until you get a load of that entitled prick."

"What?" Lola says.

Thea shoots Lola a quick look of confirmation, but doesn't get a chance to elaborate before Allgood jumps in.

"Forget the past, Thea. Forget what happened between us. Just think about the future that you guys can have. All of you, together. Considering your less-than-savory prospects back on Earth, I think this is a rather magnanimous offer I'm making."

Then to the rest of the crew, he adds, "This ship doesn't deserve to be stripped and melted down. That's why I saved it. It deserves to fly, just like you. And if you're smart enough to say yes, you can all keep doing what you do best. That's what I'm offering you."

Just as he wraps up, the lift pings behind them and starts to descend.

"And if we say no?" Thea asks.

He glances around the cargo bay, wrinkling his nose. "Well, it won't be easy, but I'm sure I can find someone else to fly her. We can reinforce the nose and use her as a plow in small swarms or have her taxi junk away from our trawlers. Grunt stuff. She might last a few years doing that."

"You're a real fucker, Allgood," Rory says.

The look of derision that Allgood gives Rory is rare. Few people manage to stand firm in the face of Rory's obstinance. "Careful, Mr. Abernathy," he says. "My generosity has its limits."

Thea jumps in, sensing things are about to get even worse than they already are. "You're not leaving us a lot of outs here," she says. "You know I couldn't stand the idea of my dad's ship in yours or anyone else's hands. None of us could."

"I do know that, yes," he admits.

"We could stay together?" Beetle asks Allgood. "That's a guarantee."

Allgood moves over to the lift, which has started to rise again. "Life is full of uncertainty. But it doesn't benefit me, or the Conglomerate, to break up a team as effective as yours. There is, however, one condition."

"What's that?" Thea asks.

The lift stops, and the door opens.

"You're a man down," Allgood says. "So I took the liberty of filling the post."

Darcey comes around to where everyone is gathered in the

cargo bay. She has a bag slung over her shoulder and is wearing regular civilian clothes.

Allgood snags the bottle of wine from Thea's slack hand and takes a swig as he boards the lift. But not before offering his parting shot.

"Welcome to the Conglomerate."

The End
Book 2

Acknowledgments

Middles are hard. Writing the second book in this trilogy—one long middle—gave me a whole new appreciation for that fact. And being stuck in the middle of the middle? Pure despair. But I didn't go through it alone.

To my family, especially my wife and children: The novelty of my writing surely wore off long ago. By now, this odd hobby (obsession?) is just something I do—something you've patiently endured for years. Your quiet acceptance, even when it must test your patience, means the world to me. Thank you.

Pete Ralston, Jim Brandenburger, Chris Matarazzo, and Blair Wisner—your friendship and unwavering support drive me to keep chasing this dream. I hope to entertain you for the rest of my days. And to Scott Warnock, the man who brought us together and still keeps us connected—meeting you changed my life's trajectory. My eternal gratitude. Now, garçon, bring the pudding. The monkey is hungry!

For Evan Young—pie and burgers on the table, always.

David Gatewood, my editor—I've praised your genius in every book, and I'll do it again. But "editor" barely captures your role in my writing life. "Lodestar" feels more fitting, even if it's a bit on the nose for a sci-fi writer. Thank you.

About the Author

Lou Iovino was born in Philadelphia, Pennsylvania. He splits his time between working in advertising, writing, and teaching and lives in New Jersey with his wife and two sons.

For more information, visit www.louiovino.com. You can also find him on the following social channels:

RECKONING

LOU IOVINO

RARE
EARTH
TRILOGY
VOLUME
TWO

A NOVEL